MARY-BETH HUGHES

Wavemaker II

March 9. 2002

For Karen,

Best wishes,

[signature]

Atlantic Monthly Press
New York

Copyright © 2002 by Mary-Beth Hughes

All rights reserved. No part of this book may be reproduced in any form or by
any electronic or mechanical means, including information storage and
retrieval systems, without permission in writing from the publisher, except by
a reviewer, who may quote brief passages in a review. Any members of
educational institutions wishing to photocopy part or all of the work for
classroom use, or publishers who would like to obtain permission to include
the work in an anthology, should send their inquiries to Grove/Atlantic, Inc.,
841 Broadway, New York, NY 10003.

This is a work of fiction. Names, characters, places, and incidents are the product of the
author's imagination or are used fictiously. The estate of Roy M. Cohn has not
authorized this work.

Published simultaneously in Canada
Printed in the United States of America

FIRST EDITION

Library of Congress Cataloging-in-Publication Data

Hughes, Mary-Beth.
Wavemaker II / Mary-Beth Hughes. —1st ed.
p. cm.
ISBN 0-87113-835-2
1. Cohn, Roy M.—Fiction.   2. Cohn, Roy M.—Friends and associates—Fiction.
3. Prisoners' families—Fiction.   4. New York (N.Y.)—Fiction.   I. Title:
Wavemaker 2.   II. Title: Wavemaker Two.   III. Title.
PS3608.U56 W38 2002
813'.6—dc21   2001045872

Atlantic Monthly Press
841 Broadway
New York, NY 10003

02 03 04 05   10 9 8 7 6 5 4 3 2 1

For my mother and father,
and for Paulie.
Peace and Love.

Memorial Day, 1964

The marshals looked like ordinary men. They were not in good shape, they did not have wary eyes. Their man was not handcuffed to either of them, and when the steak was served they ate with appetite. Both men took the beer that was offered. After dinner they drank Scotch. They drove a blue car, not a black one; an Impala. They bit corn off the cob in a yard full of old trees: holly, sycamore, oak, pine. A hill sloped down to a creek, more than that, a small channel, wide and deep enough for pleasure boats to come back and forth and dock in the slips. Each yard had a slip, and at this house a Boston Whaler was tied up.

The hostess was young, about twenty-eight or twenty-nine, and pretty, with blond streaks in her hair and the top pulled back and pinned. She wore a Chinese jacket with silk frog closures. And when she bent down, one of the marshals, but not both, looked to the gap left between those closures for a glimpse of her lacy brassiere. The other marshal was thinking of his boy. His son was slow in school and might have to go to summer classes. The marshal and his wife fought about this. At every chance, each hit the other surely and swiftly with the evidence that the boy's poor progress could be traced back to the accused. The marshal believed his wife's slow brain cells had diluted his own good stock and produced a son who couldn't think his way out of the first grade.

The second man watched the pretty hostess with some pleasure. When their ward got up from the plastic latticework of his recliner and walked up the back steps to the porch, neither marshal blinked. The hostess refilled their glasses from a small bar set away from the heat of the grill. More Scotch. The evening was warm, and a velvet light settled on the lawn and the trees. At nightfall, they'd be leaving. Now the woman followed her husband up the steps and into the house. Their two children, William Junior and Ann Louise—Bo and Lou-Lou—stayed out on the lawn under the care of the next-door neighbors, the Maguires.

The marshal with the slow son looked at the two children lying a short distance away on grass as smooth as a carpet. The children had their cheeks to the blades of grass, and when they pressed their faces, small hectic weaves imprinted there. They were listening to the worms. They could hear the rumble of earth moving. The boy's eyes were red with blood, more than bloodshot, almost filled where the whites should be. When his sister looked at him, confirming the loud worms, she looked beyond those terrible bruises and her brother laughed, then coughed. There are worse things than being stupid, the marshal thought. And he had the first kind thought for his wife in some time. He thought of her pregnant, visiting her folks on another Memorial Day when he'd been working, what else. He'd traveled down to the shore to be with them at the end of a long, tedious day with a felon who couldn't keep his mouth shut. A foul-tongued sick fuck. The marshal's mind was dead. He rode the local train down through about a hundred shore towns and arrived in Manasquan. His mother-in-law, stout as a bull, met him at the station in the green Chevrolet.

In the driveway, his father-in-law had the saw out. The stogie in his mouth was soaked. He bobbed his head toward the side yard. Behind the honeysuckle, the marshal's wife sat on the low, thick branch of an oak tree, but still—he ran. What do you think you're doing? She yawned, in no danger. He could see the shape of her belly, a white pear that erased completely, for the time being, all the things the felon had said, and he was so grateful to her he held out his hand for her swinging leg and kissed her heel and ankle and her toes all around the rubber V of her flip-flop.

Inside the house, Kay Clemens saw the cake would take a while to thaw. When she first got the word that Will was coming home for a visit, she bought a cake, then froze it, because they might be late and the cake would dry out. But they were right on time and now everyone would be drunk before she could serve it. It might be good if her husband was drunk, good and bad. Eight weeks since he'd been home. He didn't even like cake. What was she thinking.

She wandered through the house, a long ranch style, with a layout of airy, sunny, low-ceilinged rooms, interweaving one into the next: dining, living, study, guest, master, and here he was, sitting head in his hands at the edge of his side of their bed, just as he used to sit most mornings waiting for black coffee in a mug. She was up at six anyway, on her third cup by the time he stirred. Now she wondered, What did he do? How did his day begin?

Will? she said. Dear heart. But her husband did not move. She sat beside him on the bed and smoothed down the silk jacket and tucked her hands beneath her thighs and waited. She stood up and listened in the doorway. She closed the door, flipped down the little hook lock. She sat beside her husband again and placed a hand against the curve of his neck. The smell of his clothing was so sharp, a desperate clean, and she thought about finding a shirt that was softer, a golf shirt maybe, from the drawerful he had, maybe something blue. She thought of his shirts but held still. She could smell the soap he used, which had no perfume, a kind of scent like shoe polish in a tin.

Her husband didn't say anything. She withdrew her cheek and hands, and started with the frog closures on her jacket. Her husband released his head from his palms and, still looking down, watched the top of her instep sliding slightly in the black embroidered sandal. He watched her fingers push at the knots, then watched as she dropped the jacket back off her shoulders to the bed. She sat still, not doing anything, wearing the kind of brassiere she often wore, a full-coverage affair that clasped at the waist level in the back. Her belly rounded out just beneath the stiff ruff. She unzipped her black silk toreador trousers. Lifted her bottom

off the bed just long enough to shimmy them off her hips. Dropped
the trousers down to her sandaled feet. Started to lift her feet, then
left them there, swaddled in black. She looked at the puddle of
fabric. He looked at her ribbed, cinched waist. He looked to the
cups, a bull's-eye effect in stitching, and her shoulders, rounded
slightly, not interrupted by bone.

Outside the door, there was a commotion coming toward them,
like a beehive cracked open and the bees gaining volume and den-
sity, they could hear footsteps coming through the house. Hey, hey,
came the voices, and Gert Maguire was knocking lightly on the
door. Kay, she said. She kept the syllable tight, deliberately unem-
phatic. Kay heard Gert's footsteps move away from the door. And
quickly, quickly, back into her clothes, God, now, not everything
buttoned. A frantic back look to her husband, and she was pressing
hard at the hook on the door. Gert stood in the front foyer beyond
the small corridor that led to the master suite. Red Maguire was
on the phone with the pediatrician, who'd meet them at the hospital; the ambulance was already on the way, and the men who
drove it, men Kay Clemens routinely brought gifts to, New York
strip steaks by the dozen.

Past Gert, and followed by Gert, out through the living, dining, pantry, kitchen, porch to the yard to her son, Bo, held steady
in the arms of a United States marshal. Down two steps, her frog
clasps not quite done but who was watching now, and she knelt by
her son and slowly took him from the man, brought her baby into
her arms, her boy whose eyes were not quite closed. He was not
conscious, How long, she said, how long? It would be the first thing
anyone needed to know. The ambulance made its rude, loud way,
backing up the gravel drive, backing onto the grass, and the emergency team, her friends, were beside her, oxygen first, then a stretcher.
Kay kissed her daughter, Lou-Lou, who did not cry, and glanced at
Gert to arrange all things in that glance: her daughter's homework,
sleep, school the next day. And then she stepped into the back of the
ambulance in time to see the heart monitor register a beat strong

enough, strong enough at least for her son to make it in time, once again, to the hospital. They would go local then, the next day, move him to New York.

Will Clemens stood at the top of the brick step. He looked at the wracked gravel, the tire marks on the lawn, and his mouth twisted, he pressed the heel of a hand to his eye.

Lou-Lou moved toward her father. One marshal put his hands in his pockets, took them out, then slipped past Will on the steps to make a phone call in the kitchen. When he came back, he said to the marshal with the interest in Kay's brassiere: Let's take a look at the water. The two walked down the gentle slope past the sycamore trees to watch the pleasure boats return at sundown to their slips.

When the marshals climbed back up the hill after a protracted observation of a thirty-five-foot trimaran, Will and Lou-Lou were seated on the screened porch. The Maguires tidied up. They dismantled the grill, collapsed the bar, wrapped the leftovers, loaded the dishwasher. The marshals both needed to use the facilities, and Gert directed them to the children's bath through the den. One looked over the bookshelves while waiting for his partner: all leather-bound sets, no mysteries, no magazines, no newspapers. A big television, cabinet console. Three golf trophies, the type a club gives for no real reason. The marshals traded places. In the yellow bathroom, almost by rote, the second man slid open the mirrored medicine cabinet: a battalion of clear plastic, all made out to the boy in care of the mother, more than he'd ever seen in a home, this was extraordinary. He didn't touch any but bent closer to read the dates, dosages, then drew the mirror closed. The house was so quiet. The street too. A cul-de-sac without a lot of traffic. It was getting dark.

The marshals made their way back to the porch. So, we'll give it a minute. They sat down at the glass-top table, both folding their hands as if in casual prayer. Will swatted at something buzzing around his head. In the twilight, the Maguires were walking through the pine trees, across the yards, already pretty far gone.

Lou-Lou, between them, knocked into Gert's hip. Gert reached around, pulled her closer. Will didn't watch. The insect had his full attention. No one spoke. Ten, fifteen minutes passed this way.

The phone rang. Will sat still. The marshal stood, looked at Will, then crossed to the door and into the house. He picked up on the seventh ring. Yes, sir. Got it. Okay. Okay. Yes, sir. Goodbye.

He stood in the door frame, All right, we're going to the hospital, and he nodded several times. Will said, Oh God, and tried not to cry, and said, Two seconds, and went back through the kitchen, dining room, living room, den to the children's bath, opened the same mirrored cabinet and emptied one vial from an uppermost shelf into the stiff paraffin-scented pocket of his shirt.

They closed the doors, snapped out the lights. Will sat in the backseat of the blue car without restraint. He thought he could still smell the charcoal fire in the air as they pulled out of the drive. The marshal on the passenger side fumbled with the spinning top, reached out to attach it to the roof. This took a moment or two. At the end of the road, the driver released the siren. They ran every light.

June 3

It was a small dinner in an apartment that stared into the Met, peeked in at the national treasures. At one tall window, a telescope big enough to spot Pluto was set up. Roy looked through it: columns. And on the marble pedestal next to the telescope, a hand of God, Rodin, that anyone could hold.

Roy thought Esther looked a little odd tonight and wished she'd stop sewing her own clothes. Or at least stop wearing them to the gatherings with the big gazoos. But then she was here, and that was more important. And if she wanted to wear an orange velvet turtleneck with sleeves like a bat from Transylvania, wasn't it her prerogative.

Roy adjusted the tight collar on his shirt, something from Turnbull & Asser. He knew about them already, before anyone. And Esther had helped him. She was very involved with fashion, and very soon she would be fashion, a woman whose clothing line sold in Saks Fifth Avenue. Her own label. Her own atelier off Seventh where the furs rolled on carts just like the dead animals down on Gansevoort. It was in the works.

Roy's mother, Muddy, liked Esther, and how could she not? Sylvia Horner's youngest. Muddy knew Esther from the time she was not very smart in kindergarten. What was all that? Roy was much older, six, seven years, that put him in seventh grade when all the trouble happened to Esther, and never much since. So Esther was in the girls' bathroom at the little day school, not Horace Mann where her three brothers had gone. She wasn't that bright, let's face it, her mother knew right away. And pretty was a matter of taste.

Esther was small in her class and young, like Roy had been. And she was the last in a family of big boys, boys who had a lot of balls. It was a family that made itself known. Muddy knew the boys and steered Roy out of their purview, sensing things would not go well, no alliance there, no mutual interests, those big Horner boys with the heavy shoulders, all of them. But the girl, she had her mother's heart. She had a face like a snake charmer drawing all the best nuances, all the little mental dances, out of the mothers. The mothers looked at her and thought, Not smart, not pretty, and smiled watching her face anyway, big round eyes full of feeling, and they would chuckle, seeing something of themselves there, and they liked her for that, they all did, before the incident, which wasn't large but stayed with them and changed their minds, except for Muddy, who was deeper.

Of course the incident was sexual, a kindergarten sex scandal. The mothers hovered and even briefly demanded the child be removed. She was a public contaminant. But Muddy Cohn intervened, she'd said a word or two as a favor to Sylvia Horner, and the whole thing, tiny, was forgotten at the top. But not in the minds of the mothers. They never looked for their own generous, unsatisfied hearts in the homely face again.

Here it is: In the lavatory for the smallest schoolgirls, kindergartners through second-graders, Esther was found with a sky-blue crayon pushed very slightly into her tiny vagina. The crime? It didn't appear to be a new trick. Who told her she had a vagina?

Esther's kindergarten teacher, Mrs. Lopato, always too worried for her own good, a heart attack in the making, had the misfortune of an unruly class that year, a bunch of gangsters, seventeen boys and seven girls. She'd complained to the principal, Mr. Haberman, for a redistribution of gender. Nothing doing.

Mrs. Lopato, harassed, sick to death of all the shoving and pushing, couldn't sleep at night. At four in the morning she scrubbed her spotless living room while Mr. Lopato slept. She scrubbed and schemed, but in the daylight, driving her black Ford into the teachers' lot, she remembered, wearily, that kindness was the teacher's mightiest weapon. She climbed out of the too low driver's seat and straightened her plaid wool skirt on heavy thighs, thighs that made her tired to contemplate. Mrs. Lopato was close to thirty-nine, thirty-nine in April and childless. Kindergarten was beginning to be a strain. Soon after this day she'd decide to quit altogether and leave Mr. Lopato and move to southern California. She'd learn to serve Bloody Marys on Sunday mornings on a small deck jutting out over the Pacific Rim. It was beautiful there, and when she thought of the Bronx, which she seldom did, it was as if that part of her life were completed, she thought of little ugly Esther Kinder and her blue crayon and she thanked her.

But before the good news, the bad. There was a lot of mischief that day in Mrs. Lopato's kindergarten classroom. And why, she thought for the thousandth time, had she been given a room into which sunlight crept for about thirty minutes a day, a basement room for tiny children, whose idea was this? Mrs. Busansky, with a class of twelve girls and eight boys, all quiet geniuses, what could it matter to her, but Mrs. Busansky had the room upstairs that was practically an atrium. And what did Mr. Haberman, the principal, say when she complained? Close to amenities. What amenities? The boiler room? Children don't learn in a basement.

On this day, the boys were laying siege to the coat closet, and finally Mrs. Lopato put her foot down, detention, detention for everyone, in the middle of the school day. And what exactly was detention? Detention was nothing, the absence of everything: learning, movement, fun. A strong measure perhaps for kindergarten, but necessary. Every day the class would have detention until they could learn to behave. Somehow Mrs. Lopato was able to enforce this. The children sat, heads down on their tiny desks. Mrs. Lopato turned out the lights and sat down at her own desk, which looked like an ocean liner compared to theirs. She sat on her teacher's wooden chair, and her wool skirt scratched at her heavy thighs, and she felt the trembling weariness of too little sleep for too many nights and closed her eyes. When she awoke, a shocked four minutes later, nothing had changed. The children were still in their seats, heads down. Some had fallen asleep too in the dark, hot room. As Mrs. Lopato's panic subsided, she noticed an empty chair in the girls' row. Sheila, Carol, Becky, Helen, Sarah, Judy, Esther. Esther?

There was a rule. A rule she remembered even now: Never leave the classroom unattended. So sent her most reliable boy with a note to Mr. Haberman. Come, she wrote, bring Mrs. Felix and Moe, the handyman. Her worst fear—the boiler room. She imagined little Esther burned beyond recognition, her poor face, it was too awful. Too awful, the door was never locked. And Moe had never been forced to do so. Why? Well, this would be a terrible lesson for them all.

The principal arrived in the darkened classroom and raised his nearly hairless eyebrows. What's going on here, the brows asked, and Mrs. Lopato took charge, she knew how to handle this. She gestured to Mrs. Felix with round hand motions to sit at the big desk. She took the principal and the handyman into the hallway. The boiler room, she whispered, a child is missing. What's with the lights, Mr. Haberman asked, some problem with the electricals? She ignored him, he was a foul man who shaved his own eyebrows. She led the way to the boiler room, stopping to let Moe precede her when she reached the wide-open metal door. She could smell herself. She stank like an old blanket. She could taste blood in the back of her throat.

Nothing, Moe said, you're nuts. She was relieved. Okay, where? Mrs. Lopato felt almost lighthearted, as if she'd mastered a fancy dance step. The child wasn't burned or maimed, the situation was turning radically for the better. Esther was in the building. She had to be, Moe kept all the outside doors locked. The men skulked along the cement corridor, looking left and right, as if the child were leaning against the wall and they just needed to look harder. Idiots, thought Mrs. Lopato. Mr. Haberman pushed through the swing door of the lavatory for the littlest girls. He had that kind of authority in his own school, and soon, very soon, before Moe could even say Holy Jesus—the other thing that stayed with Mrs. Lopato, the mystery of that utterance—the primary mystery was solved. Little Esther had her underpants, a thick cream-colored cotton—too heavy for a little girl, thought Mrs. Lopato, germs could roost in such hot, heavy underpants—these were down around Esther's bony ankles as she sat on the tile floor, a dusty place, Moe dealt in half-measures as a cleaner as in all else. Esther's knees fell out to the side, in a position that Mrs. Lopato would later learn, in southern California, was a variant of the goddess position in yoga. So the view was clear to Esther's tiny vagina and the crayon there. Esther's hands rested on the floor beside her hips. And she smiled calmly at the adults shivering above her.

Here's the worst part: Without consultation, Mr. Haberman bent down and removed the crayon, put it in his pocket, and left the room. Esther began to wail, a shrieking, mournful cry that Mrs. Lopato on the occasional lonely night over the Pacific tries to remember, thinks she should remember, but can't. She only remembers the face: ugly, crushed, lonely for life. Esther Kinder.

Now Roy watched Esther leaning into the placid face of the senator's wife, Ruth Harbottle, looking like a vision of Halloween. Esther was his friend. She was his date. Roy was wondering if there were going to be any speeches, because that would be interesting. Nate was here. No speech happening, he looked too calm. Albert? Nope. Roy pondered his own cummerbund, released his throat once more from his collar. He was thinking he'd do it. It was the right crowd.

He didn't say anything to Esther, who might get flustered and flap her crazy arms. He stood up and walked to the window, where he was backdropped by Corinthian columns, very classical. He touched the hand of God as a goodwill gesture to the host, who owed him a lot of money. No throat clearing, instead he compressed his mouth and looked irritated, and that got people's attention. A little ribbing about the state of his bowels, which struck

Esther as unbearably funny. Ruth Harbottle did a little simulated back patting, then led Esther off to a powder room. Now Roy heard the news about his sexual prowess. This seemed to produce a bad taste in his mouth, his lips puffed out as if he were checking his teeth, and then they parted while his tongue explored the lower left quadrant. Roy had a very thick tongue. Very pink. The room went quiet, Roy touched the hand of God again, said, Have we met? And he was off.

He was going to tell a story, so he started in right away with the groundwork, and this bothered his stomach, this need to do it right: There's a friend of mine who is in trouble.

That's the definition of a friend of yours!

This from Albert, who should be keeping his mouth shut, who should be grateful down to his pathetic joint that he was here at all. Then let me say, this is a friend I don't deserve to have. No one countered this. Some people looked at Albert. He was not as smart as he needed to be most of the time. A weak guy, carried along. So this friend has a beautiful wife, Roy said, two beautiful children, a boy and a girl—a son and a daughter. And the wife? She looks like a movie star, but not a fake, the real thing, a lady. Okay, good.

Esther returned from the powder room, chastened. Mrs. Harbottle held her by the wrist. Roy winked at her and smiled. Esther nodded back, took a long drink of water, then signaled the serving woman for more. Good, nice, perfect. So this movie-star wife is a dream to my friend. She grew up by the seashore with a nanny and a gardener and blond curly hair like Shirley Temple that the nanny does up in a different ribbon every day. Roy gave the serving woman the tiniest glance. She summed it up. And my friend sees this beauty, is introduced to her by a priest, for godsakes, on her seventeenth birthday. And it doesn't matter that his father hasn't held a job in a decade, and that his mother is raising his eight brothers by sheer will. They haven't seen a loose nickel in the house since the Depression. Doesn't matter. He sees her. All is equal. He gets a summer job at a local seaside resort hotel tending bar. On Sunday nights he bribes the concierge to send three quarters of his earnings to his mother by Western Union, and uses the rest to take out the girl. Everything goes.

A year or so later the two are married. Very nicely. The priest who made the introduction does the honors. And when they come home from Bermuda, the girl's father sets up his new son-in-law as a vice president. And that's when we meet.

What is he? Vice president of your ass?

Roy didn't blink. Like a bird's, his head swiveled toward the perceived noise of this comment. No, said Roy, directly to Mrs. Harbottle, as if it were she who'd spoken, as if she'd asked for a little clarification. Roy almost addressed her by name, almost said: Ruth, dear, he was the director of marketing for a company that made safe products for children, things that wouldn't warp their minds or burst into flames or break and do bodily harm. But that would be overkill. So he just looked into Ruth Harbottle's eyes and said, Toys, a toy company. And within the year he'd bought his mother a house and was picking up the mortgage. Still the father never budged from the divan, didn't need to.

So what happens? The perfect setup, you know it. Two kids, girl, boy, a house on the water, everyone's happy, boy gets sick. Roy paused. He needed to say this right. He rested his thumb on the hand of God and tapped for a moment. His tongue checked again into the lower left quadrant. A kind of sick we barely know about. (This delivered to Senator Harbottle.) A kind of sick our government is just beginning to fund the answers to. And what next? This man, my friend, who is beside himself, as is his wife, though they are keeping the illness low-key, not too many people know, these two are in a kind of hell. But the good officers of the United States Attorney's office, Southern District, ignore that. They come to my friend, as they have come to so many others, others who by the way have not refused their invitation to testify. Roy didn't need to look at Albert to let this sink in, everyone knew that story. And when these officers, in a judge's chambers, ask my friend if he prefers to testify against me or to *lose his good standing,* that's the vernacular, he declines to testify. In fact, it goes further, he takes the stand on my behalf. You know this guy. I don't need to say his name. No need to mention names (this directly to Esther). So he takes the stand. And right after he steps down, he is arrested, on the spot, by federal marshals. This is a man, a loyal friend, the sole support of his mother, a loving husband, the father to a son who is gravely ill.

There was a long silence. Roy turned to the window, looked at the spotlit steps of the museum, it was pretty true what he'd said, mostly true, some telescoping here, some timing adjustment there. A couple of dramatic embellishments. It was close to ten o'clock. The cars sped below on Fifth Avenue when they got the chance. Roy turned back to the quiet room and said: And now that boy is dying and my friend is in jail, and nothing can be done. What kind of country is this where honesty and hard work and decency are punished like that. You tell me.

In the morning all the papers ran the story as if it were hard news. Roy sipped iced tea. He hadn't mentioned any names, made a point of that, but there was Will Clemens, spelled correctly, in boldface in every edition. A big mistake. A problem. But not one he could solve today. He'd call Charlie Peeko after noon and see if the boat was fixed yet. But only after twelve o'clock; he'd give the captain a chance to get it right.

June 4

The phone rang like crazy, but nothing from Will. Did he read the paper? Kay didn't know. The first thing she did was try to reach him. She went through the warden's office but got no further than a secretary, tired and unhelpful. Will would be very angry, Kay knew. He was on a business trip. And Bo was being tested for allergies. That's what they'd told almost everyone except, of course, the school, the first-aid squad, and the Maguires.

All day, lots of calls from odd people: the golf pro, Will's tailor, the owner of the hardware store, both town newspapers, Cecilia Gardella, chair of the local American Cancer Society. She wondered if Kay would speak at a luncheon.

Will's mother, Rita, had phoned, beside herself, and now she was on a train out of Baltimore on her way to Rumson. Nothing from Kay's father, and that silence made her sad. Even though he was cruising to some uncharted place off the coast of Sweden, even so, she'd rehearsed the vocabulary all day in her head. She could explain. He would understand if she told him everything. But now she was too wiped out.

Kay wrapped a dish towel around the receiver and dropped it on the kitchen table. Then eyed the buzzing lump, uncertain. Maybe she should keep the line open. What if the hospital tried to call? Maybe just five minutes of peace and then she'd put it back on. Five minutes. Carmen slipped by with a stack of freshly ironed sheets. Her father's housekeeper was on loan *until the little buster rallied.* Before Carmen left for the day, she'd cut up citrus fruit and bake a chicken.

Kay stepped out on the porch, pulled the door shut behind her, curled up in the corner chair, hugged a throw pillow tight to her chest. It smelled like onion grass. Lou-Lou probably had her feet all over it when Kay wasn't looking. Down across the water, Hank Ruddy steered his boat smack into the dock, a real moron. Basic spatial calculations eluded him. Her father was a true sailor. When would he take her sailing again, she missed that. They could go to Nantucket, sail off toward the blues, just like when she was a little girl. Pure heaven. But lately she brought a set of problems with her that he seemed unwilling to discuss. Ever since her mother died, he couldn't talk about illness, ever, not at all. So instead, he sent Carmen to do the laundry. And when Bo was first diagnosed, misdiagnosed, Kay said allergies, perhaps severe, and her father opened a line of credit. No questions asked, and she'd been grateful. But now she wanted his questions, she was ready, she needed to give him some answers.

I'm ready now, missus. Carmen stood with her purse on her arm. Oh my God. Where had all the time gone? Kay said, Good night, Carmen. Thank you. And ran into the kitchen to reconnect the telephone. She jabbed at the cradle a couple of times until she got a dial tone, then called Gert Maguire: I'm so sorry. I think I was abducted or something. Maybe Hank Ruddy swept me away and I didn't notice.

You'd notice. Don't worry, Lou-Lou's fine. She's watching some crap with the boys. You want her home?

Definitely. And Rita's coming.

Tonight?

Carmen made a chicken, I think.

I'll send something with Lou-Lou. No, I'll walk her over.

I'm building a monument to you right now.

Kay tapped at the phone again and dialed the hospital, hard to get through this late in the afternoon. They started serving dinner at four. Finally someone answered, breathless, and Kay asked to speak to Hollis, Bo's favorite nurse. Just listening to all the grind and screech made her throat constrict. What was wrong with her, had she fallen asleep? Hollis came on the line: Hey

Mrs. C.! How're you doing? She sounded happy to hear from Kay. Amazing.

Is everything okay? she asked, grateful for that happy voice, relieved, jealous, grateful. Is Bo okay?

Fine. Better. He ate a lot of dinner. He seems a little quiet.

Quiet? She'd come home very late the night before to be with Lou-Lou after all the upheaval, but Lou-Lou was at Gert's as usual, and she, Kay, was nowhere. Not with her son, her daughter, her husband, her father, herself. She tried to listen to the good woman who was speaking.

Yes, quiet, Hollis said. Easy. Sleepy.

Why sleepy.

A tiny fever, but it's down, much lower. He's better already.

Oh boy. I'll be right back in tomorrow. Will I see you, Hollis? I'll be here.

His grandmother will come with me. Probably. I'm not sure.

Well, good. Don't worry, Kay. Do you want to speak to Bo? Yes. Yes.

Always early, everywhere she went, Rita Clemens stood on the platform at the Red Bank train station and watched the commuters' wives drive up, park (engine idling), apply lipsticks, subdue children. The southbound 5:38 approached with a double hoot and clattering of gates. A sprig of music poured out of an Oldsmobile and was drowned out by the arriving locomotive. A swarm of men, some young and handsome, pointed faces to the cars. Women stepped onto the curb, pretty legs bare, bright lips curved to kiss the air. Others sat tight, looked over their shoulders for the quickest way out of this mess.

Five minutes later it was silent and still, just a whoosh of the occasional car passing. Kay probably had the time wrong. But Rita would not call the house or sit down on the bench. She watched the curve of the track ahead until it wound over the road, out of sight. Maybe she could get the train straight to Woeburne from here, see Will. She'd find out all that.

Just this morning at Staubitz's market, cold-cut order half filled, Patsy Staubitz pushed out the top of the Dutch door behind her husband's new slicer with a New York newspaper in her hand. She'd been waiting, her face like an open trap. Now Rita, don't be upset, she said. Too wound up by half. Rita straightened her handbag on her wrist, found her wallet to pay fast and go. She did not enjoy this side of Patsy, not much at all, though knew her to be better in other ways. Good to the school, helped out there. Said, Fine, Jay, that's plenty for today.

You won't have a scrap left by tomorrow! he said.

Leave it for now. And she had a ten-dollar bill on the counter. That'll be all. She'd make a meat loaf, and her husband could do sandwiches from it when he pleased.

All weekend he'll be working the back side of the old house on Treehorn Road, Rita said, you know that place. So I won't see him, it'll go bad.

Wait, Rita, you may find him home. You take a look here.

And this Patsy Staubitz had no children. That was part of it, and Rita understood. She took hold of the newspaper held out over the wet joint of ham. Patsy's face a step down now in satisfaction. A query burst open there. Rita could not answer until she saw and, when she did see, read her son's name in a story that made little sense, she felt only silence, which disappointed Patsy.

Rita read it again.

I can have this?

Patsy Staubitz nodded, then shook her head. Transaction concluded, and a few conclusions already reached about what Rita Clemens might be thinking just now, though she said nothing.

I'll just take what you've got, Jay.

No trouble. He scribbled a list of numbers on the brown paper, broke her bill, poured the change into her palm. Glanced to his wife. Her jaw opened a bit.

Rita found her husband at the far end of Treehorn Road, where the tar turned to dirt and the house he worked on looked made of patches of partial houses. Jack Clemens was at the top of an extension ladder, leaning into the uncertain chimney that was half crumbled onto a gambrel roof. Next winter a fire would be safe there. He could be relied on. Everyone knew to use him for these things.

Hey Cowgirl. Lou-Lou Clemens had her nose in Gert's side pocket, and it looked like she'd gained about ten pounds since the morning, was that possible? Kay kissed Lou-Lou's brown hair, took a sniff. Like a bad onion. She must be rubbing her head in the grass. Tub for you, lady. And all business.

Go. Go. Go, Gert said, as if cheering for a team, but Lou-Lou's nose stayed buried in her pocket.

Whatcha got in there?

Come on, pronto. Ann Louise. Get the lead out. Kay's voice had moved entirely out of the appeasing zone. Now.

Gert peeled Lou-Lou's face away from her jeans. Come on, turnip. Do what your mother said. Ta-dum.

Lou-Lou moved off at last toward the bath. Pink Danskin pants tight in the bottom, strained at the seam. Sweetheart, you need help?

Uh-uh.

I have a genius for reunions. Don't you think? Generally speaking, a mother with gifts. Kay poured two Scotches. Arranged five Ritz crackers on a plate.

Only a minute, said Gert. Got the menfolk gnawing at the furniture.

Red's home for dinner?

Did I tell you he's become a runner?

Like a track star?

Yes, but around the block, late at night, when he can't sleep. It's good for circulation and insomnia. So he says.

I didn't know he had insomnia.

Me neither.

Observant, madame, Kay said, and yawned wide.

I get in bed, I'm gone.

Lucky. I get in bed. That's a bad story. You don't want to hear it.

You're so right. Gert laughed a bunch of hiccups in a row, as if something was funny. Gert Maguire, next-door neighbor, childhood friend, the most faithful, unquestioning supporter during this whole nightmare. Kay could barely stand to look at her. Porch or den?

Porch. Then I gotta go.

Not a soul at the station besides Rita, standing like a statue by the bench. Kay angled the Thunderbird to the platform. Lou-Lou was out and running, arms wide, wet hair flopping, calling *Meemaw, Meemaw,* before Kay could get the gear shift into park. She assessed the hug as she put out her cigarette, waved the smoke out the window. They looked like weird twins. The kind of girl-child most likely to be produced by Jack and Rita Clemens was her Lou-Lou. Rita hugged Lou-Lou like she knew that, felt it herself. Gert had mentioned something about something the nuns had said about Lou-Lou feeling downcast and not really in line for a lot of attention, and so was acting up, in fact, had thrown her shoe across a room and hit someone. That would hurt. Already, and only nine years old, her feet were bigger than Kay's. Rita was built that way too, big limbs, strong hands. Kay brushed off her slim pink linen skirt and swiveled out of the car. Lou-Lou was becoming a hip-clinger. Mother! Let me help you!

Rita Clemens juggled an overnight bag and Lou-Lou all on one side. Kay caught Lou-Lou by the hand, shouldered the bag, and kissed Rita, touched the warm dark hair with her lips. In the car, Lou-Lou did all the talking and Kay looked ahead, trying to remember now what she'd planned to say.

* * *

Behind the door of the master bathroom, there was a long, narrow closet where Kay hid all the things she maintained her appearance with that she didn't want Will to see. She looked into that hidden inventory now, assessing. Trying to know what she could live without if she had to. She just didn't want to be here any more. She was thinking maybe it would be best to camp out somewhere neutral until Bo recovered. She'd lived in this house with Will for ten years, and everything she did here she'd done too many times before. If nothing else was obvious, it was that she needed to start thinking, start living, in new ways. She'd let go of some of these devices: depilatory kit, electric curlers, douche, hair color, manicure kit. She'd try natural, the way the kids were doing in California, see if that would clear her mind.

There was the lightest tapping sound in the bedroom, like a squirrel gnawing. Kay looked around. Rita stood in the doorway of the bedroom; when she saw Kay's face, she wriggled her fingers and took a seat on the slipper chair. So, she said. Rough times.

Not so bad.

Rita squinted at her like she was a lying child.

Not so good.

I want to help, so does Jack.

I know you do, I do. But I'm managing, it's working out.

We could take Lou-Lou with us.

Well, right now she's in school. And Gert's a good egg. And I'm back and forth. She'll be okay.

I could come here.

And leave Jack Clemens to fend for himself? Unlikely. That would be the end of me in his eyes. Kay closed the closet door.

Rita didn't answer. She brushed a speck from her lap.

We'll be okay, you'll see. And she noticed that Rita was watching her, not directly but in the side-view mirror over the vanity. She straightened her chin. Rita, you'll see.

What about a good lawyer. I know you don't put a lot of stock in anyone outside of New York, but we've got a man you two might consider, he's known Will since he was a baby. That might count for something.

Kay made a face like she was considering, but she was thinking about the time right after Will and she were married. She was almost nineteen. They were looking to escape Rita's house in Maryland on a Saturday morning when Jack Clemens woke up sour in the head, a mouth on him, from a lot of card playing the night before. Rita answered everything Jack said with a tap of her spatula against the skillet, a Morse code of displeasure. Then she said to Kay: Your father seems such a gentleman. Jack Clemens studied Will and his new bride sitting with a newspaper spread wide on the table. Jack looked like the source of his problem was just now occurring to him. Will took Kay by the arm and led her out through the backyards in the bright unbroken sun down to the boatyard behind some shack, to sit beneath a briny hull on two sawhorses. He rubbed sand on her knees; it smelled like chalk. You don't want this, said Will. But apparently she did.

And then he did something with his tongue, right in the boatyard, hidden away, her skirt pushed high on her hips, a poof around her waist. And he told her: Cunnilingus. Labia. That was funny. And that was their deal for a long time, he'd bring home whatever he could come up with, she'd let him show her, and she'd be surprised. What was he learning now.

Rita patted the silky trim on the slipper chair. What about Roy. What's this business about Roy.

I think Roy was just trying to help. Will's going to be mad now.

Mad? I should think so.

Maybe we should be thinking about sleep. A long day ahead, as they say.

It's only seven o'clock. Lou-Lou hasn't had dinner yet.

Yes, well.

Honey, I'm not trying to hurt you.

No, no, of course not.

Only one sliver of ice, shaped like a guitar pick, floated in the tumbler of Scotch. Kay lit a mosquito candle too late. Scratched at her neck. She could hear the knocking of a boat tied too loose down on the water. Probably Hank Ruddy's. The moron. It was midnight. Lou-Lou and Rita were sleeping, both in the guest room. She'd taken a peek to see, twin heads turned into the pillowcases. Lou-Lou looked happy.

Kay let the sliver of ice melt on the tip of her tongue. Outside the screen, in the blackness, she heard a crackle, pinecones underfoot, then a panting for breath. Jesus! She jumped up, spilled her drink down her blouse. The latch wasn't even hooked on the door. Jesus, who's there, she yelled really loud, maybe she'd wake up Gert.

Shh. Shh. Kay. It's me.

Me? Who the hell?

Red. Red. I'm sorry, jeez, really sorry. I just thought you were awake and everything.

Red?

Don't worry. I'm just out, that's all, and I saw you. How're you doing?

I don't know.

I haven't seen you in days. And I was thinking about you. About you guys, just how and stuff, things were going, and I hope.

Oh. We're fine.

Great. Great. Can I come in?

I'm on my way to bed.

Just a little water would be great. Red pushed through the screen door. Hair matted around his ears like he'd been licked. Face all damp.

You're soaked.

Ten rounds already. Here to McKim's and back.

Wait here.

Kay dumped her empty tumbler on the counter inside, then headed for the laundry to shed her blouse. She stunk now. She wiped the dampness from her chest with a towel. She stripped off her wet bra and looked in the dryer for something. Empty. Carmen would never leave an unfolded load inside. One of Will's old sweatshirts was in the ragbag. She took that out, it smelled like mothballs, which was better than Scotch.

She came back out with water for Red and more Scotch for her, but before she could hand it over, Red's own hands, like silky claws, hard and smooth and very big, were stroking with an emphatic upward push along her waist. Kay skittered back, again spilling. Hey. Quit it.

But Red kept on, took away the glasses. He sipped the Scotch, watching her eyes. And she was interested. For a moment she forgot to stop him, forgot to start screaming really loud, and wondered if she'd already awakened Rita, and what would that be like. Such a blankness started and the thought of Rita's tapping spatula. The boat knocking down below. But Red was pulling the sweatshirt away from her damp again skin, and again the hands found her waistband, and her belt loop, and the snap on her cotton shorts.

Wait. Wait just a minute here. But her neighbor was deaf and uninventive. He lifted her up, arms right around her hips, and carried her like a sack to the rod-iron sofa, and slid her onto the waterproof cushions, and pulled down her shorts and panties. Shorts, begone. He said that. And Kay laughed. But, really, this is, she said. Ridiculous.

And he dropped his own baggy shorts, looked made of plastic, and he was wearing a jockstrap which had angled his erection out to the high left. Kay couldn't say anything for the moment, let him peel that thing off and mount her, as if she had never learned a thing. She lay there with her legs splayed, thought maybe

I'm being repaired. That was the idea, an overdue maintenance, a clumsy repairman, but honest and adequate. She listened for her mother-in-law, for her friend, for her daughter. She closed her eyes and didn't look. Felt the hands laid tidy and warm and heavy around her breasts. Thought about starting over. Thought I am so beautiful he cannot believe I have come into his humble shop. Soon she would be a clean slate.

June 5

Will Clemens discovered a way to wet his soap and slowly, so not
to create a lather, get the bar to issue a slick, gelatinous sludge.
He could use it with the comb of his fingers to scoop his hair back
out of his eyes. When he first entered Woeburne two months ago,
it was like being inducted into the marines. He'd been hosed,
prodded, vaccinated, shaved, and barbered in a way that gave him
a moon face, but now his hair was growing back.

At the start he was also given a sack of personal goods and clothing. Some of which were replenished on a regular basis by fat
Pasteur—the housekeeper, they called him, the chief guard of cell
block *Kentucky,* where Will and the other executives were housed.
Every other Sunday, Pasteur delivered: one cake of pea-green soap
that smelled like bacon, four washcloths, two bath towels, a miniature unlabeled tube of aqua-colored tongue-burning toothpaste,
but no razors. Razors got a special treatment. Handles wrapped
in masking tape, owner's names written in Magic Marker, all kept
together in a wicker basket under lock and key.

Every day, after the eleven o'clock head count, Pasteur escorted
the eighteen men living on Will's cell block to the john and
brought the basket of razors with him. They shaved in silence,
looking into the long slab of marbled mercury above the sinks.
No talking allowed when the razors were in their hands. Once
Pasteur had collected them, rinsed and wiped, in his basket, they
were free to say something.

Will thought these precautions excessive for his group: the
short-termers, the accidentals, the compos mentis deluxe. But
Pasteur had trained with the mental defectives, which was the
majority population at Woeburne. This was the designated stopping place for New York criminals whose first motive was an

emotional disorder, not necessarily including malice. Some of the mental defectives were heartbroken. Pasteur had learned to be consistent in his methods, to be strict, and not to let any talking excite melancholy when a sharp edge was at hand. Razors were impossible to get, except out of Pasteur's basket, but everything else, and certainly soap, could be bartered for.

Kentucky block was located on the upper-right tier, overlooking the central atrium. A glass and iron ceiling arched twenty more feet above, and through the haze of thirty years of accumulated muck, *Kentucky* was often radiant with filtered sun and stippled blue skies. The dirt functioned like a scrim and subtly patterned the light that came through. Will thought the artists had anticipated just that. The whole place had been built by Works Progress Administration artists during the Depression. Woeburne was filled with odd details. But the sound could be appalling. Rain sounded like an atomic bomb, and hail like shrapnel fire, and this was a bad thing for the veterans among the mental defectives, which were almost all. Will was a veteran. Stationed in Korea, after the peace, as a mail courier. He carried letters in a canvas sack by bicycle from the airstrip to the mail table at the tiny base camp. Sometimes he sorted it and put it in the correct pigeonholes, sometimes he was busy and stuffed it into a locker in the room with the weight bench and barbell, never used. No one ever complained. It was more relaxing not to have a lot of news from home.

Right before his discharge, Will's sergeant was doing a few sit-ups to get in shape before going stateside, and he opened one of the lockers, just by chance, and the mail cascaded all around his feet. This was only a minor problem. The enlisted men read their old letters like novels. Will almost wanted to suggest something like that here at Woeburne. Novels were in short supply, worse than razors.

Will did not want to read his mail. It was the contrast that killed him. The blue-gray edge on Kay's notepaper, that's what made him want to find a razor, want to get very melancholy and raid Pasteur's basket. So he started a storage system. By chance, he procured an empty can from the mess where he worked— Persephone's cherries, one of those wild brands that must sell only to prisons and locked-down institutions, because on the open market no one would buy them. Companies where the product names were cribbed from the homework of high school students. Persephone's cherries were in fact red tasteless bulbs suspended in a sugar mulch. Brodie, the chief cook, liked to dump a few kilos into gelatin and call it dessert. But the label was even more perverse than the contents. A bent-over agrarian worker, clearly from nineteenth-century northern Europe, caught in a suspended wag of a backside like a cave entrance, huge and dark and U-shaped. This agricultural hussy had round hands like spoons with which she dug in a field. Cherries grow on trees. There were no trees on the label.

Will studied the huge brown-skirted backside. He would have put a single blossoming branch on side A, and on side B, the identical branch with fruit dangling, supple, ready for plucking. And maybe, but this might be pushing it, he'd put a dimpled hand reaching for, but not touching, the bottom-most dew-lapped globe. Illustrate *desire*. Better always than a fruit *in* the hand. But for now, into the existing can, Will consigned his unopened letters and his emphatic desire not to read them until he was out of here.

Most days Will's job doing food preparation in the kitchen was so boring that the seconds multiplied and crammed into each other in such a way as to cause an explosion of unconsciousness. He was seized by the need to sleep. Outside the dry-goods pantry, against a back wall, pallets of canned food, clams in brine, ravioli, and fruit, were stacked ten feet high with access alleys in between. Just the cocoon of metal and wood, a little resting place, a man on the lookout might see. Will was not exactly indispensable. His schedule, as he knew from his brief time in industry, was counterproductive. He worked for about two hours, just getting into the rhythm of peeling carrots and potatoes for a thousand, when he was called for a head count upstairs, and the daily shave. He returned in time to serve lunch, leaving the vegetables to oxidize in piles, carrots turning leathery, potatoes brown. Back to *Kentucky* after lunch to be counted again. He didn't return to the cavernous underground kitchen until two or later to finish off the work. By three o'clock, frustration with the shoddy quality of his labor made him crave sleep. The uncountable seconds and the stairs and the high dark brick vaulted ceiling all conspired. There, in between the pallets, he could rest.

There was a jokester at Woeburne named Sammy Finlandor who had a bit of a crush on him. Will was savvy about these things, knew all the signs from his stay in Korea. And he took a middle line. Loneliness likes attention, and Will was lonely. Sammy Finlandor looked at Will with eyes that watched and appreciated, and took in the wave of Will's soaped black hair and the curve of his lip. Will felt a little better just to have a watcher. He trusted Sammy, a fellow exec, a fellow kitchen aide, not to give him any trouble. And when he slept between the pallets, he felt, as much as he felt anything, that Sammy might even warn him if trouble came by. He felt the wedge of insurance a bit of awe provided.

One day Sammy Finlandor was rinsing off the mountain of carrots and potatoes alone. This always took at least an hour, and by the time forty-five minutes had elapsed, Sammy was ready to renew the verve that watching Will Clemens's wily hands slipping white lumps beneath the spray brought. This is how Will understood what happened, what he explained to himself later. Sammy said the devil made him do it. Made him tiptoe past old Chef Brodie's dessert station, where red globs plopped into steaming vats of Jell-O, and made him finger one empty can of Persephone's cherries. Sammy rinsed the pilfered item under the spray intended for potatoes, not easy to do unnoticed, because the can was the size of a portable latrine. He filled it up with water. On the highest pallet of clams in brine, Sammy deployed his joke.

He perched the can on the southwest corner above Will's innocent sleep cove. Sammy attached a string to the toe of Will's perfectly polished prison-issued oxford with rubber sole. He made a
gentle incision in the rubber with a potato peeler, creating a flap
that would irritate Will for the remainder of his stay. He tied the
other end of the string around the horizon line on the label. The
prank was only mildly successful. When Will's dreams of ships
tipping and rolling caused his own feet to mimic the motion, the
can toppled, as intended, soaking only his socks and shoes.

Will carried the offending can attached to him upstairs to *Kentucky* for the four o'clock head count. He rolled the can under his
cot into the shadow and stood in his doorway until Pasteur
hobbled by, giving him the nod. Then he worked to detach the
string from the nicked rubber sole. By the time he found a dry
pair of socks and curtailed the damage to the polish on his shoes,
Will could see a good use for the can. This was his chief strength,
really, as Will saw himself. He had so many weaknesses, things
he had to persuade himself not to ruminate on. In so many ways
he was a terrible person. He knew that. Look at all the suffering
he had caused around him. Like a pied piper of misery. But one
good thing about Will: Given a moment, he could always spot
the most elegant use for something. The simplest idea, always the
best. And he could find it when everyone else was getting complicated and calling it thinking.

~

It had been a year, maybe more, since Rita had seen her grandson. She scanned back over that time for clues, things that might
have signaled what had happened to him. That's what the shock
did. She loved Bo and was with him, but at the same time her
mind flipped through past moments like a deck of cards: phone
calls, canceled plans, odd tones of voice, strange weather, air smelling wet and decayed. All the clues that might have been there
that she hadn't noticed. And each possible clue had emotions like
colors, said she could choose this one and run with it: anger, grief,
guilt, fear. Anger again. She'd been deceived, over and over. But
that was a gaudy choice to make.

Bo's eyelashes had become transparent where they'd once been
a sandy blond around his gray-blue eyes; now the white lashes
were sparse and delicate. Blue veins traced beneath the nearly
translucent skin of his face and scalp. She sat with him at a low
green plastic table in the waiting area of the pediatric treatment
clinic three floors below his hospital room. She smoothed out
sheets of construction paper. Out by the elevators, Kay was in the
phone booth, calling Roy. And Rita didn't know why. Hadn't he
done enough harm? But she couldn't get through to Kay. That
was taking time.

Rita showed Bo how to cut a chain of paper dolls. And now he
was the angry one, impatient. His white fingers wound through
the purple plastic blunt-tipped scissors and cut wildly. Each time
he finished a little stack of men, he'd snip the hands apart. He
couldn't understand how to keep the paper men together.

Here Bo. Look here, kiddo.

No. I'm stupid. Bo tossed the scissors. They bounced on the
blue linoleum. His bloodshot eyes looked teary.

There's a trick. We'll do it together. Like this.

There weren't any other children waiting. When Kay left to make her call, two little girls, both outpatients, had Bo giggling. Now Rita could see them through the glass barrier, inside, lying in leather loungers that looked like dentist's chairs. Their mothers sat beside them, one read *McCall's,* the other closed her eyes and chewed gum.

Rita picked up the scissors, made the gesture of dusting them off. Come on, baby doll. Bo let his grandmother put her worn-looking fingers on his, let her work the scissors through the folded paper with him. What happened to your skin, Meemaw?

I don't know, sweetheart, here, here's the place we leave alone so we keep the fold. That's how they stay together. There you go.

Bo pulled apart a row of barrel-bodied men, four of them with flat heads.

Now you can color them any way you want. Rita pushed a bright yellow bucket full of peeled and broken crayons over to Bo.

Kay made her first try for Dan Dunlop, the finder-keeper, the man who actually got things done in Roy's office, before seven this morning. Always in first, always available; today, for once, he was impossible to reach. So she hopped the 8:12 train to Manhattan anyway, with Rita and her suitcase. At every pay phone from the Red Bank train station to New York Hospital, Kay tried to get an answer.

She stopped pacing in front of the elevators and looked at the wall clock, 11:25. Bo's test would be soon. Any minute, Hollis would stick her head out the door and say: Where are you! And then it would be a while before she could call Dan again.

But now some other melodrama was unfolding in the phone booth. Kay let a woman use the telephone, and she wasn't giving it back. This made Kay furious. This made her throat prickle, like only a good scream would relieve the itch: This phone is for emergencies, not for conversations! She wanted to interrupt the subdued sobbing and say hurry, hurry, for godsakes, just hurry. You can do that at home. What would she do with Rita if Dan didn't get them a hotel room? She couldn't take her back to New Jersey. She needed to stay away from New Jersey for a little while, for everyone's good.

The door peeled open on the booth, and the small woman in the cream-colored dress stepped out and blocked the entrance while she dug in her bag for a handkerchief. Oh, she said and looked up at Kay, searched her eyes. Kay stood as still as she could, tried to keep the recoil out of her face. She could not do this. She wouldn't be the catcher for this woman's heartache. Forget it. The woman found the handkerchief, blue-and-gray-striped, it belonged to a man. She put it up against her face like she was breathing in chloroform. Thank you, she said to Kay, looking down, thank you very much, and she stepped over to the elevator doors as if waiting, but didn't push the button.

Kay moved into the booth, closed the door, sat down, closed her eyes, lifted the receiver, depressed the button with her wedding-ring finger, started counting backward from fifty, at thirteen she opened her eyes, dropped the dime, and began dialing the number of Roy's office for the thirteenth time that day. Alice, the receptionist, picked up on the fifth ring.

Alice, Alice, Alice, it's Kay Clemens, give me Dan, will you?

Dan Dunlop came on the line all nervous cheer: Kay, my girl! How's everything? I'll bet *you* have some questions.

Dan, I just need a hotel room for tonight, maybe longer, and I have Will's mother with me.

Tonight?

Right, said Kay. She opened and closed the seashell clasp on her purse.

Um. Well. I'll call the St. Regis. Just like before.

What do I do?

Nothing. Meet me there at five, how's that? said Dan. Is that going to be all right?

Kay could hear someone in his office talking loudly. In her closed-in booth, with all the pebbled glass, it sounded to her as if someone were standing on a mountain and yodeling, the sound echoed and bounced in her ear: Dan, Dan, Dan.

Someone wants you. Is that Roy?

No. No problem. All right, five it is, glad to hear from you, Kay. Ciao.

Ciao, Kay said, good-bye, and she put down the receiver, sat for a moment, then pushed out of the booth. The woman in the cream-colored dress had vanished.

In the children's waiting room, someone had kicked over the toy box. Kay stepped on a pink hollow cube and crushed it. Plastic pieces were scattered everywhere, banked up against the furniture. Did you do that, Bo?

No. The twins did it.

The twins?

Look. Bo held up a loop of orange cutouts.

Beautiful! Kay cupped Bo's head with her hands, stroked the peach fuzz. You did that yourself?

Yup.

Wow. How're things, Meemaw?

I think we're doing just fine here, isn't that right?

Bo nodded and pressed the men flat on the table. Colored one of the heads aquamarine blue over the orange. Kay took a seat at the tiny table, decided not to pick up any toys. Just like Lou-Lou, said Bo, coloring one leg forest green.

She misses you, guy. We've got to get you home to see her.

Hollis leaned into the door. Hey there, partner. We're ready for you. Sexy, lovely girl, Kay thought, done up in her cowboy boots, a bright red sweater beneath the standard clinic smock. Today Hollis had made a special trip down from ten, Bo's usual ward, to assist. The last time they'd tried this test, a lumbar puncture to check spinal fluid, he'd gotten so hysterical they had a hard time getting a clear result. Bo loved Hollis. They hoped he'd stay calm with her present. How we doing? Whatcha got there, Bo? Hollis straightened up and smiled at Rita, smiled perfect, even teeth, everyone was crazy about Hollis.

Rita tipped out of her toddler chair, stood up, found her balance. She glanced at Kay, *you're not going to like this,* then gave Hollis the direct question. Give me the straight dope here, what's the story with my grandson?

Oh, boy, do I see the resemblance, said Hollis, looking only at Rita, especially the eyes, and she smiled.

Just tell me, please.

Well, Bo is very sick, but we keep looking for ways to help. His program is experimental, anything that might make a difference, he's first in line. Hollis paused, nodded, watched Rita's face. Today is mostly a test, a marker to check for progress. We'll take a sample of his spinal fluid, and while he's under a local, we'll give him vincristine. It's a chemotherapy.

Rita looked back at Kay. It wasn't much different from what Kay had said already.

Everyone here thinks a lot of Bo. I'll show you some other things he made, later, if you like. Hollis pulled a plastic cap out of her pocket and began fitting it over her ponytail.

No, said Bo.

Kay, said Hollis, ripping open a packet of sterile gloves, could you give me a hand?

Come on, sweetheart, said Kay, she bent down to lift Bo out of the chair. He wrapped his feet around the blue plastic legs. Come on, honey, you've done this a million times.

No, said Bo, and he started to whimper, his face flushed and bright.

What is it? Rita asked. What's wrong?

Hollis waved to someone down the hall, called out, Okay, then turned back to Rita: It's the test, he doesn't like it, no one does.

Right, Bo? But we'll be quick, and then it will be all over. You'll see. Dr. Fred is waiting.

Bo was breathing hard and blinking back tears. Kay frowned and knelt down next to him, pulled him to her. Come on, angel, I'll go with you, come on now. Bo looked into Kay's face and she lifted him into her arms and stood up. Hey, ballet! She carried her small, beautiful son past Rita, past Hollis, to the procedure area down the hall off the main space. She would never forgive herself for this.

Dr. Fred followed her in. Kay, he said. Hello, Bo. Let's see. He placed Bo up on the examining table. He held a penlight to Bo's left eye, which had cleared, was looking better, much better, Kay wanted to hear. Looks good, pal. Let's—see—the—other, ah, good. Dr. Fred needed a lot of room. He moved around the table to the back. Kay stepped aside, keeping her smile on Bo. Maybe you could wait outside, Kay? Nope. Dr. Fred inhaled. Okay. Hollis? Give me a gauze pad. Right there, in the left drawer. Thanks. He wiped his glasses, tossed the pad in the waste pail. Bo, could you let go of Mommy's hand? Bo was shivering, said, I'm hungry. We'll get you something good to eat as soon as we get back upstairs, Hollis said, I'll call the kitchen. Bo, could you let go of Mommy and lie on your side for me? Good. Kay stepped around Dr. Fred to the head of the examining table.

The room was hot and smelled like too much disinfectant. Kay crouched lower so Bo could see her face without turning his head. Scissors soaked in a blue fluid just to her left. Just like at the barber, she said. Sweetheart, she said. Bo watched her eyes. Kay smiled at him, thought of a lullaby in her head. Dr. Fred lifted Bo's pajama top and pulled the elastic on the trousers. Hollis? Dr. Fred said. Hollis got a sheet. Laid it at the foot of the examining table, shimmied Bo's pajama bottoms off, then covered his legs. You okay there, slugger? Dr. Fred lifted the sheet to swab the skin over Bo's lowest vertebrae. His spine was a little reef of bone. He was so frail. Kay looked into his eyes. Sweetheart. And Bo watched back. Frightened.

Hollis handed Dr. Fred the syringe, and quicker than Kay could change her expression, the anesthetic had gone into Bo's hip, and he was shrieking. A burn flashed out under his skin, and she hadn't warned him. Bo screamed, but Hollis had anticipated it, and she held his hips firm and rubbed down the muscle. They waited for the numbing to set in, then a second needle bored into the bone. Bo cried and said they were breaking his back, Hollis held him tight, Dr. Fred withdrew the plunger and the barrel filled with fluid. Bo screamed and Kay wanted to scream right along with him. She swallowed her horror and put her face down to his. Touched his cheek. You'll be okay. Very soon. You'll be okay. The hurt will stop in a minute.

The third needle was only a pressure to Bo, and his crying softened, his breathing settled. Hollis looked away, lifted her hands from Bo's hips. It had been a clean take. Nothing had gone wrong. Hollis put a sterile strip on Bo and gently, carefully wrapped him in a cotton blanket. There you go. He might fall asleep, Kay.

Kay had her head resting next to Bo's. Kay kept saying yes, yes. Yes, what? Hollis said. Let me get you a chair, Kay. Dr. Fred opened the door to leave. I'll see you in a little while. Kay stood up, hand on Bo's head, his eyes were closing already. Yes, thank you, she said. She would go crazy. She was crazy already. Here, Mommy. Hollis came back holding a red chair. Here, you sit until he falls asleep, and then we'll move him upstairs.

Outside in the children's waiting room, Rita said a novena straight to the Blessed Virgin. She had a small, creased prayer book pressed flat on the table next to the cutout colored-in men. Hollis brought Rita water in a paper cone.

On the sidewalk just beyond the entrance to New York Hospital, Mrs. Millstein, the Sabrette hot-dog lady, was open for business as always, even though it had been raining off and on all day. Kay relied on her.

Adorable dress. Mrs. Millstein waved her tongs at Kay's blue linen. Such a nice girl, said Mrs. Millstein, nodding. She searched out a cream soda for Rita from the ice chest. In my location, I know.

You getting any customers in this mess, Mrs. Millstein? I'll take a Tab, if you've got one.

See what I mean? A gem!

Oh! Oh! Wait! Kay yelled and leaped off the curb and into the stopped traffic on York Avenue. A Checker cab was dislodging an elderly passenger on the other side. Kay ducked in and out of four lanes of cars and made it to the curb just as the light changed.

She's gonna get herself killed that way! And over a cab ride. Better to wait and take your chances, I always say.

Kay slapped her hand on the wet hood of the taxi as if to hold it in place. She waved to Rita. Come on!

Now, don't you do what she did. Mrs. Millstein took back the cream soda. No charge, you didn't open it. She pointed with the can. There's the crosswalk, that's what it's there for.

When the light changed again, Rita crossed the avenue holding her small suitcase in her arms like a baby.

Inside the cab Kay directed the driver to the St. Regis Hotel and sat back in the seat just as it started to pour again. They were a little early, but not much. Rita patted down the dark fabric around her knees. She looked done in. A drink, a bath, a bed. Kay knew the drill. And the sooner, the better. Upstairs in Bo's room, Rita had been perfect, lining up all the Snoopies for magic tricks and jokes. And when Bo dozed off for good, they tiptoed out, two leaden fairies. She'd get Rita squared away, then come back to the hospital in time for the test results. If she didn't loiter, things got lost, delayed, Kay believed that still.

What kind of a name is Hollis for a Catholic girl? Rita gave Kay an anxious look.

You think she's Catholic?

She *told* me, said Rita.

Well, she can call herself truck or pinecone or Achilles. She's a godsend. She's the best thing going in that hospital.

Rita nodded, leaned against the door, looked out through the downpour.

I'm sorry. Kay touched her hand. You know what? I think it helps her. It helps to have a strange name.

Rita patted Kay's hand in return. You must be planning to visit Will on Monday.

Monday?

And I'd like to go with you. If that's all right. I'd like to do that.

Kay put her fingertips to her mouth.

His birthday?

Yes, of course. Kay nodded. But I'm not going. No. Will definitely wouldn't want it.

That can't be.

It's true. But maybe we could try to reach him tomorrow. There are certain times to call. We could make sure to do that.

Rita said nothing and studied Kay's steady eyes and then her profile and then, when she turned completely away, the back of her head. Rita looked at Kay, at the streaky blond hair, all sunlight even in this dismal old cab on a gray day, and felt she understood very little about this girl. Nothing at all, really, after all these years. They rode the next ten blocks in silence.

On Fifth Avenue, Kay checked her wallet for cash. Two days ago Jerry Henderson had called from the bank to raise a flag, that's what he said, Just raising a flag here, Kay, just thought you needed to know. He would cover everything she'd already written, but she'd have to sell something. Just give him a buzz when she had her ducks in a row. The windshield wipers barely cleared the glass. Mother of God, said the cabbie. Did you ever see so much water?

The doorman at the St. Regis unfurled the tent-size umbrella over Rita's bent head as Kay grabbed the bags. Here, she said, leading Rita to the first silk chair inside the revolving door, here, sit and dry off, I'll see if our room is ready. Kay stepped across the marble floor to the gold and ivory front desk, manned by a tall, thin boy whose bad complexion made his lips crack in the corners. Kay looked to his eyes, away from the mess of his face, and said her name. He pulled open the register and sighed. I'm afraid not, Mrs. Clemens.

There must be some mistake. Perhaps Mr. Dunlop put the reservation in his own name. He called for me. He called to make the booking. Mr. Daniel Dunlop.

No. I'm afraid not.

But you aren't looking.

Mrs. Clemens.

Perhaps Mr. Franklin, the manager, could help me.

Mr. Franklin will return next Monday and will certainly help you.

Kay read the name engraved on the gold band dipping from his lapel: Crispin Philpot.

Mr. Philpot, we haven't met before, but I'm a frequent guest at the St. Regis.

Mrs. Clemens, you are not a guest of the St. Regis today. He turned away to fluff a waiting flower arrangement.

A small ring of pain began to throb behind her right eye. She glanced back at Rita, who slumped into the silk madrigals and reindeer. Kay had about fourteen dollars in cash. Her father was on a cruise on the Baltic Sea. Her husband was in prison upstate. Her son was unconscious in the hospital twenty blocks north. Her daughter was eating herself into a linebacker on the Jersey Shore. Her mother-in-law was losing her bearings in the lobby of a hotel run by a scarred teenager in his apprentice course on abuse of power. These inventories were not helpful. She pushed her wet hair off her forehead. I'll be back, Mr. Philpot.

Kay knelt down in front of Rita and touched her knees, the hem of her dress soaked despite everything. Well, I'd hoped for martinis in bed. Rita patted her hand. But I think instead we might check out the cathedral. It's only a couple of blocks away. And it will be warm and dry. In the meantime, I'll find out from Dan what the snag is here.

Is there a problem? Maybe I could do something.

No. No.

Kay parked their bags with the doorman and gave him ten of her fourteen dollars. Lofted her cardigan above Rita's head and sailed down Fifth Avenue until they gained the side entrance of St. Patrick's. The vestibule was slick and dark and damp, but inside, Mass was already in progress. Incense spiraled down from the altar, the priest in plain green silks climbed the pulpit for the homily. Rita found a pew up close. Kay whispered that she'd return when she'd sorted things out and left Rita there. Outside, beneath the dripping eaves, she smoked four cigarettes and watched the rain pour down.

Now well past the appointed hour, Kay let the doorman battle the elements to get her back inside the St. Regis, where she hoped to find Dan Dunlop. The lobby was deserted, even Crispin Philpot had abandoned his post. A bellhop slunk into shadow and vanished. Then, in a distant corner, tucked away from the potential bustle of the entrance and front desk and elevators, Kay spotted one foot tapping, like the movement of a cat. A shiny black patent-leather loafer tapped away, visible just beyond the bounds of the high green sofa. She edged closer and craned around the velvet curve. It was Roy. Head wrapped in a pair of puffy earphones. He spoke in a whisper into a full-size microphone connected by a thick cord to a black plastic box in his lap.

What are you doing here? Kay touched his shoulder. What are you doing?

Kay. Darling. Roy pushed the plastic box and the microphone and the headset aside. Come and sit down. You're here. Sorry. Listen, you're here. Sit. Sit down. What do you think? Frank Reilly's idea. Better than a pad and very portable. Where's Rita? Roy waved toward the front desk. He stood and waved. Crispin Philpot rose up from behind the counter and scuttled across the marble floor. So, said Roy, tell me everything.

There's a big problem here, Kay said.

Not really.

She looked mid-lobby to the frown looming toward her on Crispin Philpot's face. Here he comes, she said, he's not very nice.

How important is personality, really. When you get right down to it. Net-net.

What are you talking about?

Roy pointed to an alligator briefcase by his feet. Without a word, Crispin Philpot bent toward it like a lover. Kay watched him carry the case away and suddenly felt she would cry, almost like a sneeze coming. She touched the sleeve of Roy's jacket, just to hold something. What is this? I've never seen anything like it.

Summer-weight angora. Esther's idea. Itches like the devil.

Very bunny.

Don't let Esther hear you say that. He glanced toward the wall as if afraid. He glanced at tall Crispin Philpot entering the service elevator with the alligator valise. Esther only likes to know I look distinguished. Anything else gets the wooden ear.

In general, Roy liked mothers. He liked his own mother very much, and he was partial to other mothers, gave them the benefit of the doubt. Almost always. There were probably some exceptions. But while Will was in this time of inconvenience, Roy had been making it up to him, sending little things to Rita Clemens, subtle things so she wouldn't always know. And he'd covered a couple of—not exactly indiscretions, but lapses, for Jack Clemens as well. This was Dan's job, and he was good with the details.

When Roy went to find Rita, he entered St. Patrick's Cathedral through the chancel. It was an entrance not too many people knew about, mostly used by brides and clergy and actually inconvenient in the rain, but Roy used it anyway. Rita didn't see him coming. Mass was over, and Rita was walking the stations of the cross. Marking time before some very graphic depictions of a very violent story. Roy didn't really get the appeal. The Jews did it better, he thought. Installed directly in the blood cells. If you were looking for a good time on this earth, in this life, look elsewhere. He felt it in himself, but a lot of him didn't believe it. A low-level conflict.

Poor Rita Clemens turned a face as wretched as anything carved on the wall. Oh Roy, she said. How could you.

Rita, dear. He gestured toward a pew. That boy, that mother's son, convinced her to sit where he pointed. Just to give him a minute of her time.

All right, she'd listen to what he had to say.

They edged together, all the way in, close to the column, in full view of the altar and the acolyte in white surplice who snuffed each gold-tipped candle. Roy held Rita's hand still in his own.

Mostly what he wanted to say was this: There was a vendetta, she knew what that meant. It was aimed at him, not Will, from high places, she knew who they were. As hard as that was to believe, it was true. And her son had done the right thing, resisted irresistible pressure, and in doing so, had taken a fall. This was not to save Roy's hide, as some had suggested. His skin wasn't worth a minute of Will's time. Will had done what he did because he was a decent man who couldn't be forced to lie. Roy would not forget. No matter what happened, even if he himself was in jail, as a lot of people were predicting, he might even say hoping, and for a lot longer than Will Clemens. Roy would not let this brave thing her son had done become a faded, forgotten memory. Did Rita understand?

Rita Clemens waited a long time before she nodded.

Bo was lucky enough to get Mrs. Westerfield for his first-grade teacher at Holy Cross. Although Bo had attended school for only fifteen full days, and it was June, he was still a favorite with Mrs. Westerfield. Lou-Lou knew that. If Mrs. Westerfield lined up her class in the yard at the end of recess, she'd take her eyes off the malcontents, the troublemakers, and say: Hello Lou-Lou! And how's our Bo doing? Lou-Lou would always answer that Bo was doing very well, thank you. And Mrs. Westerfield would smile in a very special way, a prayerful way, as if she were a saint showering down a few blessings on Lou-Lou, malcontent, troublemaker, to be transmitted to Bo, her brother.

Lou-Lou soaked up all the good attention she could get, but she knew—couldn't help but know—that Mrs. Westerfield didn't care for her half as much as she did for Bo. Lou-Lou had been transferred from Sister Charitina's first grade into Mrs. Westerfield's class two years before because Sister Charitina was getting older. She looked to be about ninety, and she had no tolerance for loud, obstreperous, joke-telling little girls. When Lou-Lou landed in Mrs. Westerfield's lap, she knew she was in the right place because Mrs. Westerfield was so beautiful. Her beehive hair was salt- and-pepper-colored, she had strong crinkles around her brown eyes, and she was bone-thin, a wire hanger, with legs she twined around each other when she sat in the low chair during reading time. No one sat in her actual lap because she was too skinny. But Lou-Lou often imagined herself there, cradled in the plaid of her skirt, touching the hem. In reality, Lou-Lou was often in the corner, or out in the hallway, or waiting to see Sister Mary Arthur, the principal.

Lou-Lou was fat, or at least that's what her mother said, and that was another reason Mrs. Westerfield preferred Bo, who was vastly underweight, just the way she was. Sometimes Lou-Lou wondered if Mrs. Westerfield was sick too, and the thought brought tears, tears that bordered on a drag-down kind of crying. She wouldn't start because it would be very hard to stop, so if it happened during chapel, if she saw Mrs. Westerfield's bony white hand touching the head of some good boy, Lou-Lou would lay her own head down on the pew in front of her and pray first not to cry and then to be thin someday so that Mrs. Westerfield would like her too.

When Bo started school, it was a big production. Mrs. Westerfield even got Mrs. Oates, the principal's assistant, to watch her class *on the first day of school* so that she could talk things over with Lou-Lou's mom, get to know Bo in a special way. But Lou-Lou knew Bo was just not that interesting. He didn't talk much. He liked to make models but not paint them. He put decals on instead. In a fort situation he was useless, couldn't build, couldn't guard. He was good at card games, especially war and old maid. He was patient with clay, seldom squished things halfway through an idea. He had a good laugh, that was a very good thing about him, she had to admit, but still.

And now Bo had the worst attendance record in the entire history of Holy Cross School. And everyone loved him anyway. At least in the lower school, kindergarten through third grade. He was like a movie star. Sister Mary Arthur liked to lead decades of the rosary about him over the loudspeaker. She'd hitch on to the microphone like she was leading campfire songs: All right now, boys and girls, here's one for Bo. The third-graders, Lou-Lou's classmates, and the whole rest of the school all had to stop what they were doing and recite out loud, standing still beside their desks, hands pressed together, fingertips pointing to the ceiling. There were some kids who liked it, Anthony Hoffman, Catherine McCarthy, who felt they were doing some saintly stuff, but for the most part, Lou-Lou got slit-eyed, unhappy looks during these sessions and people didn't talk to her much in the yard, besides Mrs. Westerfield, that is.

One day in January, Bo had been well enough to come to school. So at lunchtime their mom brought him in. Kay found Lou-Lou sitting on the end of the slide stuffing snow into her boots. What are you doing?

Nothing.

Why don't you run around a little, that's what recess is for. Did you drink your Tab?

Lou-Lou nodded.

Bo is with Mrs. Westerfield.

Lou-Lou scanned the play yard but couldn't see them.

I want you to help Bo on the bus this afternoon, you have to take care of him, he's never been on it before. Gert will pick you up at the stop because I have to do some bank stuff. Okay? Okay. And listen, if Rufus comes? You tell Sister Mary Arthur right away. He doesn't work for us anymore. You are not to talk to him. I love you, run around a little.

Her mother's car coat had a nice swing to it, like a bell, ding-dong, ding-dong, all the way across the yard to her Thunderbird. Her mother was thinking hard with her head down and forgot to wave. Lou-Lou put some more snow in her boots.

At a quarter to three Mrs. Westerfield arrived with Bo, leading him by the hand. Bo looked tired. His baseball hat was on crooked, and before she handed him over to Sister Barbara, Mrs. Westerfield straightened out the brim, pulled it tight on his skull. Good-bye, little soldier, she said, as if she wouldn't see him again for a long time, which turned out to be true, then she kissed him on each cheek. Bo smiled and laughed, his good laugh. So even though Mrs. Westerfield was already halfway out the door, she had to pirouette, do an about-face. She ran back to Bo and swept him up in her arms and hugged him tight, a rocking, swaying hug with an extra kiss on the landing. She nodded a brief military nod at Sister Barbara, then disappeared. The class was speechless, Lou-Lou most of all. No one had ever seen Mrs. Westerfield pick up anything larger than an eraser, much less a *child.* Bo was the only one unmoved by this, he just smiled and waved at Lou-Lou: There she was! He shuffled down the aisle to her desk. Lou-Lou could barely remember her own name at the moment. Mrs. Westerfield. Mrs. Westerfield. Lou-Lou stood to give Bo her seat. Sister Barbara signaled her row. Lou-Lou went to the closet to collect her coat. She put on her wet boots. She felt like crying, but this was a bad place to start. When her class was ready to line up for the bus, she took Bo by the hand. He wasn't wearing any mittens. She searched his pockets and found the blue ones. Here, Bo, she said.

Ann Louise Clemens, are you shopping for a detention? We can keep the whole class here until you finish your discussion. Then Sister Barbara let them go.

On the bus, Lou-Lou found an empty seat for the two of them near the back. She sat by the window because she wanted to look out and ignore people as much as possible. Everyone, especially the big kids, the fifth- and sixth-graders, stared at them getting on. Everyone always stared at them when they were together, she was fat, he was thin. Lou-Lou ignored them.

The bus started in silence, but then in an instant the shrieking began, yelling, screaming kids fighting, then someone, some big boy, took Bo's hat. He tossed it forward and someone caught it and tossed it higher, up toward the front. Bo's little bluish hands were up on his scalp. Oh, oh, he said, get it, Lou-Lou, and Lou-Lou looked ahead. It was Marky Kennedy. Hey Telly Savalas, he said, hey Yul Brynner, hey Easter egg, and Bo cried, and Lou-Lou sat still. She saw the hat, now all dirty with slush on the rubber-grooved mat of the aisle. The hat was smashed there, up near the bus driver. Marky Kennedy, star of the sixth-grade basketball team, kicked it back two rows: Hey golf-ball head, hey! What's the matter with your brother, you eat all his food? Lou-Lou didn't say anything. You eat all his *hair*? She kept still. Bo cried and cried, he was starting to cough with his crying, it was the bad dragging cry she tried to avoid always. Bo was crying. Ping-Pong head. Pool ball. Bo cried harder, then he was choking. Before Lou-Lou knew it, Bo was throwing up all over her uniform, all over her boots. His mittens were soaked and there was blood there, too. He's sick! He's sick! the big boys yelled to the driver. Pull over. And Lou-Lou held on to Bo's head. Stop, Bo, she whispered, it was the only thing she said. And he kept crying until the police came and the ambulance and their mother.

June 6

Esther Kinder and Merrill Mandel stretched out on the long curved white leather cushion at the stern of the *Wavemaker II*. Both wore tiny bikinis, something Esther had mailed in from France, *in an envelope,* that was the trick. The bikinis were made of blue airmail paper. At the boat basin, this seemed inappropriate. Roy thought maybe Captain Charlie Peeko should be issuing some kind of dress code, a what-to-wear-on-board statement. Roy was too weary to do it himself.

All night he'd been up with Dan Dunlop and Frank Reilly. Looking at briefs. Depositions. Back issues of *Esquire.* In a week they'd be back in court. They were trying to find a way out of the hole the prosecution had been making deeper and deeper since the mistrial in April. Now he needed a break. You just took a break, said Dan. Call me if you have a problem, said Roy.

Roy had a summer cold. Muddy had a cold. Frank Reilly had a cold. Kay, he didn't want to think about Kay. He had to work something out there. Not a good situation. Charlie Peeko came up on deck with the sandwiches and the Tabs. What were they waiting for? Engine trouble, but soon they'd be pushing off. Fine, said Roy. And picked up a sandwich and peeled back the protein bread. What is this? He plucked a little green caper from the mush. Roy popped it in his mouth, then spit it out. Disgusting! You trying to cover something up?

A change of pace, that's all.

No changes necessary, Captain. We can forget about changes.

Roy was bored. He had to admit it, and if no one else was coming on this small adventure, it hardly seemed worth doing. You think we should call Kay?

Of course we should call Kay, said Merrill. She raised a small pale hand to shade her eyes. Do I think she'll want to come sit in this inferno? No, I do not. Merrill frowned at Roy like he'd personally delivered the heat and humidity.

I suppose you're right. Anyone else?

And that child should be with her mother.

What are you talking about? Kay's at the hospital day and night.

I mean the other child, Lou-Lou. Why doesn't Kay just bring her in? I'll keep her with me and Susie. No trouble.

Make the offer.

You think I haven't? Merrill leaned back into the white leather, then plucked her forearms up off the seat cushion as if burned. Ouch!

Esther kept her eyes closed. Roy studied her face. His peacemaker. Merrill was a genius on everyone else's life. Gorgeous, though, you had to give her that.

Esther made a big sleepy yawn.

Ship-to-shore. Great idea. Roy went up to the bridge and started cranking the ship-to-shore radio. Why not just use the phone? said Charlie Peeko. I haven't even turned on the engines yet.

Mind your own business. Yes! Roy Cohn here, Miss Campanella. Yes. How are you? Get me Will Clemens, would you? I appreciate that. I'm sure that's important, yes. But it is also important that I speak to him. Bad connection, yes. I'm calling from aboard a ship, the *Titanic*. No, that's a joke. Charlie Peeko rolled his eyes. Roy waved him off: Don't you have a rudder to break somewhere? Charlie ducked under the doorway, six foot four, too tall for everything. Too dark too, that hair looked fake. Yes! Warden Flagmeyer. Roy Cohn here. Fine, sir. Yes sir, and you? Yes, glad to hear it. On shipboard, sir, that's correct. Yes. I will. Thank you.

The signal faded in and out. How hard could it be to call upstate from the Seventy-ninth Street boat basin? Roy watched

Charlie Peeko roll back the tarp on the Boston Whaler. It was the rescue boat that Roy used mostly for waterskiing. Now Charlie was mucking with that engine too. Look at that big dope, the radio waves were probably getting stuck in his thick head. Hello? Hello? Will! Yes, yes, hello. I know. It's just business. It'll work. Don't be angry. You'll see. What? I can't hear you. Yes! She's here in town today. Or last night, yes, I saw her. We said a little prayer together at St. Patrick's. Ha-ha. You think that's funny? I think something good happened there. You'll see. Kay? Kay's okay. No, she's not angry. Not really. Just a little. You know what? I've got Merrill Mandel on board, looking like a pinup, she's strutting around, just your regular luncheon distraction. She's asking for you! That's why I called. They're wearing onionskin stationery! Can you hear me? Hello? Hello? Hello? Charlie Peeko smacked his head against the propeller of the outboard. He stood holding his face in his hands. Roy reconnected the handset to the radio. Obviously he wouldn't get a clear connection today. He had barely heard Will. But it was really a pump-up call, not informational. He could only hope, *maybe,* that that had already happened. Roy would have to track down Sammy Finlandor and find out.

The next day, Esther Kinder smoothed down the last plaid quilted dirndl on a model, then finally, after nearly forty-five minutes of excruciating discipline, she allowed herself to go to the curtain. The violins were playing "Ode to Joy." Sixteen first-rate students, stars of their Juilliard class, they were perfect. They sounded like angels out there on her special day, and even better, it sounded like a crowd.

Where had Roy found this velvet? It smelled like cheese. Esther felt her stomach turn as she pried through the heavy drapes. Nerves, nerves, you just gotta be strong. So there's never been a fashion show at the Stork Club, so this was the first. And what an event! She could hear it, she could feel it, she could smell it. Not just the Roquefort of the drapes, she could smell the oysters and the champagne. She knew it was all happening. She felt these things in her blood. One eye, just one eye to the break in the drape, that's all she'd allow herself, then she'd give the signal to the maestro for *Swan Lake,* and her girls, her models, each a bona fide ballerina, would start the fashion extravaganza. Roy's idea: fall-collection casual wear on toe shoes, *Swan Lake,* only the happy parts, oysters (found in bodies of water, though not necessarily lakes per se), and the Stork Club, also a bird, much like the swan in that it's mostly decorative. Everything's a theme. You have to tie things together, make a package, and it's irresistible, who can refuse to buy. Will had taught Roy all about that. And he was right. About this he was right.

Esther let her artist's eye take the peek. Oh my God, a full house, but who's that in the front row? Not the movie stars. Not Audrey Hepburn, who Roy had *promised,* but the Carlitto brothers! There: Lennie, Lou, and Micky, the less successful Carlittos at that. And if their square fat selves weren't enough, all spread out, legs akimbo, there was Muddy, wearing a dress calculated to make anything Esther could come up with look like a barbecue. This was her debut? Gangsters and a chop to the jugular delivered fresh by fate's messenger, Dora Cohn. What would ever change? Why had she been so stupid.

Esther was hyperventilating, she was going to faint. She let go of the drape and shimmied down to the rigged runway floor. She sat, fists to her eyes, until one of her ballerinas, *en pointe,* clomped over to her. The show must go on? the girl asked. A brain the size of a caper, Esther thought. What show? You see who's out there? The girl stuck her perfect oval face through the crack in the velvet. Umm, she said, cute. Esther blinked up. Cute?

Yeah, I'll take the one in the middle, the bald guy with the big jewels.

That's Roy!

Esther jumped up, grabbing the girl by her tiny arm. Oh no, that's Lennie. Roy's not bald. All right. All right! She waved to the tallest Juilliard student. "Ode to Joy" soared to a swift conclusion. The first notes of the *Swan Lake* overture sounded, a dozen ballerinas in black watch banged into position, and when the curtain rose, they bounced to the tips of their toes and began running in place, passing footballs back and forth—Roy's idea, football: synonymous with fall. But they were klutzes, these ballerinas. The balls slipped through their hands like greased hot dogs and they had to stop their *pas de bourrés* and squat to pick them up. There was a sickening stillness out there beneath the soaring violins. And then, all at once, a pounding applause. Cameras began snapping. The red-hot bulbs rolled under the seats. The audience clapped in time to the music. The buyers from Saks and Bonwit's and Bendel's and Best, Lord & Taylor, and Bergdorf Goodman were writing things down. Scratching out orders on the little swan-shaped pads that Roy's receptionist, Alice, had carved with an X-Acto knife. Roy's idea. He was an artist. She had to admit it. The ballerinas finally stopped dropping the footballs and found the beat. Success, success, success. She could feel it, she could see it, she could smell it.

June 8

So complex was Gert Maguire's daily routine that by eleven o'clock some mornings she crept into her private sewing room and pulled the quilt on the daybed up over her head to block out the buzz of the neighborhood mowers, the ringing telephone, and the vacuum grinding through room after room. Mrs. Mackey came Tuesdays and Thursdays to scour the place, while Gert repaired school clothes. Her boys burst out of their apparel on a regular basis. She mended on the machine she'd once used to sew couturier knockoffs. She could do that—walk into Dior and go home with the dress she liked best in her head. But after the third baby, she lost interest in the engineering secret behind a wasp waist. Now she was into boats, sort of. What she really wanted to do was build houses. She thought about joists and beams and sprung floors. She liked wood. She'd look into that as soon as Nathaniel went to college.

And she was a chef. She made, served, or packed ten separate, complete meals every morning before seven-thirty. All of her sons were athletes, requiring vast proportions and exact ratios of protein to carbohydrate. They had deep preferences on the scales of hot to cold and soft to crunchy. Red was less demanding, but ever since he'd taken up night running, he wanted pancakes. And because his was a sensitive palate, a mix was out of the question. After she fed her boys, she drove them, sometimes before sunrise, to their various sporting commitments. Then she got Red squared away and out the door. Lou-Lou's was the last lunch to make, the last bus stop to drive to.

On this morning Lou-Lou wandered into the kitchen; her mother called it the grotto because of its fake brick walls. For almost half an hour, from 7:30 to 7:55 every morning, Lou-Lou had Gert all to herself. Gert was leaning over the dishwasher, loading in buttery plates. Lou-Lou often needed a little overhaul in her appearance, a dish sponge to her uniform, a spritz of water to calm down her hair, but today Gert was distracted.

We've got to get a move on, she said. Gert was all dressed up with white lace stockings. Lou-Lou knew from her mother that these were articles of clothing grown women wore at their peril. Gert's legs were thicker than Lou-Lou's mother's, and bigger certainly than Mrs. Westerfield's. But Lou-Lou thought Gert looked nice, like a big Heidi, and she said so.

You look nice too, carrot. Gert often called Lou-Lou the name of a vegetable when she was feeling affectionate. But now Gert had her attention elsewhere, she couldn't see her. Lou-Lou had chalk on her uniform, chocolate on her sleeve, her hair hadn't been combed in two days.

You ready? said Gert.

It was only 7:35. Lou-Lou just stared. What had she done? Chop-chop, soldier. She was standing by the door. Gert was mistaking Lou-Lou for one of her boys. In the driveway, Lou-Lou slid into the passenger seat of the Volkswagen bug, tucked her lunch into her book bag. She was hungry. Gert hadn't mentioned breakfast, but she never did, for Lou-Lou the cereals were there for the taking. Lou-Lou looked at Gert's profile. Tight curls pressed down on Gert's head like springs on the whirlicopter ejectors her boys rigged to launch gravel.

Lou-Lou was the only child who traveled from this bus stop to Holy Cross. It was right on the town border, the last stop in the afternoon, the first in the morning. Smitty Sutphin, the bus driver, always had a joke for her, the same joke, said she was the early bird and that she should cut back on the worms. Sleep in there once in a while, kid. Smitty would choke himself laughing so hard, then he'd catch Lou-Lou's eye, like he was asking her a question: Eh? Eh? When Lou-Lou nodded, just out of politeness, he could release himself, laugh all over again, and repeat the punch line a few more times: Good worm-hunting season, spring'll do it to you, gotta cut back. But then the challenges of the road would catch his attention, always some new asshole out there reinventing the rules, and he'd forget about Lou-Lou for a while.

Gert dropped her off. Sorry not to sit today, chum. After Lou-Lou was out of the car, Gert leaned over and rolled down the window so Lou-Lou could see her bright eyes. Bye-bye. Lou-Lou watched the VW take the corner like a roadster in a race, then she squatted down on the curb. The cement was cool on her legs, the lawn still dewy. The road smelled like oranges and clam chowder. A small gray spider flattened itself into the crack in the curb. It wasn't even eight o'clock. Smitty wouldn't be here to get her for a while, so Lou-Lou unlatched her book bag. Her folded untouched homework was near the top, she reached deeper to her lunch now on the bottom. She started working backward from dessert. When she was done with the ham sandwich, Smitty still wasn't anywhere close. Lou-Lou brushed the crumbs off her navy blue jumper, left the lunch bag crumpled on the curb, she didn't need it. She took one last look for Smitty, then gave up, she started to walk. She knew a shortcut. She'd be home in no time.

The whole town was on Gert's schedule, busy, inside somewhere. Barely a car had passed and she'd been walking a while, twenty minutes or so. She was on Conover Lane, a little curving road of brand-new houses, split-levels and ranches, some with naked lawns, only a few blades of grass here and there. The rain last night left skinny rivers between the anthills. Lou-Lou stopped to watch fat black ants wriggle up the Ruddys' front walk. The Ruddys had a boat in their slip bigger than their house. And across the water, about five houses down, she could see her own house, and the porch where her mother would be sitting if she was home. Ruddy was the one name she knew on Conover Lane, Gert had told her it was a house of woe.

Later she found out what Gert meant from Gert's oldest loudmouth son, Andrew. The Ruddys' only child, Stella, a girl Lou-Lou's own age, had been born with a hole in her heart. She couldn't go to school and she couldn't go out to play because the exertion would kill her right away. Lou-Lou stood in front of the Ruddy house, where black ants congregated and scattered. She looked to the closed windows with white blinds swiveled tight, even on this hot gray day. Lou-Lou stared for a while until she figured out where Stella might be, based on her experience in her own house, and in Gert's. Lou-Lou gave that window her full attention. She put her hands on her chest, trying to feel if perhaps her own heart had a hole in it and that was why she had this feeling about Stella. Lou-Lou stared and stared. Finally she thought she saw a tiny crack in the blinds. Stella was seeing her, communicating, and in that precise second, Lou-Lou felt a pounding ache in her chest. For a moment she thought she would die instantly, then the sun broke through the clouds, the whole street lit up: the Ruddys' house, the anthills, the wet dirt, even her own house far away, everything was swamped with light, then the light closed, disappeared, and the pain was gone.

Lou-Lou saw a vision of Stella frolicking in the yard. She had transparent hair with light streaking out like Christmas-tree tinsel. She was throwing legless Barbies at the ants to bomb them. And Lou-Lou knew she had healed Stella, was certain of it, by concentrating all of her attention, just as Mrs. Westerfield said, *attention and intention,* she had done it. Lou-Lou was a saint, what a discovery. At last she was good at something.

After a decent interval, Lou-Lou moved on. She had to break the news to Gert first. She knew Gert would be pleased, and besides, Lou-Lou wouldn't have to go to school anymore, which would ease up Gert's schedule. It started to rain a little. Lou-Lou closed her eyes, bowed her head, and said a special prayer turning the rain into holy water that would fix up the bad grass on Conover Lane.

Lou-Lou wanted to get home now. She took the shortcut through McKim's farm, through the orchard. Mr. McKim was in his kitchen. Lou-Lou could see him through the wide old-fashioned window. His house was the oldest in the neighborhood.

Conover Lane had been built on his farmland. He hated children and sometimes chased them with a squirrel gun. She knew this from Andrew also. He was bitter, Andrew said, because Mrs. McKim had died at a young and beautiful age. Lou-Lou crept through the orchard from tree trunk to tree trunk, hiding behind each skinny tree. On such a glum day as this, her dark uniform should help her melt right in, but she knew her body flopped out on either side, and if Mr. McKim saw her, she'd be a Christian martyr before anyone knew she was a saint.

Lou-Lou was halfway through the orchard when the back door opened and Mr. McKim stepped out onto the porch. He unzipped his fly and pulled a dark ribbon out and started to pee. Lou-Lou quit hiding and took off at a dead run. Hey! Hey! What do you think you're doing? Get back here, you little monster. I see you. I know who you are. Lou-Lou was wheezing when she burst through the hedge that cut up her arms and face. She was out of bounds here, off his property, but maybe he'd hunt her down anyway with his gun. Cars whirled by on the big road. But she ran across, horns screeching at her, tires skidding. She ran into her own street, breathless and hurt.

Lou-Lou dragged her book bag down the street to Gert's driveway. She tried the garage door first, then all the rest. The house was completely locked up. This was unusual in Lou-Lou's experience, but then she'd never been home from school unannounced before. Lou-Lou walked the whole way around the house again. All the lights were out and she didn't see any movement. A dark red pickup rumbled down the lane. A farm truck! Lou-Lou dove into Gert's ornamental holly. The truck slowed down, almost to a halt. She couldn't see the driver from the ground. She'd make a break for her own house. Hurling herself out of the holly, she scrambled across the lawns, through the pine trees, to the back porch where her mother always sat.

Just like Gert's house, the door was locked. All the windows looked sealed. Standing now in the driveway, she could hear the low rev of the engine coming closer, and then the gravel began to pop. She spotted a seam of air beneath one of the garage doors. Lou-Lou yanked on the pull but couldn't budge it. She lay down on the cement apron and pushed up as hard as she could. It gave about a foot and she rolled under just as the truck pulled around the back. She hid behind the lawn mower and the red truck ground to a stop. Someone slammed a hollow-sounding door. She saw muddy boots standing at the garage door; the wearer pulled on the handle. Shit, he said. And walked away. She heard two loud thumps and then the engine exploding like bullets. A plume of smoke burst out the back end and sifted into the garage, a streaky blue poison, with the smell of an Easter egg boiled overtime. The truck rumbled away. Lou-Lou stood on the seat of the lawn mower to see out the high oblong windows. Two new rubber garbage pails lay tipped over in the white gravel.

It was hot in the garage, but not as hot as outside. Lou-Lou went into the Deepfreeze and pulled out a couple of Fudgsicles. She applied one medicinally to the scratch on her cheek from Mr. McKim's bushes. She dragged her book bag over to the filing cabinets, where she could get a purchase on the bottom drawers and get up to the old billiard table stored in the rafters. The legs hung down below. Lou-Lou wriggled onto the knobbed table and squeezed down into the darkest corner. She curled up there, her legs tucked in. She pulled her uniform tight around the backs of her thighs. She sucked as slowly as possible on the Fudgsicles. This would be her shrine. She would have many visions here. She'd have to stay a while. When the pops were done, she twisted the wrappers around the sticks like flowers, then rubbed her cheek into the dusty green baize and fell asleep.

Gert Maguire drove swiftly down curving Rumson Road. She'd decided to make an unscheduled visit to her husband's office that morning. With the boys all needing her so much, and now that Lou-Lou was part of their household—well, she loved her boys and cared for Lou-Lou, and besides wanted to help, but the time with her husband was being eaten away. She barely saw him, and never alone unless he was asleep or slipping out the bedroom door for a midnight run. Before the intervention of a priest or an advice column told her what to do, Gert would inaugurate the random drop-in at the Maguire Real Estate Agency on River Road. Before the passion between them eroded entirely. After all, the place was romantic, an old-style Rumson house, creamy yellow, late Victorian, white gingerbread trim. And from the second floor, from Red's office, it was easy to spot the Navesink River.

Red was lounging against the window, watching a strange barge huff down the channel, when his secretary and general receptionist, young Mrs. Fallon, entered with a three-part knock. She announced that Gert was in the opportunity area below. Yes, Mrs. Fallon, I'll be two minutes, just two. Mrs. Fallon nodded without giving him her eyes. She had an aversion to looking at him when he spoke that Red found mildly arousing. It was as if she were listening to him say dirty things and not stopping him entirely, letting him talk but not. It was great. And she was a blonde. He'd always felt an affinity to blondes, being a partial blond himself. A blend-head, his sons called him.

Red Maguire adjusted the angle of his chin. He let his bottom teeth surmount his top, correcting the slightest, largely imaginary, recession of his jawline. He coughed to draw Mrs. Fallon's eyes upward to his face. When he had her looking straight at him, he released his jaw and said in a low, profoundly unsuggestive voice: Thank you, Mrs. Fallon. She vanished immediately.

Red adjusted his trousers. He was both happy and dismayed. Happy to have this little erotic charge at the workplace, keeping him sharp. But dismayed, now concerned that his wife would find his arousal odd. Red stepped into the adjacent washroom, just to give himself a little splash of no-nonsense. But he left the door ajar, and peeking through the crack, his wife found him there.

Gert wasted no time. She let herself in and shut the door. Red was confused and uncertain how to proceed, but Gert's mouth was on his in a second, her hand to his fly. Still kissing, she opened her blouse, unlatched her skirt and let it drop to the floor. Gert pushed down Red's trousers and his skivvies. She closed the toilet seat. Sit here, she said. She straddled his knees. Panties and lace stockings now lassoed her calves. She did a quick evaluation, worked for a minute improving his erection, then took a firm grip of the lavatory and pushed herself onto him. She wriggled, right, left, right, left. After a while, he cried out: Holy Mother! Gert clapped her hand to his mouth: Shhh! Then she was off his lap and pulling up her lingerie. She turned away to fasten her skirt. Gert grabbed her blouse, opened the door, exited, and closed it without saying good-bye.

For a long time, Red Maguire sat on the john, wondering what had come over his wife, wondering if she was planning to make a habit of this. He wondered if young Mrs. Fallon had heard anything and tried to decide if that would be a good thing or a bad thing.

Bo searched for Hollis in the art-activity room at the old end of the tenth floor in the late afternoon. No one was there, but that was okay. He let the door swing shut and took a look around. He was a free agent today, cut loose from the IV. Cereal for breakfast, soup for lunch, and no throwing up. Bo had never been in the art-activity room alone before. He was seldom alone anywhere. Even at home, even when he was sleeping, Lou-Lou would come in and edge herself into the bed between him and the wall. She didn't hug, she just liked to sleep next to his ribs. Sometimes at the hospital he missed her, sometimes not.

Bo pried open the Tupperware container of green Play-Doh. It smelled like an alcohol swab. The play-nurse, Mrs. Coxcomb, doused all their community objects, all the things they played with together, in disinfectant. Bo had learned that anything could make him sick. Before he knew it, a germ could wriggle its way into his body and he'd be *out like a light,* Mrs. Coxcomb said. He knew that, but he just couldn't care about it. Bo dug the medicinal Play-Doh out of the container and made a pan-cake on the floor. He took off his baseball slippers and stuck his foot in the green mound. He pulled it out. Very nice. Bo found some tongue depressors still wrapped in paper and made a fork effect along the top, extending each of his five toes. Bo was prob-ably the best artist on the pediatric hematology ward, but he tried to be modest about it. Michelle, a bad artist, made rips in her paintings. She'd slap on the paint, the paper would get soggy and tear. Other times she'd just bleed on them, which would also wreck them, and then Mrs. Coxcomb would hustle Michelle out of there, Michelle screaming to *put her down now.* But Bo didn't let that ruin his concentration, and when

Michelle was back, starting over with a clean slate in art, Bo always gave her a hand.

He wished he could find Hollis. Sometimes when she wasn't busy, she played cards in here with him. Her square fingernails would tap on the deck, calling to her lucky card: the two of diamonds. Bo decided to explore the big windows. Be a Christopher Columbus of the hospital, Mrs. Westerfield said. Bo was an adventurer. Stay away from the windows, Mrs. Coxcomb said. She was extremely nervous for an expert in fun and art.

Bo crossed to the windows anyway. His skeleton didn't hurt so much, he was cruising, he was sliding, he put his hands on two separate panes. No electricity, which was good. Far, far below, the East River curled and shivered. The tiny boats barely moved. Bo scanned the water for the *Wavemaker II,* easy to spot because its lifeboat was a Boston Whaler. You never knew when it would sail on by. It could be down there this second, waiting for Bo and for Michelle.

Actually, if it was there, Michelle probably wouldn't want to go. The last time Captain Peeko pulled up to the electrical station across the highway, two orderlies with sweaty faces carried Bo and Michelle through the underground tunnels, which were too narrow to navigate with wheelchairs. They emerged under the loud cranking gears, and Michelle was afraid of electrocution. But Uncle Roy said it was all talk and no action, meaning the sound was loud but the generator was really underpowered, even if the emergency it was built for came. Michelle cried. In the Boston Whaler that carried them out from the dock, in Captain Peeko's strong arms, she cried. And when the *Wavemaker II* sailed away down the channel, Michelle looked up at the cliff of stone and glass that was New York Hospital and wept like she was leaving Disneyland.

The trip was very short. They barely glimpsed the Statue of Liberty. Captain Peeko served the tuna sandwiches, Michelle threw up. When Uncle Roy strapped on his water skis and jumped overboard,

Michelle said he would be eaten alive by invisible red fish. She was from Tampa and knew all about them.

Bo pushed away from the window. He sat on the floor next to his Play-Doh footprint and listened to the hum, a sort of sonic constant at the hospital. Nothing could drown it out. Herman, the pet experimental rat, clawed at his cage, but that was a minor sound. Bo tried to remember how long he had been at the hospital but couldn't. His mother had been here all the time, and then she went home for a day, and then she came back with Meemaw, and now she was gone again but would come back tomorrow, Hollis said, and then maybe Bo could go home. Lots of people asked Bo what he would be. When? Bo asked at first, but not anymore. It was a question only to say hello.

Herman was snapping his tiny teeth on the bars of his cage. Herman, the rescued experimental rat, had been given more chemotherapy ounce for ounce than Bo, and more kinds, said Hollis. Even though Herman smelled of pee and sawdust, Hollis let him crawl on her shoulder and nibble her loop earring when they played cards. Herman's main body was white, but his eyes and nose and tail were pink. Even the cobalt? Did he get the cobalt? Yep, said Hollis in a drawl, just like a cowgirl, and she stole the good one-eyed jack right out of Bo's hand. She pulled Herman's miniature fingers away from her neat black ponytail.

Now Herman chewed so hard and clawed so fast he looked desperate. Herman had no voice, so he could not cry. Bo inched closer to Herman without standing up. He just slid along the floor on his bathrobe. Hey Herman. Did you turn into a *dog*? This was a compliment. Pure flattery. Herman was an irritable rat, actually a poor choice for the art-activity room pet. Hey there Herman. Arf!

Herman did a quick spin, biting his tail. What's wrong, kiddo? Maybe Herman just needed a lucky break. Bo put his finger next to the cage, just to see what Herman would do. He was a known biter, something that drove Mrs. Coxcomb crazy. Herman's nose vibrated like a machine, sniffing at a hundred miles per hour. Bo put his finger closer and felt Herman's cool dry nose bouncing on his fingertip. Come on out, Herman, you just need some company. Hey Lassie, here boy, come on Lassie.

Bo unlatched the cage door. Herman tore out, ran around the pet table about twenty times, then took a wild leap to the floor. He landed, Bo the explorer was interested to see, on all four paws at once. Herman ignored Bo. Come here! Lassie, here boy! Herman scrabbled across the floor. He couldn't get much traction but made it to Bo's green footprint. Good boy! It's a bomb! Herman sniffed at the disinfected Play-Doh, then headed straight for Bo's feet. Lassie! The bomb's over there. Herman nibbled on Bo's pajama leg. You gotta save us. Come on, you can do it, boy! Was Lassie a girl? Good dog. Herman was in Bo's lap, burrowing into Bo's belly. Bo wrapped his hands around Herman's trembling body. There, there boy, don't worry. The bomb won't go off, actually it's fixed. You fixed it! Just the sight of you was enough.

The swing doors opened and fat Clarissa the night nurse stood there, arms stacked on her big belly. Well, here you are, she said. Clarissa's cheeks had bright pink spots right in the middle of each. Bo, did you let that piece of vermin loose again? That is irritating. Hand him over. No. I'm not going to touch him, I mean just put him back where he belongs and come have your dinner.

Did Hollis go home?

About an hour ago. Come on. Let's get going.

Here Lassie. Bo stroked Herman's quivering red ears, stood up, and carried him to the cage. Go to sleep now, Lassie.

If that's Lassie, we're all in trouble.

What's for dinner, Clarissa? Bo made a pile of dry sawdust and dropped Herman on top. Herman rolled over and clawed at his own nose.

Chicken à la king.

Michelle's favorite!

Michelle's not here, Bo.

Bo looked at Clarissa, she was pulling at something on the skin of her engagement-ring finger. A tiny blue diamond poked out of four gold prongs and she scratched all around it. Clarissa liked to say she's had a rash since the minute that guy popped the question. You ready yet, Bo?

Well, it's still her favorite, you know.

Any day now, Bo.

~

There was no point in having a really excellent automobile, something truly fine, especially calibrated for speed, if Peter was going to stay within the speed limit. Roy always admonished Peter, said: Get the lead out, Rev it up! But not today. The weather was lousy. He'd just relax, let the scenery go by, think things through. He hadn't done enough of that lately, and though he hated to admit it, things were out of hand. But soon he'd remedy all that.

Outside New Haven in only three hours! And weren't they going to upstate New York? A world record in mediocre driving. How had Peter ever become a chauffeur? Because Roy had made him one, that's how. He had no one to blame, etc. They'd get to Woeburne eventually. Today was Will Clemens's thirty-fourth birthday, and Roy would celebrate whether Will wanted him to or not. And word from Sammy Finlandor was that Will did not. The story? Will was unhappy. Roy had promised protection from prosecution and now Will was in jail. Roy had promised protection from the press and now all the national syndicates were waxing their violins over Will's trouble. Roy's interpretation. And promises were important. Promises were a sacred trust and vow. Now what.

Peter took an odd route through New Haven, through the ghetto, for godsakes. What am I doing here? Roy tapped on the glass. Roy was surrounded by dark-faced people, everywhere he looked, on every corner, every sidewalk, leaning in doorways, smiling, not smiling. And now Peter was driving at a crawl, the least forward motion possible without actually stopping. What is this, Peter? What's the message here? A shortcut? I see. My understanding is that shortcuts are about speed, not agendas. Agendas, that's right. Could we move on, please? I'd like to get there before July.

Peter moved on. The scenery got sadder, poorer. Roy closed his eyes. Not today. No civics lessons today, Peter. We've discussed this. The car came to a halt. Roy blinked, sat up, leaned toward the glass divider: Enough! But it was a traffic light turned red.

A man crossing the intersection took a radical turn and came right up to Roy's window, put a huge hand to the passenger handle, and yanked. Locked! Roy's heart fluttered. Step on it, Peter. But the light was still red. A slow light. A law-abiding driver. Just run the fucking light, Peter. The man put hand over hand across Roy's window, up to the roof of the car, hand over hand down the back window to the trunk, like he was patting it down, slowly, slower than Peter's acceleration foot. The man made a bridge from one side of the car to the other. Hand, hand, hand, big as basketballs, making soft thuds as if weighted. He reached the opposite side and then released the dark blue limousine from his care. The light went green. Peter got a move on. What was that? What was that? Can you tell me?

Lord if I know, Mr. Cohn.

Roy shut his eyes, angry beyond words.

All right, Roy said to Peter in the parking lot, they really overdid it with the razor wire here, I won't be long. Don't go anywhere. Peter gave Roy a look of sweet incomprehension, as if going anywhere would never occur to him. But lately, Roy knew the truth, Peter had been taking little unexplained trips, maybe even running some kind of business on the side. Roy would find out soon enough. Just wait, please. That's your job. In fact, it's your job description. Can you do that for me? Peter smiled even more sweetly. He was beautiful. Really a perfect face, if there were such a thing. Roy felt something like the taste of apple at the back of his tongue, a prickle under the collar, he wriggled as if loose mites were squirming in there. Okay.

Oh, the present. He forgot. Peter? Open the trunk, please. There was a black cardboard box, and in the box Roy dug around until he found the long red jewel case from Cartier. A tank watch, who wouldn't want one. Will was in the tank. It was a great gift. Why not. Roy made his way along the stone footpath to an arched entrance, gift in hand. He knocked. He knocked harder, looked back over his shoulder to Peter. Peter was in the car, in the driver's seat, taking a long pull off a paper cup of coffee he'd bought hours ago on the Upper East Side. Roy could taste that stale coffee, and he was thinking that, I can taste it from here, when the metal door swung wide and an officer of the law asked him his business. Roy gave the warden's name, Flagmeyer, and his own. He was escorted immediately down a long, dark corridor to a dark, curved staircase. Peter and the taste of his cold coffee vanished completely. Forgotten.

The warden was an ugly man. Roy concluded quickly that the main problem was the warden's teeth. They looked filed down and coated with brown varnish. The man's upper cheeks were swollen and red. Dry, flecked skin surrounded eyes the color of grilled organ meat. Roy didn't like to look at him but did, made himself, and got right to the point. Nice to see you, sir. You're looking well. And Mr. Clemens. I imagine everything there is just fine?

Not quite, said Warden Flagmeyer, averting his strange eyes, not speaking to Roy per se but directing himself to a sallow houseplant struggling under the weight of a blue ribbon at the corner of his blotter. The man had a mahogany desk, just as Roy's father had. The judge. This seemed unfair. This seemed wrong. And Roy was suddenly angry for the second time in a short day. What do you mean; not quite, he thundered. The warden, twice his size, grossly overweight in fact, seemed to blossom under the assault. He smiled. Let's take it easy, shall we? Warden Flagmeyer pointed to a chair.

No, we shan't take it easy. Not until you explain yourself, here and now. But Roy took a seat. He stared hard at the fat warden. Roy's look indicated a whole catalog of unpleasantness to come, and the warden took his own seat, something carved and elaborate. He sat on the edge like a giddy sophomore on a first date, and he smiled again. Roy was beside himself. Who was this asshole? He'd call the governor, have the guy annihilated. The warden coughed, something nice and tubercular. And Roy calmed down. Made himself. Roy took a deep breath, what really was the problem here? Roy needed a vacation, that was all. Right after the retrial, assuming events unfolded as they should. The pressure was big, so the minutiae were getting to him. So tell me, Warden Flagmeyer, tell me everything. Now Roy was smiling too. A vulnerable smile, like it cost him a lot, revealed too much. The warden watched him, then said: Will Clemens has not been kept separate from other prisoners, he has not been given special food or special privileges. He has not had additional access to a television or more frequent visits from his wife. He will not be paroled early, as the judge has already made abundantly clear, and you cannot see him today.

You don't say.

Oh, but I do.

Roy studied the ugly grinning warden for a full minute. Under whose orders, he asked, as if the time had not elapsed.

Under these. The warden pulled a sheet of thick embossed stationery from his pen drawer, not from a file, and placed it on the mahogany desk. Roy spotted the letterhead. Corrupt bastard. He checked the signature for the girly paranoid scrawl. Roy sighed. He eyed the warden as if he'd seen some kind of light, which in a way he had. His whole situation was even more deeply twisted than he had imagined. All right. Please see that Will Clemens gets this, he said, standing, pulling the watch box from his pocket. Roy propped it against the dying African violet. I want to hear all about it when I come back. Which will be soon.

I promise you. I want to hear just how much he likes it. Please ask your guard to show me out of here. Roy didn't bother to look at the ugly face again.

In the car he asked Peter for the remainder of the coffee, which tasted like shit. The turnpike, Peter, he said, straight home now. No detours.

The windshield wiper kept sticking on Gert's Volkswagen. A swath of watery murk doused her field of vision. She stared ahead, waiting for a blotch of yellow to appear. She was thinking of her husband, who was very sensitive, took things to heart. She saw the look on his face when she left today: stunned, a little lost, what a man. Gert straightened her pale green cotton skirt, gave it a tug. Nothing funny, she felt like laughing, where was the bus? Half past three, soon. It should be soon. And then what would Lou-Lou want to do. Maybe Gert would take her to Gascon's market, Lou-Lou didn't mind errands, not like her mother, the queen.

Kay the royal terror. Spoiled from day one. And growing up, Gert's house had been her kingdom. Gert's mother had only boys until Gert. The aftermath, her father called her, her brothers called her afterbirth and showed her bloody photos from their father's medical textbooks. There you are, bloodface. Kay, even tiny, knew how to circumvent such tags. Gert's brother Dwight called Kay an infected pimple, Kay put her butterfly hands on each of Dwight's fat cheeks and squeezed until he was breathless.

Lou-Lou woke up again in the late afternoon. It was hotter near the roof and she'd been dozing off and on all day, like she was sick, like she was Bo, or maybe Stella, the girl with the hole in her heart. She curled tighter around her book bag. There wasn't much room or give, the dusty green baize of the billiard table smelled like the cattails down by the water, like something living that had died. She was hungry now, which made the smell stronger, worse. She listened, then felt her way down off the table, her foot missed the window ledge and she fell down hard, scraping her thigh on the filing cabinet. She didn't cry, she knew the rules about that.

She hid the blood from herself so she didn't have to think about it. She edged along the concrete floor, between the piles of boxes and tools, not arranged in any way. The light came in big squares through the high windows. She bounced from square to square. She smacked into the lawn mower, and this time she did cry. Very loud. Outside she heard the gravel and the thumps of the garbage cans being thrown against the door. She stopped.

With a metallic grind the door began to rise. Lou-Lou watched the figure of Rufus Johnsilver, the handyman, appear gradually. Rufus! Did you come to find me?

Lou-Lou girl. What in the world? How'd you get stuck in here? I'm here on purpose.

You ready to come out on purpose? What are you crying about? Rufus put his hand to Lou-Lou's cheek, plucked a tear, shaping his fingers like it was a flower. Don't you cry, Lou-Lou. I'll get you over to Mrs. Maguire. She's probably worrying about you.

Rufus took Lou-Lou's book bag and her hand and walked across the lawns, through the pine trees, to Gert's door, where he knocked and called. No answer. We'll have to just do for ourselves, I guess. They headed back to Lou-Lou's house, where Rufus had fixed the locks and knew how to break them. The kitchen looked as if Lou-Lou's mother had just left a moment before. It was a museum to her departure, a stick of butter left out to soften, a pan in the sink soaking the residue of scrambled eggs, tags from the dry cleaner on the kitchen table, ballet slippers under the chair. No evidence of Meemaw, who wasn't supposed to know about Bo, so she was operating like a ghost. No traces. Lou-Lou felt confused about her, confused that her smart, kind grandmother hadn't just known something was wrong. Rufus studied the contents of the icebox with his arms folded. Her father said Rufus liked to collect credit cards. Something about bureaus, and when her father stood by his bureau looking in the top drawer, Lou-Lou had come in without saying hello, without knocking, and her father turned, arms crossed just like Rufus now, only her father had no clothes on, but Lou-Lou was just looking at his face, wasn't thinking so much, except for bureaus and credit cards, Christmas cards, birthday cards. Her father yelled loud, to get out, get out, and she hid in the easiest place to look, under her own bed, and she heard his footsteps, but he never found her. Rufus found her. Well, Lou-Lou, I don't know what to fix you from this group. Not a whole lot here to work with.

Also Lou-Lou knew that Rufus was in some kind of trouble with her mother. She remembered the rule about going to Sister Mary Arthur if Rufus tried to pick her up at school. A school rule. She wondered when her mother would be back, she put her feet on the ballet slippers, squished them down.

Gert always thought that Smitty Sutphin was a lousy guy, knew it by looking at him, but when he didn't show up by four-fifteen, she began to fear he was a criminal guy. She snapped the Volkswagen into gear and started down the winding road to Holy Cross School at full speed, where one of those nuns had better have Lou-Lou in detention or Gert was going to kill someone.

Gert looked frantic racing into the principal's office, she'd already been to Lou-Lou's empty classroom. She tugged on her skirt, trying to make it stop bunching between her thighs while she explained the problem to Mrs. Oates, who barely nodded, come to Holy Cross after a long career in public service. Mrs. Oates looked at Gert as if she was hysterical, and that kind of excess was a language Mrs. Oates, for one, didn't respond to.

Just tell me if she's here. Did she get on the bus?

One moment, please, let me try Sister Barbara. Mrs. Oates nodded toward a wooden chair. Gert bobbed and yanked but then understood that until she sat, Mrs. Oates would not proceed.

Where's Sister Mary Arthur? Let me talk to her. Please.

She's on retreat.

Retreat! Jesus!

Mrs. Oates replaced the microphone for the intercom on her desk. She opened the file she'd been studying when Gert came in. Gert sat back in the chair. Call her, please.

Mrs. Oates depressed the button, spoke into the padded knob, then ducked her head down into her filing cabinet. Gert knew that Mrs. Oates didn't like her one bit. But Sister Barbara did. Dear child! Gert was red in the face and shaking. Sister, did Ann Louise Clemens get on the bus this afternoon? Mrs. Maguire, Ann Louise wasn't in school today, I assumed you knew. And then Sister Barbara looked as stunned as Gert. Never came? My God, my God, my God. Gert saw herself dropping Lou-Lou at the curb. Christ, what had she been thinking. Gert had wanted time to herself, just one damned minute, and look what happened. Sister Barbara pressed her entire hand on top of Mrs. Oates's open file to arrest her attention. The police, Mrs. Oates. Please call the police.

The train slipped through the Amboys, sunset lavender, cattails high. It was Will's birthday and Kay hadn't even talked to him. Rita's novena lay open in her lap, a new rosary from St. Patrick's, red. Was there a symbol here? Everything had meaning for Kay some days. It was a discomfort. The lab coat on a volunteer, the scissors held open or closed by the attending physician before snipping a bandage, the name Fordenhoff, pediatric oncologist, the name Ray, neurologist. The color of Rita's rosary. Kay was working hard, scanning the signs, knowing when to go and when to stop, because if she could get it all right, her son would survive this time. A year ago, she didn't even know it was possible to work this hard. What would she do when Bo was well and Will was home. Run for president, Roy said.

Here's how she found out Bo was in trouble. She and Will flew to California on a Pan American flight that lasted ten hours. They arrived in Los Angeles and went straight to the Beverly Hills Hotel, straight to the Polo Lounge, as if they hadn't had enough to drink in the air. But it was very good, she remembered this, the feeling of the cool thin glass in her hand and the comfort of the tall chair, a chair that wasn't vibrating, and some dislocated scent of sweetness, something luscious and close. Coconut. The lounge was filled with tan women, women in white with bold-looking teeth and hair set high; through this forest came a page holding at shoulder height a chalkboard, and he called her name. Then delivered a telephone. She picked up the receiver, smiled her own bold smile—Will was playing a game with her—but instead of the messenger of fun, it was Gert's voice, full of the same old worry for nothing. We just got here, you goat, what are you trailing me for. Gert didn't laugh, and Kay's glass went warm in her hand.

She looked to Will. She watched Will for the assurance that nothing Gert said would change anything. In profile, as he was now, he was most remote, it was his eyes she wanted to see.

There was a fall. A fall off the swing set, but Bo may have hit his head, and the girl, the nice girl they'd brought into their home to take care of the children and study at the local college, she called Gert right away, because Bo was slow to rise.

Where is he now? Let me talk to him.

Will had moved into the crowd and wore the chivalrous look of a man secretly bored by these beautiful women, irresistible, she watched the eyes turn, watched them watch him. A high-haired girl stopped him with a something, a question, a thought she needed to share. Highest hair, highest bosom, Kay watched her husband's eyes assess and release. Gert was talking about the emergency room.

Gert. The swing set is so little. It's for midgets.

He had trouble walking.

Kay was confused. It didn't make sense. Bo was big, already five, and the swing set was tiny, they'd outgrown it, she was getting rid of it. She just hadn't gotten around to asking Rufus to take it down and bring it to the dump. Falling off that swing set would be like falling off a throw cushion on the floor.

I don't get it.

We took him to the emergency room.

Gert, way overboard, how could he be that hurt?

They're keeping him overnight.

But why? Christ, the minute her back was turned, Gert was playing doctor. Will edged through the crowd. He bounced ever so slightly on the balls of his feet. He looked quick and slim, and when he slid sideways between two dark-eyed blondes, Kay watched his hips.

Why would they keep him? And where's Lou-Lou? Kay suddenly felt incredibly drunk, smashed.

They're keeping him for some test, they want to take a look at something. He's having a little trouble walking.

Kay flagged the page and directed him to fetch her husband, to peel him off the woman in the Pucci blouse. I don't get it. Her head had turned to stone. I don't get it, she said, and heard Gert breathe in, take a moment for rephrasing. Will clapped his hands on her knees, pressed them lightly as if he were going to pull them apart right here right now in the Polo Lounge of the Beverly Hills Hotel, he looked high and happy. Kay touched his wrist, said, Jesus, put the receiver at her neck, it slipped down and dangled off the bar by its cord. She moved her heavy stone face toward him, put her forehead to his mouth. Christ. I think I have to go home. And he held her as if she were only drunk and sick and that was the problem.

Rufus had water boiling for spag etti and Lou-Lou's feet were on the table, as she was never allowed to do, when the police pulled into the driveway, the blue spiraling light rippling bright into the kitchen. They heard the gravel crunch and the loud whine and crackle of the police radio. Lou-Lou was accustomed to emergency vehicles, but no one was home, so this must be a mistake. A loud angry banging on the porch door. HELLO. HELLO. HELLO. Rufus must have flipped the latch. HELLO. Now the tear of dry wood, that screech. Let's hide! But Rufus already had the same idea. He knocked over Kay's ladder-back chair, already running. Out through the dining room into the living room, his big body, long arms ranging out. Lou-Lou followed him to the front door. But now there was banging there too. Rufus plunged toward the master bedroom. Okay. Lou-Lou would hide in the other direction. In the playroom. She raced through to the den and out again to the last room in the long house. She pushed up the switch for the light. Shut it off again right away. That would be a clue.

The room was a mess, she'd have to be careful. Stacks of paper bags full of stuff for Bo, stuff he barely looked at. All the kids in school, through the sixth grade, had written cards, drawn pictures. More than once. There were whole periods assigned to making stuff for Bo. Holy pictures, for the most part. Pictures of heaven. They made Lou-Lou's mother so angry she put them in here out of sight. Until the bonfire in the schoolyard, she said. But she didn't really have the heart to throw them out. And the games, toys, GI Joes, LEGOs, every possible stuffed animal, all that came from the parents.

Lou-Lou pulled out a stuffed leopard and took it to farthest corner of the room, to the daybed with the baby quilt, got underneath the old leaping-lamb pattern and let only her eyes and the leopard eyes show. The door to the playroom crashed open into the wall. Lou-Lou's mother hated that, told Bo and Lou-Lou to always open doors gently. Now the man was smashing it open wider as if he couldn't fit his whole self inside. Come out, you fucking pervert. Get the fuck out now. The man felt along the wall for a switch but just missed it, set low for Bo and Lou-Lou's reach. Even though his flashlight was bright, he tripped over the first bag of heaven drawings. Fuck. He shone his torch on the bed, then up the wall too fast. His light was crazy, flying all over, not landing in any one place. He kicked over another bag. Reckless. That's what her mother would say. Reckless, thoughtless, careless. Less of everything. He slammed his hand into the wall, right into the circus poster, smacking the elephant. Another voice yelled from the porch: Hey, O'Connor, I see something out here. In the yard. The man kicked his way out of the room.

Lou-Lou heard someone crying. It wasn't Rufus, his voice was low, very low. It was Gert. Lou-Lou edged out of her hiding place and slowly picked her way across the playroom. Sweat smell like a rag for cleaning in the air, that angry guy had a stink about him. Gert was fumbling with a knob on the stove. And then, startled, almost burned her hand. Lou-Lou. All over! I've been all over town for you. I can't believe you would do this. Gert's face was mottled like a cat had clawed her. The men shouted down by the water, Over here! Over here! Lou-Lou pressed into Gert's skirt, held the pocket. Thick. All of Gert's things were thick to hold.

Who put the water on, Lou-Lou?

Lou-Lou shrugged. Gert hated that, her boys weren't allowed to shrug, and usually not Lou-Lou either. Outside, the police flashlights bobbed in reeds like enormous lightning bugs. She knew Rufus would never go down there. He was afraid of the eels. Evil creatures, he told her. The men with the lights barked *fuck* at each other. They were chasing fish. Lou-Lou stood on the porch waiting for Gert to make all her phone calls, to stop the search. And Rufus slipped out beyond the brand-new garbage pails, a brief flash of blue light on his face. He vanished into the pine trees. The police came up out of the reeds only when Gert yelled out for them: She's here, she's safe. But they looked like they didn't believe Gert, or didn't care. Finding Lou-Lou had ceased to be the point. They didn't ask any quest ons beyond the one about her being hurt, she wasn't. They stepped into their vehicle and, without turning off the flashing blue light, backed down the drive.

Roy just needed a little peace. Marital whispers, judicial torpe-does. Basically, he could take it, but peace never hurt. So he came directly to the boat. He'd circle Manhattan. A casual surveillance until Frank Reilly called in with the latest news from downtown. No one's happy in a courtroom in the summer. Every day brought a new hassle.

But when Peter dropped Roy at the basin, Captain Peeko said Merrill Mandel had phoned. She had a problem. She was already on her way. Now she balanced a can of Tab on her kneecap, no hands. Grace incarnate, her husband used to say. And Roy was inclined to agree. He felt around for a throw pillow to give himself some dig-nity. He looked at Merrill, then looked beyond her to the gray-green sky and the puckered black river. How about a swim?

Roy, that river's a cesspool. Let's go inside.

All the other boats were shrouded for a downpour. Roy nod-ded. Okay. Inside.

Merrill ducked her blond curls in the entry to the salon. White leather sofas glowed in the gray light. A family of Czechoslova-kians kept things up, made sure no speck of dirt ever became a permanent blemish. Merrill kicked off her sandals, nestled into the sofa. In the damp, the room smelled of lemon wax and Merrill's Fleur de Lis.

Okay. Roy squatted down on the ottoman, changed his mind, leaned against the bar. So what's bugging you?

That's a good question. I *like* it. She ran her small hands along the seams of a throw cushion, then checked the next.

Something wrong? Someone drop a sandwich?

He's on to us. Merrill caressed a hand-sewn zipper. She tried to pry the hidden tab free.

What are you doing?

You'll see. Merrill pursed her lips—perfect really, oblong like a magenta hot-dog bun, puffy on the top *and* the bottom—near the corner of the cushion and whispered: I'm on the boat with Roy and there's nothing you can do about it.

Merrill?

It's over. D-I-V-O-R-C-E. You creep. You midget mafioso. She flung the pillow across the room, then dropped her face into her hands and wept.

Merrill. Sweetheart. Roy sidestepped the pillow and approached the sofa. Merrill?

Merrill thrust her legs out straight, toes pointed, and lifted her arms above her head, damp eyes searched the ceiling. Her body made a very pleasant V. Roy had seen her do this before, and it always got to him.

Merrill, darling. Please. Try words.

It was this posture that had won the heart of her ex-husband. One look and Sid Mandel whisked Merrill permanently off the balance beam. She collapsed her pose and stood u̧ Sid knows all about us, honey boy, and it's not a healthy bit of information, not for you, not for me.

Come on now. Roy took her by the wrist. Led her to the puffiest chair, the one Charlie Brown and Sable liked best. They were at the vet today, getting shampooed. Here now. Sit. Sit and breathe a little.

Merrill took a couple of shallow breaths. There was a captivating rise and fall of her bosom. Roy's hand was on her white lace shoulder. Esther could take a look at this kind of workmanship. Deep breath now. Roy knew divorce was like combat. Sometimes there were flashbacks. Okay, now. Relax.

Merrill closed her eyes. Roy was free to study her face in repose. Her pale lids were touched with an icy blue shadow. He knew her bedroom played off this extraordinary palette. Pale silk spread, vast creamy carpet, tiny cupid sconces with violet-blue ribbons on their asses. Sid loved that. The last visit, a visit Roy had to terminate, Sid plucked a blue satin souvenir and ate it while two semiarmed Pinkerton cops waited in the foyer for him to swallow. So. What's really going on?

Susie.

What about her?

Susie can't get into kindergarten, she's a dope.

Don't say that.

She is, she's thick. *Just like her father!* Merrill yelled to the throw pillow.

Roy moved the pillow to the other end of the coffee table. Let's keep this in confidence. So what happened? You tried the school, what school by the way, and they just said no? That's it?

Merrill sighed, recrossed her legs.

So you took her down to school and the principal said?

Susie took a test in the school library. Two hours with a repressed person sticking pegs into holes.

What repressed person?

A nun! A sister of charity flunked Susie in IQ. Can you imagine?

Roy scratched his neck. He checked out his lower left molars with his tongue. He finished Merrill's diet soda. So. This is a Catholic IQ test? With saints?

No saints, just pegs.

All right, give me a minute. Just one minute.

Merrill's eyes darkened with sadness, with injustice. She should have been a movie star, but she was too busy for the big screen.

One minute. Roy stood up. He needed some air. He needed to think. Contrary to logic, sometimes being with Merrill was like taking a high-potency sleeping pill.

Out on the aft deck the rain had slowed to a wet atmosphere, nothing coming down, just cold steam. Disgusting. Now the river was a bright viscous green. Roy leaned out and adjusted the flag, made sure the stripes hung straight. What could he do. He could get the name of the principal, or the nun with the pegs, and put in a call to the diocese. Shouldn't be a big deal. Wasn't the point of being a Catholic that brains didn't matter, spirit was all? Crazy spirit trumped. He could think of several examples. Hadn't he been called to tame those spirits once too often? And look where it got him. Anyway. Susie. She could peg any hole she put her mind to, the nun had only distracted her.

In school Roy had known his own troubles with distraction. At Columbia, it was Gerald Meecham. And at Horace Mann, it was Dun Wickford, then Perry Santimeyer. Talkers, cutups, tall boys. All charisma. Roy wanted to see how the world looked through those special eyes. What did they feel, what did they know? And it kept him from things. Sometimes he got Bs and Cs. The equivalent still happened, he hated to admit it. Sometimes he just couldn't concentrate. Though who would believe it if he said so.

The water smelled like an anchovy, really vile. Roy pushed back from the rail but then spotted his captain on land. He thought Charlie Peeko was on the boat, but no, there he was, outside the office hut with the basin manager, a true crook. Charlie gestured toward Roy, and the manager, slimy-eyed dope, gave Roy the benefit of his slow reflexes. Was the guy alive? Charlie, Roy shouted. But they were too far away. Well, he'd find out soon enough. Something was definitely wrong.

Out through the barnacle-ridden doorway slipped a new figure. A head-down, limp-armed type with hair like a slab of butter. Fourteen years old, Roy guessed, the kid looked wet. And even dopier than the father, who clapped him on the back. They started back down the ramp to the dock, Charlie and the boy. From the size of those feet, landing every which way, Charlie Peeko was lucky a misplaced foot didn't pop him in the drink.

They took the gangplank for Roy's sake. What was the use of having one if everyone stepped on board wherever they felt like it? Charlie Peeko wore that annoying smirk of satisfaction that, so far, Roy had failed to erase.

Roy?

Captain Peeko?

Mr. Cohn. I'd like to introduce Dirk Kegel, the new first mate.

Excuse me. Captain Peeko. We're docked in the Hudson River. We are planning, at most, a trip to the Statue of Liberty in the next two months, we need a first mate for this? We already have the entire Karpochnicj family acting as steward. No reflection on your abilities intended, Mr. Kegel. You'll pardon us for a moment.

The boy watched the planks of the deck very carefully. He had long, beautiful hands like a pianist's, and a soft mouth, the kind that drew a mother's attention. Made her think her child was still a child.

Dirk Kegel.

Yes sir?

All right. All right. Tell me something about your prior experience.

I'm a straight-A student at Bronx Science, sir.

That will certainly be a big help on board. What's the plan here, Captain?

We'll be doing a lot of prep for the fall. And Dirk is good with children.

Children?

Yes.

You've got to be kidding me. Roy gave Charlie Peeko a long stare. You truly amaze me. No wonder Merrill's in there talking to lamps. It's rude to eavesdrop. Is this news to you?

Now Captain Peeko studied the planks too. Roy shook his head. Unbelievable, Roy said. Kirk?

Dirk, sir.

Dirk. Do you know anything about pegs?

Excuse me, sir?

Pegs. IQ pegs.

No sir, but I'm willing to give it my best shot. The boy had a neck like a statue's, white and corded. He glanced up at Roy briefly, a look full of wonder.

What was that, Dirk?

Pegs, sir.

That's right. So, you're willing to try.

The boy gave a downcast nod.

Well, I guess that has to be good enough. That's all we can really ask. Isn't that right, Captain Peeko. Fine. Do whatever you want, you always do. Go ahead. Give Merrill the good news and then give Mr. Kegel the tour. And in my next life, if I'm lucky, I'm coming back as Charlie Peeko.

That night Roy had a dream. His office was decimated. The wrecking ball had come and gone, and only the floor was left, and rubble where the carpet had been. Roy could see the night sky, the roof had been blown away. Directly above, a full moon. Roy lay down on the filthy mattress. On his right was Frank Reilly, on his left a miniature bride no bigger than a paper clip. Frank would know what to do.

Roy was the first to spot the birds. Look, said Roy, and nudged Frank. Big webbed feet, feathered bellies, and red underparts, coiled like fists. Roy reached for Frank's arm. He knew what should be done, knew it before Frank did. Roy woke up. For a long time he lay there trying to remember exactly what he'd come up with.

Muddy was all alone in the kitchen. She'd made her own toast and the room smelled of burned caraway seeds from the rye. She wore a peau de soie quilted night jacket and a full-length lavender nightgown. Matching lavender mules, a dozen tiny hand-tied bows spanning each instep. Usually Mrs. Levy brought a tray to Muddy's bedroom with the mail and several newspapers, but Mrs. Levy had caught the flu, the worst ever—always worse when it comes in the summertime—and none of the cousins could be prevailed upon to come and serve on such short notice. Roy hadn't seen his mother at breakfast since his father died. He smiled as he opened the refrigerator. He wasn't much for breakfast himself, so the occasion was rare. He would try to get Muddy to interpret. This wouldn't be easy. Muddy loathed dreams, especially in the morning. Maybe a little chitchat first.

Roy brought a crusty tin of caviar to the table. Who knew how old it was. Mrs. Levy could not be taught to keep only fresh food, a wartime mentality Muddy indulged. A plate, Roy, Muddy said, now we are living in the twentieth century, something I meant to mention.

Roy put the little tin on a saucer. He used Muddy's good silver fluted grapefruit spoon to hack the crusty black bubbles from the sides. He craved that salt and licked his lips just slightly, his tongue already thickened by it. Muddy did the same thing, and she wasn't mocking him. Her tongue swept out across her planed lower lip, a long, slow exploration and then back inside again. Muddy's lower lip had a pressed-down shape as if she'd stacked a couple of bricks there for a decade or so.

When he was in kindergarten, Roy asked his mother why he had no brothers. Everyone had brothers, it seemed, but him. Muddy said—and this was at breakfast too—that when Roy was a baby, he had eaten them in their cribs. Roy thought about that. And then he looked at her, and he looked at her mouth. It was much wider than his own, and if anyone had eaten any brothers, it was her. He could see the brothers, popped in like snacks, their little boots flattening and widening her lower lip as they went. That Roy had been left alone was a double message: He was too good, he wasn't good enough. Any given second he toggled between the two self-assessments. Even now, age thirty-five, in a kitchen he paid for, he dodged back and forth without words, like a pulse in his brain, and it kept him safe. In this way, Muddy and Roy got along.

Always the last to know.

What's that? asked Muddy. You're mumbling again.

Between husbands and wives, either side, always the last to know the first thing about the other.

This is a subject you want to hold forth on?

I heard a crazy story last night, Roy said.

No dreams.

It's a true story. A husband and wife.

What could be more boring.

Not always.

No. True. Mine is a fatalist's outlook. Muddy sighed. You are right. Go on.

It involves a famous film director.

So?

All right. The director's wife is in the park one day.

What director, David Lean?

I thought it didn't matter.

Why should it matter to me?

Exactly. The director's wife is in the park, and she sees an old woman running, really fast. Roy paused to chip out a little more caviar.

Don't tell me. She's being chased? And I know who's doing the chasing. That the police don't arrest on sight, it's really a scandal. What's so hard to figure here?

Well, this old woman is running for her health.

How old is she?

Much older than anyone we know.

Is this a story about Roberto Rossellini? I won't listen to trash, Roy.

It's not him.

Fine. Go on.

You sure?

Yes.

So the wife goes home to her husband and says: I'm forty years old and I feel like I'm a hundred. She convinces him that they should start running too.

Is he faithful?

How should I know.

You know. You know. If her husband is faithful, a hundred is a long way off. If not, well, these things are like old fish. They stink up everything!

What about ducks or birds?

Excuse me?

Never mind.

Roy.

I don't think this story is so interesting to you.

Are you looking for a debate? There are teams you can join. Yes, even at your age, it's not too late.

Let me just tell you this one part. They start running. The husband thinks it's an excellent idea. First they run to Fifth Avenue. Then they run to the boat pond. Finally they start running in circles around the pond, ten, twenty, thirty times. After a while the wife notices—

She sees a lot. Not always a good practice.

Yes. She notices that they are running on an incline. All the time, one leg is bending more than the other. She tells the husband. She says, We should go in the other direction, even things out. And you know what the husband says?

Muddy shrugs. Husbands don't usually say so much.

He says: This is the way we run. That's it! And then he takes off in the usual direction. The wife turns around and goes the other way. When her husband passes her, he doesn't acknowledge her. She said it was the first time in their twenty years of marriage that she thought maybe he wasn't so flexible. What do you think?

Muddy brushed the toast crumbs to the center of her plate. You call this a story? Tell me something, Roy. Is marriage on your mind?

No.

You are not thinking you will marry Sylvia Horner's daughter. That would be a mistake like you don't know mistakes before today.

No, it's just a story, but I think there's something in it.

You do.

Yes. What does the story tell you, pretend it's a dream.

Not hard to pretend, the way you talk. But I'll tell you what it says, Roy. It says: Never, and I mean never, be afraid to turn around and run the other way. You tell that to Sylvia Horner's grasping daughter who thinks she can return a favor in such a way. You tell her I said so.

And Muddy pushed back from the table and planted a sharp wet kiss on his forehead before stamping out through the pantry.

June 14

It was Sunday already. A complicated day at Woeburne. For one, Pasteur was always agitated. His wife served a supper for the whole family promptly at five. And if any of the executives were lazy or clinging or sad during the visiting hours, the head count went slowly, and Pasteur arrived home late. This caused problems. Pasteur's daughter, Emily, just fifteen, cradled a deep desire for romantic adventure. If Pasteur wasn't consistent, setting an example of fealty and tenderness, all through gestures—he'd studied the importance of expression and movement—then his daughter might swirl away on the rising vapors of her bad ideas.

It was Sunday and Pasteur was distracted, thinking of Emily and her way of chewing with her mouth open, of cuddling the furniture. The way her body seemed different, looser by degrees, than the adults' in the house. Her skin more susceptible to help and harm. He thought she smelled funny. She gave off a musk of road tar and cotton candy. Pasteur believed if Mrs. Pasteur could be enrolled in a program of sustained attention, Emily might skate through the next three years or so. She'd land in adulthood as her mother had, undisturbed. Nothing agitated this protective urge like sitting in the high-back leather chair during visiting hour, watching the execs meet their outside relations. The mental defectives didn't have the same effect. It was the free will and the free desire that got Pasteur's unhappy attention.

He was trying to recall, just as a point of reference, if Mrs. Pasteur had been a lank-legged seducer in her youth, when Mrs. Will Clemens dropped her alligator purse at the check-in station. A rookie guard caressed the exterior as if feeling for breasts rather than weapons. Just the kind of thing that shot Pasteur's blood pressure to hell. The rookie chatted away, telling Mrs. Clemens his life story, while a line built up behind her. Pasteur pushed out of his chair just as the rookie came to his senses. Mrs. Clemens floated in the entryway looking for her husband. Pasteur looked too and realized only in that moment, that Will Clemens was missing.

There was a special system for dividing the prisoners receiving Sunday guests from the prisoners who were not. It involved what Pasteur liked to think of as a humane ruse. A distraction of his own devising. The prisoners unlikely to be visited were saved from despair. They could pluck a sealed deck of bicycle cards from an open box on Pasteur's desk. Pasteur paid for these himself. Anyone with a deck could find a seat in the education room. A hearts tournament there was loosely supervised by one of Pasteur's juniors in command. At the end of each month, Pasteur gave the lucky lowest scorer, prorated for days played, a Bundt cake baked by his own Emily.

Warden Flagmeyer agreed that some men on *Kentucky* benefited from the example of a good home life. So the cakes were presented at a monthly Friday fish supper in Pasteur's rec room. His basement on Scymour Street had been fashioned with sofa, love seat, and easy chair—all upholstered in stain-resistant dark red plaid—a wet bar, and a separate exterior entrance. The lucky visitors had access only to the underground den. For the Friday-night fish suppers, card tables angled like a short string of diamonds from the wet bar to the laundry-room door and the toilet. Pasteur served the fish sticks and fries himself, but when dessert came, the invitees cocked an ear to the wooden stairs, listening for the footfalls of Emily and her mother. Mrs. Pasteur carried down the gallon container of pistachio ice cream. Then came Emily and her Bundt cake.

Will Clemens had attended only one fish supper, and Pasteur was determined he should not come again. Weeks ago there'd been a disturbance between Will Clemens and his wife that Pasteur witnessed from afar. Every Sunday she came, pretty as you'd want. And Will was often silent, head down, and that pretty girl leaned into the table like she'd bore right through it if it would get him to uncurl inside himself. Pasteur had seen this kind of thing before, but never really with such a temptation to talk. Will Clemens sat with his legs crossed, his hand moving up to his mouth to smoke. Then one Sunday Will said something that made pretty Mrs. Clemens sit straight back in her chair. Later Sammy Finlandor said that Will told her she was giving a bunch of convicts hardons. Did she enjoy that? No more mercy visits, please. Pasteur didn't really believe Sammy, who was known to lie as soon as breathe. But Mrs. Clemens didn't come back. Four Sundays in a row, Will Clemens had swept the hearts tournament without breaking a sweat.

On his winning Friday night, Emily came down the stairs, with her blond hair sculpted to a perfect flip, her hip grazing the handrail. As always, she was in a world of her own. Her mother hacked green ice cream into bowls. Emily hoisted her Bundt cake, sleepy-eyed and bored, waiting to pass it off to the winner. Pasteur wanted to say: Straighten up, a strong girl slumping around, it's a crime. But he didn't like to shame her. Shame was a poor motivator. He directed her to Will, stretched out in the red easy chair, leg over leg, cheek in one hand, two fingers of the other extended to hold a cigarette. His black hair soaped into a neat brick. Emily's eyes focused abruptly. Her hips executed a swift corkscrew maneuver that ended in a squat at Will's feet, her cake tilting off its cardboard platter. Will reached out with the hand that had held his face, caught the cake, said, Thank you, Emily. It's very nice. Emily remained squatting. Pasteur, shame or no shame, reached over, encircled the back of his daughter's neck, and brought her to her feet.

Now on this Sunday, weeks later, Pasteur found Will Clemens, just as he'd feared, in the education room, making a killing in hearts. Mister, maybe you didn't get the news, Pasteur said. Will was just dropping the deadly queen of spades on Ray Spofford, who'd never once won a Bundt. You've got a nice wife downstairs waiting to say hello to you.

Will squinted down at the paper by his wrist, perfect zero score. Such a position was a salable commodity. Knowledge Pasteur overlooked officially, but he knew Will could easily trade that slip for a carton of cigarettes or more right now. Here you go, Ray. Will pushed the score across the table and picked up Ray's and stuck it in his pocket. Okay.

Pasteur didn't know much about Will Clemens. He seemed decent, quiet, gave him no trouble. But he was a boil on Warden Flagmeyer's neck for some undisclosed reason, and now Emily couldn't stop asking about him: Is he coming for supper, is he winning, how did he know to call me Emily, is his wife a blonde and has she let herself go? These questions were an irritant. But Pasteur had cautioned himself over the years not to take his personal problems out on the men, as so many other officers did, even when they were the cause of the personal problem. There was no turning back from that kind of thinking.

Pasteur followed Will back out of the education room, down the south stairway to the reception area. Pasteur pointed to Mrs. Clemens, still standing under the archway. The rookie guard chattered away at her. Will thanked Pasteur and slowly approached his wife. The denim pants Will wore looked like they fit him, Pasteur noticed, and wondered if Will had them tailored in some way. Maybe he did it himself. When Will got close to his wife, she saw him and swiveled, something deep in the hips, just as his Emily had, and her face lit and darkened at the same moment. Will took her hand, as he had taken Emily's cake, and Mrs. Clemens was stunned into stillness in the same way. Will led her over to the nearest table, and they spoke for less than four minutes. When she stood she looked calmer, as if she'd gotten what she'd come for, and Will Clemens reached across and held his wife very briefly, kissed her, and let her go. Next to them another exec, buried in the shoulder of a massive woman, never moved. Mrs. Clemens stood watching her husband traverse the hall, his tall, slim body in his good-fitting clothes. Pasteur studied her. He knew she couldn't hear the rookie guard who spoke to her now. She watched her husband, her eyes satisfied, calm, and lost. Pasteur felt very sorry for her. He resolved to put the fix in, or to cancel the hearts altogether. This man was dangerous.

The worst time to be awake at New York Hospital was after midnight. Especially hot and thirsty and itching because no one could hear Bo, and no one he really liked was ever on duty at such a time. Even the generators, which always rumbled, were quiet. No one laughed or talked or even prayed. No priest or rabbi stood at anyone's messy bed, no one at all. Only Clarissa. And she was more sour than ever because her fiancé had taken a job laying pipe in Alaska to secure their financial future. He'd be leaving any day now.

Three different attachments exited from three different parts of Bo's body. He had a tube in his nose to move his breath, a tube attached to a permanent shunt in his arm to feed his blood, and a wired cloth disk taped to his chest under his pajamas to listen to his heart. Whatever that disk detected tapped out in green lit dots on a ticking machine with its own wheeled cart. In the green light, Bo could see the tube on his arm where all the itching was.

From the hallway, the sound of Clarissa's footsteps, splats and squeaks, came closer. Then a shadow took up the entire doorway. Bo was all alone in his room now that Jimmy was gone, Jimmy and all of his toys and all of his father's football posters.

Bo, you awake again? What did I tell you about sleep. It's more important than anything for you.

Bo lifted up the arm with the tube apparatus. The itch wakes me up.

Well, let me take a look, but no big talks now. The shadow moved out of the door and the light fell in softly, a relief, as if the darkness made him hold his breath and the air in the nose tube got caught and cold.

Here, Clarissa.

I think I can find an IV, thank you.

Clarissa moved the trolley and let the plastic tube pull tight. That smarted like a Band-Aid being readjusted. No squiggling there, mister. She flicked on the tiny light. For reading, if he knew how to read, that's what it was for. Jimmy knew how to read, and certainly Lou-Lou, though she liked to read in the dark.

Well, you're on empty here, no wonder you've got an itch. Fat Clarissa smacked her lips. Her tiny diamond sparkled like a buoy light in the swell of her big hand. You hold on there now, and I'll be right back. She turned a knob on the line, then made a fast, loud retreat down the hall. Bo heard her talking on the phone, very angry, she was calling someone incompetent. Her favorite word. Bo had heard it so often he asked Hollis what it meant. She told him funny in the head, the idea doesn't connect up with the right action. Her example had been if Bo wanted to paint an ocean blue and then got distracted and left it blank. No ocean.

Clarissa returned. She brought a tall guy with acne. He wore an intern's jacket. He looked like a sleepwalker, but his hands were softer than Bo's mother's. He put gentle, exact fingers where the tube was in the shunt, and before Bo could blink, the old tube was removed and a new one in, with a quick wet touch around the edge. The itching stopped right away. The tall boy-man tipped the tube in Bo's nose, made a slight adjustment somewhere on the line, and the little jets of air stopped pulsing so tight and cold inside his nostrils. Everything calmed down around this man. He put his warm hand over the disk on Bo's chest and kept it there, soothing everything. Bo would tell Hollis and she would be glad, and Bo was asleep before fat Clarissa made the floor squeak again or the light vanish in the door.

June 16

Merrill gave Lou-Lou a discerning once-over. Hold it right there, now. Lou-Lou stood dripping water on the ivory-colored carpet. Just hold on, little lamb. Lou-Lou tucked the velvety towel tighter around her belly and stood at attention. Merrill reached for the tiny gold Blessed Virgin medal that hung around Lou-Lou's neck, a recent gift from her grandmother, and she scrutinized it for meaning. Well, there's a bit more to be achieved in the here and now.

Susie, Merrill's daughter, lay prone, faceup in her French linen navy blue dress. Her feet in patent-leather T-straps hung just off the edge of the mauve satin cover on the king-size bed. She was five. She did not want to see *Man of la Mancha* again. Merrill gathered a handful of Lou-Lou's pixie hair and stood back. Yes, I think we can do something with this.

Merrill looked like a person on television: tiny waist, teeth whiter than her daughter's. She smiled at Lou-Lou, and Lou-Lou fell in love. Merrill bent down and rubbed petal-pink fingernails across the bumpy scarred surface of Lou-Lou's knees. Loofah! she declared, and Lou-Lou felt herself soften with wonder. Merrill could just touch her all over and turn her into someone just like herself. A small round dark-haired Merrill. Lou-Lou squinted toward Susie's face, not an inch of Merrill anywhere. Not a molecule. Not an atom. Lou-Lou saw her own atoms, just as Sister Barbara had drawn them in red chalk, jiggling all around to create the new Lou-Lou in perfect likeness to the beauty telling her to tuck in her tummy *and* her bottom, both at once. Now, breathe too, baby doll, that's right.

The doorbell sounded with a loud electronic bark. Merrill frowned and stood up straight. Shit. Took him long enough. She gave Lou-Lou one last appraising glance, then left to answer the door. Once her mother was gone, Susie closed her eyes.

Are you tired?

Susie didn't respond. But when Lou-Lou turned to find her own clothes, just as Merrill had laid them out on the paisley chair— her new dress, a variation on Susie's navy linen—Susie propped herself on her elbows and asked how long Lou-Lou planned to stay. Forever seemed a possibility. Lou-Lou shrugged.

Well, you can't have my dog. Susie lay back down. She had a teacup Yorkie who appeared only for walks. Usually he lived under the sofa in the library. Lou-Lou's mother had warned her about Susie. She explained that Susie was very lonely and missed her daddy, who lived in Chicago.

On business?

Yes, I suppose he is.

Something in her mother's face, a distraction, kept Lou-Lou from drawing the obvious parallel to her own father out loud: business. Lou-Lou nodded. Kay flipped through the magazine with an all-yellow house on the cover. The train rocked through the marshes of the Amboys, and Lou-Lou thought that business was frightening in its ability to swallow fathers whole. All dressed in white, Merrill was waiting to greet them at Pennsylvania Station. She hugged and kissed Kay as a missing father might, then Kay had to go right away to the hospital and to Bo. When she said good-bye, there were tears stuck beneath her bottom lashes but not on her cheeks.

In the limousine, Merrill had some crucial things to tell Lou-Lou about bravery. She said that Lou-Lou was naturally brave, that any feelings to the contrary were just a pestering little devil and that Lou-Lou should pay that creature no mind whatsoever. Her voice was like a harmonica, a happy song in it all the time. Her ideas just burst out that way. She had some things to say about her daughter, Susie, who was at ballet school until three o'clock. Susie was an extraordinary girl, and Merrill knew that for Lou-Lou a very special friendship was waiting in the wings. That's why Lou-Lou would stay with Merrill instead of at the hotel with her mother. Sisters of the heart, Merrill said with certainty, knocking on her beautiful white blouse, I can feel it already.

She had some further thoughts about the vital importance of a good dress when the thorns of life reach out for you, and that's why she directed the driver to Saks before they did another thing. Lou-Lou understood that questions would slow Merrill down. She smiled and wondered which thorns were reaching for her as they crawled along Fifth Avenue. The car smelled like the leather of her father's good wallet and like a whole garden of flowers, but that was Merrill.

There must be a lot going on in the foyer. Whoever rang the buzzer was keeping Merrill very busy, laughing and cooing almost. Lou-Lou wondered if she should just go ahead and dress herself. Merrill would have other chances to change her into a beauty. She edged her fanny onto the paisley chair and started wrestling with the spider-fine white lace stockings Merrill had chosen for her. She was a girl, more a girl than ever before, something that everybody liked all the time.

My father is in business too, Lou-Lou whispered to Susie's closed eyelids.

Your father's in jail, Susie whispered back.

Lou-Lou regarded the upside-down face for a second. Business, she said.

Jail. Susie didn't bother to open her eyes. Jail, jail, jail, she sang like a Tweety Bird, high and chirpy, an imitation of her mother's beautiful voice. Jail, jail.

Not so! Merrill stood now in the doorway. Not so, and no more stupid talk out of you, young lady.

I heard you on the phone. Susie's puffy mouth began to tremble.

You heard wrong.

Susie burst into tears without moving an inch from her position on the bed. Her face reddened and she howled a little: Oh, oh, oh.

Lying hurts, doesn't it. Her mother's voice had changed. Now Merrill was laying down a few more observations on life, just as in the car. And Susie cried on, as if she'd only been suffering a long pause and was picking up the beat. Lonely, thought Lou-Lou. And lying always causes crying, that much was a certainty.

I think we've had just about enough drama for one day, you'll wear us all out for the theater. Come on now. Merrill displayed a fan of three tickets and fluttered them toward her heart-shaped face. All her blond hair flowed back from her forehead in a perfect wave, tucked for a brief soft instant beneath a pale aqua grosgrain ribbon, and then a rush of blond curls. Let's get a look at you two.

The doorbell screeched again. Merrill jumped. Good Lord. Lou-Lou thought she'd never get used to the sound, or the sirens muffled and constant beyond the thick white curtains, still loud. She missed Gert in that moment, she missed the dirt pile down by the water that constituted her area of the Maguire boys' fort. The annex. But her mother wasn't speaking to Gert right now, that's why Lou-Lou was here. Gert had lost her. And no matter what Lou-Lou said about that: I helped the girl with the hole in her heart, I saw my name written by the ants and in the stars, I have a calling, her mother closed off her face, much like Susie did now lying on the bed. What was I thinking? Kay said to Merrill on the phone. She'd always known Gert was careless. For a few days Meemaw stayed with Lou-Lou, drove her to school and picked her up again at three in the Thunderbird, had snacks on the kitchen table all set when they got home, but then she needed to go back to Baltimore. Your grandfather's the biggest baby of them all, she said. On the train Kay shook her head in anger. It's better, goose, you'll see, you'll be nearby now. Merrill gave Susie a hard look, then went to answer the door again.

Jail, whispered Susie.

I know you are just lonely, I know your father is far away. Lou-Lou closed her eyes too and saw two Ls and a hyphen made of sparklers in the sky.

Merrill's limousine was being used that night by someone else, she didn't say who, so they took a taxi to the theater. Merrill said to the driver: Take the park. But the driver wanted to argue with her, he turned around and threw his hairy arm over the glass divider, his voice quaked slightly. The traffic is bad, he said, he said *bad* as if the traffic would injure them. Merrill hummed: I have my reasons. Suit yourself, the driver said. He looked at every inch of Merrill he could see. Turning back around, he repeated it, Suit yourself, as if he was saying something pleasing and wise.

When sometime later, the Tavern on the Green finally appeared, the hot smell of mulch and horse manure flowing through the open windows, when the lights rippled behind the elm tree and the road curved up and back into the city, Merrill wrapped her arms around Lou-Lou and they were soft as the petal of the best, most important flower. Lou-Lou let herself be drawn into that spot, even though Susie gave her a narrow eye. Lou-Lou fell in. And then they were out, out of the park, and shuttling down the vibrating circus of Broadway to the Beaumont Theater and all the things that happened there.

Susie was sick right away. Even in the taxi, she kept holding her stomach and saying she didn't feel so good. Merrill delivered a sharp tap to Susie's knee and said, Take a deep breath, it does wonders. But when the theater came up and all the people crowded in together in shiny groups, women in coats of satin with glimmer collars, men in dark jackets, Susie burst from the cab and doubled over toward the sidewalk. Merrill, slipping out, all in palest aqua tulle, looked unimpressed. Lou-Lou peered into Susie's tipped-over emergency-style face. She had to say, she'd seen a lot of this kind of thing, and Susie looked okay.

Now Merrill, smiling to no one in particular, grabbed Susie by her navy linen collar and yanked her upright. Susie's eyes remained squinting shut, her mouth a grim line.

Lou-Lou tried humor, as her father always advocated in difficult moments. Who poops faster than Superman? Lou-Lou inquired to the small shut face. Give up?

No. I don't give up, you stupid fuck.

Whack. Susie's head was hit so fast, Lou-Lou wasn't even sure it happened. Susie's eyes and mouth popped open. Lou-Lou thought she would shriek right in the mash of all that satin and summer trousers pressing in with cigarette smoke and steam from the sidewalk. A shriek was coming. Lou-Lou could see it starting. Merrill bent down and whispered, with her singing voice, We're talking about what you can handle. What did that mean? But Susie got serious. She nipped that scream, wherever it was, shivered out of her mother's grasp, and walked to the door, as if she had all the tickets in her hand and nothing had happened. Merrill followed with a how-dare-you expression, but when she reached the doors and Susie, a tall thin man stood, smiling a giant smile that waved like a net floating high in the air. Well, said Merrill, and planted about twelve possible meanings on the word.

Susie, peach, you remember Mr. Henning?

Susie dropped a curtsy, and Mr. Henning bowed, straightening up to open and close his teeth, beaming right into Merrill's face like she was the big steak he'd been waiting to cut into. Ding. Ding. They had barely gotten here on time, Mr. Henning and the meat feeling of him receded, as the special usher skipped them right down the aisle to the very best seats in the house. The very best. When the Man of La Mancha scrubbed his eyebrows into place, Lou-Lou could see where his real ones ended and the fake ones began. At the intermission, Merrill drank four glasses of champagne in a row with Mr. Henning and didn't return with Susie and Lou-Lou to their seats. Susie cried, head on her knees, in the best seat in the house. That and the exasperated looks of the theatergoers all around made it hard to concentrate on Dulcinea and all the sadness singing there on the stage. Finally the theater manager tiptoed down the aisle. Susie and Lou-Lou had to sit in his office, with old *Playbill*s on their laps to keep them busy. Susie cried harder still, but no one except Lou-Lou could hear her.

In the morning, Lou-Lou's special blood test was happening first thing, and although her mother and Merrill had made the arrangement when they hugged at Pennsylvania Station, Merrill had momentarily forgotten. So when Kay appeared at the door at seven-thirty as planned, just sweeping by to get Lou-Lou over to the clinic at the hospital, Mr. Henning answered the door wearing only a bargello-flame-stitch throw pillow. Merrill's still asleep, he whispered, with a wink.

In the taxi to the hospital, Lou-Lou finished dressing. Her mother was very angry because the T-strap was so difficult to buckle on Lou-Lou's new shoe. She did only half the buttons on Lou-Lou's dress before looking out the window to think. She said they were late and she would explain what was happening as soon as they got there. But when they pulled up to the awning at New York Hospital, someone else needed their cab immediately, and inside, the elevator was just about to depart, and they arrived on the seventh floor with the green walls and the long slanting ramps with strips of black sandpaper and the bolted-down chairs. The person who was supposed to meet them wasn't there. Kay told Lou-Lou to wait while she found a technician. Lou-Lou finally managed to get her shoe secured and her dress buttoned, just in time for the nurse to ask her to take them off and put on a cold green nightie.

The procedure lasted only a minute. A man with hands so large they wrapped around the entire circumference of her arm, took a blood sample from the crook of her elbow. She saw the blood, dark and thick-looking, fill the needle's barrel. While he drew the blood, he let his mouth open and his tongue lay like a tiny pink carpet six inches from Lou-Lou's eyes. He told her to keep sitting on the wheeled chair while he ducked next door to the lab. We'll do a smear right away, he said. She never saw him again. Lou-Lou held the gauze pressed for a while, then let it go; she could barely find the dot where the needle had been.

Forty-five minutes passed before the door opened and her mother entered. She kissed Lou-Lou's forehead. Come on, pumpkin, she said, put your dress on, we'll see Bo. Then she kissed her again on her hair and began handing Lou-Lou her clothes.

Lou-Lou kept a close watch for discrepancies, for oversights, while Bo counted the freckles on his body. On the television mounted high on the wall opposite the two beds, Superman was deep in the woods, spying on Lois Lane, just to make sure she was okay in that lonely cabin. Bo did not exaggerate the way Lou-Lou was said to do, but sometimes he got excited and lost count of things: trucks, days until Christmas.

Right there! She could see the shadow of a freckle in the IV bruise, peeping out from the tape. But she'd let that slide, too hard to tell. What about your nose? You have a ton on your nose.

Bo looked hurt. No, he said. They don't count.

It's an avalanche. One million, one. One million, two.

Shut up, Lou-Lou.

One million, three.

Bo tucked his nose into the elbow of his unbandaged arm. No. I can still count with my photographic memory.

No! said Bo.

A large black wolf howled just outside Lois Lane's cabin door. Lois reached for the phone, but the line was dead.

Hollis looked in a very bad mood. Her sneakers made a ripping sound on the floor, like Band-Aids coming off a knee. Are you bothering him? I'm going to bounce you if you don't cut it out. Hollis reached up and snapped off the television. Let's see, Bo, let's take a look at that arm. Hollis lifted Bo's IV arm in both hands and traced along the forearm and above the elbow like a weaver smoothing silk. She flicked her middle finger ever so lightly just above the shunt. Shit.

What? asked Lou-Lou.

Bad luck.

What's bad luck?

Sweetie pie, your mommy's out in the hall talking to Dr. Fred, do you want to get them for me?

Um, not right now.

Please?

Bo was grinning at her.

What's so funny, Mr. Million Freckles?

Now, Lou-Lou, please.

Hollis shook the bottle on the cart and watched carefully. Nothing, no movement. The vein was definitely collapsed. Jones Beach, David Hetzler chased her to the end of parking lot D, and then planted his hands on her hips like he owned them. God. She didn't know if she could find another vein. Bo, angel, is there any ache in your arm? Anything hurt?

Lou-Lou thinks I have a million freckles.

In this case, Lou-Lou is wrong.

Hollis pulled a sterile gauze packet from her pocket. She closed the clamp on the IV tube. Bo? What time is it when an elephant sits on your fence? She shimmied the plastic tubing off of the exterior end of the shunt, pinched the tube before the liquid spurt, then carefully, carefully removed the tape from his arm.

Time to get a new alarm clock.

What kind of alarm clock? Hollis took a breath in, and on the exhale, tried to pull out the shunt in one movement. Reverse archery. Hollis covered the wound fast with the sterile gauze, taped it tight, pressed all around with her fingertips.

Big Ben.

Big Ben? Hollis looked up at Bo's face. He did have a lot of freckles. Bo smiled at Hollis. Big Ben. Good answer, Bo.

After the hospital, Kay went back to Merrill's to explain. The treatment was being delayed, it turned out. She made some hand signals. Then she said Bo just wasn't ready. Merrill and Kay sat in the white deck chairs on Merrill's white brick terrace and drank iced espresso. Merrill looked sad and blue. She didn't say anything. Kay tried to explain it again, about the experiment, the bone marrow transplant, about the white cells, the need for strength. They'd be going out on a limb as it was, and now they'd have to find another donor. She might as well send Lou-Lou home.

Kay and Merrill, each stretched long in the lounge chairs, closed their eyes as if asleep. Their blond hair was pulled from their faces in identical black headbands. The late-afternoon sun made their arms and legs whiter than the bricks. Susie rubbed the bare feet of her Barbie back and forth against the cement wall, grinding away the toes. Lou-Lou drank a real Coke. Then she went into Susie's all-pink bedroom and packed her own red suitcase.

Chef Brodie's cheeks were flushed and just visible above the mound of ground chuck on his wood-block table. Pasteur gave a quick salute, then looked around for his charge. Even in the basement kitchen, sunlight striped the walls, pouring down from six-foot gashes near the ceiling. Chef Brodie in tennis sneakers stood on discarded wood pallets, but Will Clemens wore his prison oxfords, and light or no light, the stone floors chilled him. He was glad to leave the pile of Spanish onions and climb two levels to the ground floor, to the small alcove some artist had carved with a statue in mind. Two tiny sconces with bare bulbs poised to light a marble torso lit the wall phone instead. Special calls, if warranted, could be patched through to prisoners. Will thought it must be Roy. He picked up the line, gave the operator his name, and read off the number inked on every article of his clothing. It was his mother. And she was crying. Oh, Will.

It's all right, Mama, he said. This was perhaps the fourth or fifth time she'd called.

And Bo.

Yes. Will started to cough. I know.

You're not sick?

No. No. But I shouldn't stay too long on the phone. Will coughed harder, and Pasteur gave him a look from where he stood a polite distance away. Will kept coughing until he made himself gag. Rita began to cry again.

Mama, don't do that, I'm okay, please don't worry about me. I'm coming there.

No. Don't. Promise me you won't come. I'm better, at least for a while, without visitors, please. I need to go now, but we can write.

Your father too, he wants to come.

Both of you write, please.

Will said good-bye, that he loved her, then hung up the phone. Pasteur watched Will sit there hacking into his hands.

Do I need to take you over to the infirmary for that cough?

It's my head. Any head doctors?

Could be arranged.

Will did feel nuts, but it was in his body. A word about Bo and he felt a kind of bizarre misery. It started in his groin, then radiated down toward the space behind each kneecap with a slow red insistence. It stopped there, rested in an oscillating on-off pattern, then traveled upward again, reaming his hip joints, landing in the center of his sternum. His throat would swell, then his head would finally dry out like a gourd and swing with pain. This choreography was completely reliable.

Maybe you should take a small break, Pasteur said. Twenty minutes in the library, then I'll haul you back downstairs. Pasteur had read the newspapers. He didn't much care for this man with his slicked hair, or the spin Will had put on Emily, but he could feel for him. Pasteur knew about being a father.

Will nodded. Thought he had conned Pasteur, as he did everyone else, but nonetheless let himself be escorted to the carved door off the center dome. Pasteur let him in. The library was dark, smelled of mice and old paper. Well out of the sunlight and the endless blue. In off hours, the library staff was off duty. Pasteur took a swivel chair behind the center station. He had a panoramic view there of the stacks. He reached under the desk for the main light switch.

Leave them off, could you?

Sure, said Pasteur. He turned on the little desk lamp instead and picked up a bulletin to read. Will felt a little sorry for Pasteur. The other guards didn't like him. They called him the social worker, said Pasteur was administering his fat ass as therapy. Said Pasteur could always hear the sound of a stiff dick in need.

But Pasteur seemed oblivious, continued his usual methods as if they were standard. And got good results. Warden Flagmeyer let him do what he wanted.

Will took a chair at the big oak table and stared for a while at the black tape on all the spines of all the books. He waited for the dark and the dust to act medicinally. He looked at the tape and the white hand-inked titles describing things that happened slowly enough to make sense, unlike his experience, which was random, fast, and overwhelming. And then it was all hindsight. Sorting the past. Figuring. That's all anyone did here.

Here was Kay in the past: eighteen, dark blond curls tucked in amber clips shaped like poodles. White shorts. White blouse, exaggerated darts, pinpoint bra, round breasts, a nice surprise. In Sid Plowporter's borrowed truck, Kay sat in the ocher trim paint by mistake. Later, when she bent in to the soda case to pull out a Coke, the paint amoeba wriggled in the double-stitched seam of her crotch, made Will ache. At the beach, in the boardwalk shower, Kay sulked when he said her lips, little clams, were shriveled by the ocean salt. He kissed her and let the water down into her bathing suit, held out the straps to wash away the sand.

But then there was Enid Cartwoll. Enid could be found any day serving iced tea and fried oysters at Sandy's Fish Bar. She wore the insignia blouse like a child, without care. Often he caught her between chores and willing to fool around. Enid had a thing going with the cook, Swanson, a jaundiced-looking guy with long false teeth. He let her come and go. If she was gone, Swanson served the customers himself.

Enid Cartwoll didn't have a car or a driver's license, though she was nearly nineteen. She walked to Sandy's Fish Bar from the carriage-house apartment she shared with three other girls. On that walk, in the early afternoon, though Will did not like to plan such things, there was a spot, a little copse of trees, white pine and underbrush that bloomed in summer. Huge flowers like heads of cauliflower sagged along the sandy road to the tennis courts. If Will happened to be walking himself to get some fresh air after a late night's work, waking at noon, stretching his legs. If he did see her from, say, a distance of a hundred feet away, she would take that turn. A waitress rumpled already in her Sandy's Fish Bar blouse, she'd turn as if to catch a little tennis, then turn again into the heavy heads of the flowers, and there she would do something peculiar that Will could never quite shake from his head.

Will would continue along as if he'd seen nothing. He'd untuck his shirt, a breeze toying with the flap. He'd pull it down, cars would pass, he'd play with his shirt and the wind. In the drive-way to the tennis club, feet sinking in the soft ground, he'd fig-ure out which way she went, look for a torn flower. Or listen, he'd listen for a crackle in the underbrush, cup his hand over his ear to block out the swish of the wind. When he made the right choice to locate her in the midst of sand and sticks, she'd be squatting, face away, skirt curled and bunched at her waist, barefoot, her white waitress shoes lined toe to toe beside her. Her ass spread right at him, that's what he would see first. She was like a girl taking a crap, and he just happened to stumble over her.

At the librarian's station, Pasteur was caught up in the bulle-tin. Big on the benefits of study, he advocated the exploration of the stacks, such as they were, for his executives. Pasteur faithfully delivered the news of every recent acquisition. He promoted study-ing the law, said it was useful to know the system that curtailed you. Will had no interest, he already knew what curtailed him.

Once Roy took him on a business trip to Europe to meet the White Russian. Kay bought him the most beautiful luggage he'd ever seen. He hadn't known luggage could look like that, and in it she'd packed his ordinary shirts and ordinary underwear, but in Paris, the fabulous container lent them its air . What did you sell? The house? Kay put her temple to his cheek, some tea-rose scent. Nothing you'd notice, she said. What you don't know, you know.

In Paris with Roy, Will could barely breathe. Who knew the world could be so big. His bed had a fucking footstool. His ordinary laundry came delivered back to him in blue tissue. The White Russian stroked his cock with her foot under the table while eating tiny roasted birds, three to a plate. And Roy caused a big diversion, some problem with his snapper, everyone frantic, yelling in French. Will slipped away, yelling too, but no one heard. Every day, clean soft sheets that smelled of ocean water and honey.

Later, Roy wasn't there. He wasn't in the courtroom with Will that morning. No need, he said, this is just routine, a little hassling from our friends. What can they do? A sentencing hearing for a misdemeanor? What can they ask for? Frank will take care of it. We're talking misdemeanor. This is an irritant. I'll meet you for lunch. If not, dinner.

But there was confusion even before they arrived. The whole business of going at all. Earlier, there had been the advice to plead guilty, it was nothing, forget about it. And he had forgotten. Then months later, more, Bo was already sick, he got a visit from a junior attorney, an infant, asking for his testimony against Roy, which was, of course, impossible.

Off the record, the attorney said.

Can't do it, said Will, sorry.

Right away Will got the notice, delivered by a U.S. marshal, a subpoena, a sentencing date.

For what? Hiding the typewriter ribbon? This is science fiction, they're making it up as they go, said Roy.

Sentence?

Frank said it was no big deal. Teapot-tempest kind of thing.

Roy said lunch, maybe dinner, he'd know by eleven, some dope wanted justice and Roy had promised. Either way, they'd meet up later and eat.

It was a small courtroom, a miniature, like a room in Lou-Lou's dollhouse. Walls fitted with wood paneling and empty nooks too heavy for its size. A dark room with no windows. Half the space swallowed by the judge's bench, flanked by two scarred desks. Behind the one on the right sat the judge's clerk, Hiram Green, with voluptuous lips and a cough deep in his chest. On the left the bailiff arranged a calendar, moved a pair of handcuffs. It was still early, just past nine o'clock. Frank Reilly looked fresh as a young athlete, pink-cheeked, he ran ten blocks from the wrong subway station. Where's the car? Will asked.

Don't ask.

More confusion. Kay didn't hold Will's hand. She rested her hip against his and seemed calm. Her navy blue suit, and legs in soft beige stockings, so pretty. The clasp on her purse a tiny seashell.

There were others in the room as well. Scattered in the benches, maybe six men. A couple dozed, others read the paper. One gripped a briefcase in his lap. The judge entered the room from a side door, and everyone stood before the bailiff could make the announcement. Kay's purse dropped to the dirty floor. She ducked to get it and Will did too. The bailiff called his name. Frank said, Good, we'll get this over with.

Another man entered from the back through the swinging doors, blond, a baby face with heavy glasses. The bailiff stood to protest, but Hiram Green waved and coughed him down. The young man was allowed a brief private conference with Hiram, even though Will was already standing. Hiram listened to the whisper, plunged out a lower lip in response. The man left the room swiftly, glancing only once at the fellow with the briefcase. Hiram wrote something down on a sheet of yellow paper, carefully, as if working out a sketch. He handed this to the judge, who was polishing his own glasses on the sleeve of his robe. The judge read the scrap, squinted at Hiram, who squinted back, looked at Frank Reilly, looked down.

There seems to be some kind of a mix-up here. Hiram Green nodded, and the judge looked like he tasted something bad on his teeth. All right, all right, he said.

Frank stepped forward with Will to the bar, a thick wood rail-
ing, and waited. The judge cleared his throat and said it had been
brought to his attention, but then he stopped, there was a proto-
col to be observed here, a word or two from the bailiff. The judge
leaned his face toward his left hand, patted down the hair on the
top of his head. The bailiff reseated himself. The judge said, looking down all the while at the paper, Mr. Reilly, your client pleaded
guilty to a misdemeanor in the State of New York, but in this
courtroom, as you are well aware, other rules apply. He looked up
for confirmation.

Your honor, the charge to which my client pleaded is a misdemeanor.

I'm afraid not, sir. No, I think not. The circumstances reveal a
larger ramification to his actions.

Your honor, the circumstances are that my client is being used
to prove a political point far beyond his own course of action. I
also want to bring to your attention, before any kind of sentencing, the condition of this man's child, who is gravely ill. Also,
I've submitted a motion to withdraw the initial plea.

Thank you, counselor. Mr. Clemens, I have it that you entered
a plea of guilty to a conspiracy charge on October 5, 1962.

Your honor, there is an error.

Thank you, Mr. Reilly, I am addressing your client. Is that correct, Mr. Clemens?

Yes.

Were you coerced in any way to make this plea?

No.

Then I can only assume it stands.

Your honor! There is a motion to withdraw the plea.

Motion.

Yes, sir. It's right there, sir.

Hiram Green stepped back toward the bench with a file folder.
The judge looked at him, opened the manila folder, peeled off the
top document, and read it through. I see, he said. Looked to the

back of the room, patted the hair at his temple. No, motion denied. Without further—

Your honor, there's a mistake here. My client, under personal duress, pleaded guilty to a misdemeanor. By mistake. It's in the motion.

Mr. Reilly. A word to the wise, don't interrupt. It doesn't help anyone. Mr. Clemens, I am sentencing you to a year and a day. Under federal law, it is the minimum sentence, to be served in full.

Your honor, I move to set bail pending appeal.

No bail.

Your honor! This is a mistake.

Mr. Reilly, I can correct it. There's a good deal I can correct for you if you'd like me to. Within my limited powers, there are still some things that I can do. Bailiff?

The stench. From dirty laundry to garbage. The bailiff fumbled at his desk. Will felt his face go cold as he turned to Kay. Her head cocked sideways, as if someone had slapped her, she was as white as soap, his girl. The bailiff picked up the handcuffs, dropped them twice, before calling his name. William Clemens? The bailiff approached the bar, came around, holding the cuffs away from his stout body like ice-cream cones dripping. He fastened them to Will's wrists. The pink all gone from Frank's face, all color gone, he said, Will. Don't worry, don't worry.

More poor advice, counselor, said the man in the pew with the briefcase. The judge turned to Hiram Green, said, Call the next case, and took off his glasses. He stuffed all the loose papers in front of him into the folder. The bailiff led Will down the short aisle. Kay stepped forward and slammed her knee hard against the pew. Come along, now, said the bailiff. The doors swung closed behind them, taking Kay out of Will's sight. In the dark corridor, the bailiff said, Sorry to hear about your child. The remainder of the trip to West Street was silent.

When Will thought about this, it was always the very end he changed, the walk down the aisle from the bar to the double doors. Kay made it out of the bench in time. He touched her, found her face and her hands and her mouth. He knew that would have changed something. And then he thought, That's just stupid, I'm stupid, and he let her go.

Fourth of July

Esther had great plans for the puppy, knew all about the healing properties of animals, not to mention that every boy needed a dog.

Did your brothers have dogs? That's what I'd like to know. What Horner boy had a dog of his own? Roy pointed out.

Maybe they should have, maybe that was a mistake. Look at you! Look at your own experience.

Exactly.

You're not funny.

Let's wait.

You don't even know the difference between a life enhanced by a dog and a life diminished.

How about we wait for a remission, said Roy, so he can play with the dog. What do you think.

Are you taking a shower?

Yes, I'm taking a shower.

In the shower Roy could hear Esther laughing. She had to be on the phone, Muddy never made her laugh; besides, Muddy wasn't home. There were too many plants in this bathroom. It was claustrophobic. Esther said, You've got a skylight, take advantage of it, very few New Yorkers have so much sun in a bathroom. But he was definitely getting rid of the urns with the trees, no matter how much sun he had. Esther was talking poodle. A miniature poodle. And now Roy had a small canker sore just beginning, right inside his bottom lip. This thing was already stinging. He couldn't think of a single poodle he'd ever seen that wasn't high-strung. He let the warm water wash his mouth.

At the sink he got a better sense of what was hurting so much. That canker sore felt like a cattle brand. What was he eating that was doing this to his mouth. Lies, Muddy said. Swallow lies and that's what you get, a mouth full of pain. She would know. Woman who'd never had a cavity. Who never once went to the dentist to get an X ray. Lies. Whose lies had he swallowed today? Roy read the fine print on the Mercurochrome bottle.

The burgundy towel looked pretty good. Sort of good. He was losing weight, trimming down since that kid at the senator's pool party grabbed on to him and said he'd like to ride those love handles. Smart-ass wise-ass kid. How old? Fourteen? Fifteen? Where did he get the nerve. Eyes like a Bambi and a sewer mouth. A little pudgy himself, Roy noticed. Small mounds of fat behind the knees. The kid gave him a pinch, then a wink, then he tore off for the diving board as if Roy was going to chase him. He turned around with a big grin, wet doughy face, a tiny Speedo bathing suit, no jockstrap, the whole shooting match right on display. I'll ride those love handles, sir. Why think of these things. No wonder his mouth was a raw burn.

Side view, in this towel, everything looked pretty good. He could wear white trousers, even without a blazer. A robin's-egg-blue shirt, maybe a vertical stripe, not that he needed it. No tie. It was brunch. It was the Fourth of July! Maybe a red linen jacket. Too much? Roy unlocked the bathroom door. The white pants. Esther would tell him the truth. She never spared his feelings on these topics.

His oracle was lying facedown on the fur coverlet, mouth open, snoring very slightly. He could see the tops of her stockings. First she's ordering poodles, then she's having a party on the phone, now she's passed out. Stockings in this weather? Her thighs had small blue veins, like marble, like cheese. If he ever mentioned such a thing, instant homicide.

The phone rang twice. Roy stepped on Charlie Brown's ear. Oh, I'm sorry, boy, he said, and the phone stopped ringing. Charlie Brown was mewing like a baby. You're okay, buddy. Roy ruffled Charlie Brown's fur all along his back. Someone must have picked up downstairs. Esther curled over on her left side. Charlie Brown, against strict standing orders, against everything he'd ever learned at obedience school, leaped onto the bed and nestled into the sickle shape of Esther's body. Roy gave up. In the second closet he found a pair of black Italian featherweight slacks and a decent silk sweater, also black. Shrugged into both. Forget powder, forget everything. But then he remembered something, something Frank had said about the mail. He picked up the phone, the gold receiver heavier than an anvil, ridiculous, and dialed Frank's home number. Twelve rings. A wife and four kids and no one answers the phone. Downstairs he heard a loud bang, maybe Muddy was back, dropping her packages.

Roy tiptoed barefoot out of the bedroom and closed the door behind him. He leaned over the banister. All the way down, on the ground floor, across the black and white marble tiles, he caught the swift flash of one of the office assistants, someone's son who needed a job. The plus side of having the office right here in the house was the commute, ha-ha, the downside, strangers running in and out at all hours. Hello! Hey there! Who was on the phone? No answer.

All the way down the curving staircase, Roy wondered: Who hires these kids? He never saw them until they were handing him a list of law schools. A perfectly good Saturday, the Fourth of July! Must be a loser, a social outcast, a boy pushed too hard by the father. In the foyer, the marble cooled his feet. The door to the office suite was ajar, and light poured out from the overheads.

Hey, what's with all the lights? Hello? No one was in the outer area. The receptionist's desk was a beautiful old piece Roy found at auction, but Alice kept it like a trash heap. The woman had no sense of order. There was dust on the incoming mail stack, all unopened. Roy flipped through the top few envelopes just to make certain the world hadn't ended. Every lawyer in New York had a more organized secretary than he did. It was criminal. Who was gaining from this? Muddy. He'd forgotten. This favor had been in place for half a decade.

His own door had a coat of dust on it he could see from here. When everything was over, back to normal, he'd talk to Frank about a little renovation and reorganization, because this place was not conducive to clear thinking. He'd get everyone involved. Dan would have some ideas. And Esther, obviously. Of course, the guy with the taste was Will. What was he going to do about that? What a terrible problem.

Roy drew a little hangman with his finger in the dust on the Alice's desk. He wrote *Roy* under the platform. He drew a skinny little stick man holding the noose and wrote: *Bobby.* He drew a fat oblong, no head, with only one arm smacking the Bobby figure on the bean, and wrote *Justice.* There, for the permanent collection. The archives. He heard a bang in his own office. Hey! Who's there?

Roy went over and opened the door. Nothing, empty, the usual mess. But then an odd mechanical click snapped near his desk. Who's there? Who is that?

A tall blond boy with heavy black-framed glasses surfaced slowly, crouching, from behind the leather swivel chair. A Polaroid camera hung from a red strap around his neck.

What do you think you're doing?

The boy straightened. The camera extruded with a slow grind a photograph that made the room smell like iodine. Roy was looking straight into the calm eyes of a contender for Mr. Universe. The kid was a specimen of something: good diet, perfect parents, air you could breathe once in a while. Why the glasses, he wondered. What are you doing? Roy asked again, though just existing might be an acceptable answer. What's all the photo work? Are you doing some special assignment? Do you work for me?

Yes sir. No sir.

No sir? You don't work for me? Then how did you get in here.

The door was open.

The front door?

The boy nodded.

You're kidding. The front door was open, and you walked through it. Just like that.

Yes.

You just came in, there's a name for that, you know. Who do you work for?

Silence. A tall blond silent boy biting his lip with teeth like a neon sign. Did people have lips like that without surgery? So, who'd you say you work for?

Freelance.

Freelance. Your own idea to walk into my home and office and try out your new camera with documents on my desk. Any expansion on this before I call the police?

Yes. You had a phone call.

Who was it?

Her name was Kay Clemens. She just said to tell you it was a no-go.

No-go? What does that mean?

She didn't explain, Mr. Cohn.

Amazing. All right. All right. Let's see the picture. The boy tore the cover off the shot he'd just taken. It was a murky close-up of Roy's blotter and the top of a legal pad, with an indiscernible phone number wriggling out of the corner.

You need some lessons. You want the number of a neurosurgeon?

The boy looked vague.

Because that's what you have. And not even all of it. What else have you got?

The boy didn't move.

Turn around. Let me see your pockets.

The boy pulled his pockets inside out. Roy had caught him on the first shot.

Okay. Roy needed to call Kay back, needed to get ahold of Frank. Okay. Write your number down. Your name and number right here on the pad.

Excuse me, sir?

You heard me, right here, next to the neurosurgeon you're so interested in. And then get out of here.

The boy scribbled on the pad, hand shaking. He handed Roy the Polaroid photograph.

Oh? I get to keep this? That's fabulous. Listen. Do me a favor. Get some lessons before you break in next time. This hardly constitutes a souvenir. Roy nodded toward the door. The boy burst out of the room as if being chased, a lot of spring in the legs. I can't believe this.

Roy stepped around his desk to read the new writing on the legal pad. Right next to the neurosurgeon, written in a wobbly cursive: I love you. No name. No number. Oh, this kid was too much. Maybe there was a clean fingerprint on the photo. There had to be. Roy thought about that for a moment. Then he started turning out the lights. He had bigger problems to solve. He dropped the photo on Alice's desk. Maybe by New Year's, she'd ask him what it was.

Monday, noon, Roy arrived for lunch at "21." The place was dead. Maybe thirty people. And no one that interesting, but it was early and right in the shadow of a big holiday, still a holiday for some, the court wouldn't be back in session until Wednesday. And now, now when he wanted it, when he was saying, Pretend you don't know me, they were all over him. No, here, Mr. Cohn, right this way. What did he have to do to get a lousy table? When the Duchess of Windsor was with him, it wasn't a problem. He was shipped to Siberia, next to the employee restroom, until a bus-boy who'd read the *Daily News* that day, thank God, came out fiddling with his fly and recognized who'd been put where. A lot of anxious hand-wringing ensued, but now it was hopeless, he couldn't get out of the way if he tried. The Monday after the Fourth of July, he should be able to eat in the dark. Look, he said, I want peace. I want quiet.

Yes, sir! And he was being pussyfooted right into the first circle. Pay attention!

The new guy, no one he knew, maybe still in training, gave Roy a stricken look. Surely he *was* paying attention. That was his job, his vocation.

Bo moved slowly into the dining room on his mother's arm, no IV this time. He looked thin but good. You're here, sweetheart! Already! I'm just getting the table. Hello, Kay.

Roy, who had come early for once, just for this purpose, just to save this kind of hovering, couldn't get through to the imbecile in charge. Let me make it simple. A sick kid doesn't need commotion. Find me out of the way, right now, or tomorrow your whole life will be out of the way. Am I making sense?

Well, that was easy. The dope got one good look at Bo, and bam, they were barely in the restaurant. You've got the stuff, kid. And Bo laughed. Yes. And all above them the model boats, and trains, and trucks. Bo looked as far back as he could stretch and his baseball cap tumbled off. The maître d' stooped to get it, and then what?

Here, give it to me, Roy said. And get us a Dewar's on the rocks, a Tab, and a Roy Rogers.

Roy tucked the cap back on Bo's head, pulled down the visor. On you, this looks good. The whole thing makes sense. I love it. Roy patted Bo's cheek. You look great.

Bo loved this place, otherwise it was pissing Roy off. The maître d' came back with the drinks himself, making a mess. Giving the Scotch to Bo, the Roy Rogers to Roy. What was wrong with this guy? So Roy told him what he wanted, right away, to get rid of him: steak for Kay, charred and rare, tuna tartar for himself, and Bo would have a Chef Boyardee spaghetti. A flash of anguish passed through the man's eyes. Roy took mercy. Just send someone to the corner store, he said, and delivered a twenty into his hand. Already Esther must be at FAO Schwarz trying to figure out what they hadn't bought yet. She'd meet them here later, or maybe back at the hospital. Four minutes in, Roy could see this would be a short lunch.

Bo's posture wasn't so great. He sat low in his chair and studied the boats on the ceiling, and Roy studied him. Bo's face was
round with medication and his skin was white as a stone, except
where little capillaries broke across his cheeks, delicate webs of
red. His hands were swollen and still. Kay's posture wasn't so great
either. She leaned in toward Bo, in a bit of a slump, but Roy knew
she was slumping like a lion. He understood that. He'd buy her
a thousand steaks. But this lunch was a mistake. Even though now
Bo grinned at him, looked exactly like his father. And Roy was
feeling a little woozy. You know, I'll be right back, he said.

On the way out, he smacked into the maître d'. And felt he
could punch this guy, if that were the kind of thing he did. It
would be such a relief. Roy looked at the flush in this useless fawn-
ing dope's face and it made him angry. The poor distribution of
health in this world. It made him deeply angry. But he forced
himself to walk on. He had a phone call to make.

He dialed Alice from the front desk. Some good news was definitely in order here. He'd put out feelers to the top-notch doctor,
the neurogenius. He had everyone on this, a cardinal, a congress-
man, a couple of movie stars just for the hell of it, what was taking so long. The phone rang and rang. At least Will couldn't see
Bo like this. Was that a blessing? Roy didn't know. He felt so
lousy, he was beginning to wonder if he'd caught something. The
phone trilled on and on in his ear.

Just then the front door opened and in strolled Million-Dollar
Dolly, her neck like a giraffe's, from all the diamond necklaces,
some said. Today a gold trumpet hung just below her left shoulder, sparkling rocks where the keys should be. Roy! Dolly tossed
her tiny hands into the air, they landed on his shoulders as she
dispersed a gardenia aroma so liquid and intense, he thought at-
omizers were buried in her dark French twist. Roy knew six players
who claimed to be her boyfriend. Heavy hitters. Personally, Roy
thought she should take it easy. He didn't want to be around when
those chips fell. He advised marriage, when asked, when Dolly

came by, when the conversation moved that way. And she advised marriage in return. She had a good sense of humor. Beauty, a sense of humor, brains, in that order. Dolly fell back, breathless, into the wing chair and laughed about Roy *sweeping* her, etc. She twined her right leg around the left and leaned forward to twiddle the strap on a beige silk sling-back.

Roy let go of the phone. I should get you after this one, Dolly, send in the really big gun.

What are you talking about, Roy?

Just taking in the scenery, or are you meeting someone?

Someone.

Friend or foe?

The difference being?

Frank, who rarely had anything crude to say about anyone, called Dolly the Lincoln Tunnel. Anyone who came to New York, he said, went through her and paid cash. Roy knew about that, but it just didn't rankle him the way it did Frank. He picked up the phone again to dial Alice. You have a new fiancé, Dolly?

Only you, Roy. Dolly stood, fully readjusted, and kissed him on both cheeks, kisses with weight and movement and pressure exquisitely calibrated. But he leaned right out of her force field when Alice picked up the line. For godsakes, Alice. He was almost screaming. Dolly moved toward the dining room. She twirled around and waved. Roy threw back a kiss, like he was throwing a grenade.

Alice, listen, he said, then looked up to watch Dolly wriggle her way into the first section. Fine. Oh my God. He was just remembering something about Will and Dolly, a momentary thing. Nothing of any consequence. And nothing to worry about, now that he thought about it. If anyone knew how to exhibit complete disengagement, it was Dolly. Without even a signal, she'd pretend he didn't exist. Alice was talking to him.

Alice, one small thing I ask, that you answer the phone. Is that too much? Am I placing an unnecessary burden on you, because if I am, tell me. Please. Do this. Call Dr. Bronson. You haven't heard from him? All right. Call Dr. Bronson, leave a message, like before. But do it twelve times in a row. I want you to count, make lines on a paper, and tell me what his receptionist says each time. But twelve calls. And we'll see what happens. Thank you.

Now maybe he could eat in peace.

July 7

Will was most aware of the shield Pasteur created between the eighteen execs of *Kentucky* and the rest of Woeburne when Pasteur was gone. And he was nearly always gone at night. There was another guard, Martin Patton, aka Pat'em, known for running girls down between the orchards and the greenhouse, who took over most night shifts on *Kentucky*. Then the guard-station telephone rang until dawn. Martin making various arrangements with his employees. Sammy Finlandor took an enormous interest in Martin, predicted that if he played his cards right, he could retire very handsomely at forty.

Woeburne was always loudest at night, loudest and brightest. Spotlights washed out all shadow. And the sound rose from all the floors below, accrued, spiraled up to the glass roof and ricocheted down again in sharp notes, as if the roof were shattering and exploding, over and over. At night, men screamed and cried and made no more sense than howling babies, a hundred at once. The sound was deafening. More frightening than anything Will had ever heard.

All the worst things happened in the night. Things Sammy Finlandor sifted out from the fusillade of sound and defined. Someone had been doused with urine collected in a cup. Thrown on the face, the worst insult, thrown on the feet, the least. Someone had been burned, again. Lit on fire in his bed. Sammy knew the sound of the fire extinguisher, and that particular shriek of pain, the medical kit detached from the wall, the cot to carry the burn victim to the infirmary where he would wait until morning, wrapped naked in cold wet sheets, until the doctor came. One man had died this way since Will arrived. And the hanging game. The men who rigged themselves on the water pipes with a torn cloth noose, a braided bedsheet, so the guard on timed walk-bys would catch them, cut them down, and send them to the infirmary too, where night was quiet and dark. Someone's just been cut, Sammy would say into the walkway between the barred doors, Will could not see him. No one could see anyone because the bars were spaced that way. Someone's just been cut. And Sammy could tell whether the cut was cautionary, just a way of saying *I'm the one you should be thinking about.* Or a direct aggression, when someone's intestines needed to be stitched back in. Another trip to the infirmary, someone else in line for a quiet night.

All this happened on the tiers below *Kentucky:* on *Nebraska,* and *Nevada, Dakota,* and *Carolina,* where the mental defectives lived and the hard-time aggressives. On *Michigan* the cells were dorm-style, and though the most trouble happened there, nothing changed. In *Kentucky,* each executive had his own cell, just about the size of Kay Clemens's blue Thunderbird. A cot, a table, and a toilet. The toilets were relatively new, within the last six years, Sammy said.

In July the sun began to light the glass dome with a red slick just after five, and the guards would extinguish the overheads. For the hour between sunrise and first head count, Will would sleep and dream. When he awoke, Pasteur was already there. His fat ass swayed down the catwalk. He tripped his lucky key chain along the bars, a small silver bell with the sound of a baby's teething ring, before he threw the master bolt and opened *Kentucky* cell block for the business of the day.

Sammy Finlandor couldn't get the thought of Martin Patton's orchard girls out of his mind, or he couldn't stop putting them into Will's. Said these were professionals, really experts, many traveled from New York City, came here in the summer to rest and make some money. He listed the things they would do. It was as if he were trying to hypnotize Will. Sammy's experience in Martin's orchard, as far as Will knew, was limited to imagination.

Pasteur was always reluctant to change a work assignment once he had a man placed. He said that continuity calmed restless hearts. But at suppertime, Sammy studied the faces of the men assigned on a rotating schedule to the orchards and the greenhouses. Sammy saw a higher calm there, men washed clean of the accumulating irritations of Woeburne by sexual transport. He troubled Pasteur every morning, called out to him before the doors were even open. Said he was longing for air and trees, that he'd be reconditioned for the better, given just one chance. Once he even stilled the tongue of Pasteur's silver bell, caught it in his hand, so Pasteur would listen. This worked against him.

On Tuesday afternoon, Will was catnapping in the dry goods when Sammy pulled hard on the toe of his wrecked rubber sole. Get up, get up! Pasteur's looking for you. Will was confused. His inner clock was so attuned, so regulated, to the head counts and mealtimes and number of vegetables to be peeled that his stolen slumber was equally precise. He knew just when and how much. Sammy's interruption was disorienting. Will thought the place must be on fire.

But he stood up, pushed back his mussed hair. He shaved two parsnips into long white bones before Pasteur—who had been having a loud, lengthy talk with Chef Brodie about appropriate nutrition for teenage girls, Meat, said Brodie, and lots of it, builds all kinds of things—showed up at his work station. Pasteur carried a small pink message slip in his fist, the sort favored by Nancy Campanella, Warden Flagmeyer's secretary. He stood by Will's sink and read the slip again, as if to be certain. Well, he said, look's like you're about to get some sunshine. You've been reassigned to the pruning squad. Pasteur lifted one of the parsnips. You give those poor trees this kind of treatment, we won't have any apples at all.

I'm fine right here. Send Sammy, he wants to go.

Sending you, sir. Come with me.

Will handed his peeler to Sammy, who seemed unaccountably pleased. Will guessed he was hoping for a reliable assessment of

Martin's goods. Keep your hands dry, Sammy, you never know, it could happen to you.

Now, Clemens, or I tear this pink slip up.

He's coming, said Sammy.

The orchard was as romantic as any musical stage set Will had ever seen, except for the perimeter. Miles of looped razor wire spun over three steel-link fences, set one inside the next, like transparent Chinese boxes. But within, erasing that, the trees were gnarled and beautiful. None of the other executives worked in the orchard, so Pasteur's consistency was not in force here. Will saw two entirely different work crews in his afternoon cutting branches, and he never saw Martin Patton. He learned from Sammy that Warden Flagmeyer considered orchard work rehabilitative, especially for the hard-time aggressives. Temporary assignments often came out of his office, as Will's had.

The orchard had only two armed guards. Each paced three sides of an interior corridor between the fences. A fourth side, closest to the greenhouses, didn't need a guard. A trusty, a lifetime prisoner with a sense of responsibility, who had graduated to light meds, kept watch there. Although Woeburne had many interesting escape attempts in its lore, none had ever taken place in the orchard, despite its relatively mild surveillance.

The trusty who spent the most time doing apparently nothing, leaning on the back legs of a wooden library chair set out of the sun near the greenhouse, was Hank Williams. Self-named. His real name, Will learned from Sammy, was Norbert Swan, and he had killed his wife with a waffle iron on a Sunday morning. Now he was slow and mostly silent with regret. On some occasions he'd bring it up, though, and say how sad he felt that as a very young man he hadn't had more patience, hadn't known that cooking and conversation could be learned. He came to Woeburne when its doors opened, transferred from Elmira. For many years he'd been the chief sorter of scrap iron.

But Martin Patton had seen other ways that Hank Williams could be spending his time, rather than separating nuts from bolts. The men were frightened of him, frightened of his slow movements and his widespread crocodile teeth; killers of such clear intent were actually rare at Woeburne. Martin Patton put that fear to good use. He petitioned Warden Flagmeyer for a compassionate reassignment. Hank Williams was old now, his hands unsteady. So for half a decade, in the work season, from late April until the end of October, the hardback chair was set by the greenhouse.

Hank Williams sat there from nine in the morning until sundown. He was given a black metal lunch box, all the orchard workers were. And if anyone needed to use the facilities, Hank Williams directed them to three I-shaped cuts in the knit and purl of the metal fences. A man could squeeze through, one, two, three, and find accommodation on the north, shady side of the greenhouse.

Although Martin Patton was making a small fortune, he had expenses. He paid the orchard guards a straight fee for walks they cut short, eyes they kept averted. The girls worked on a per capita basis. Hank Williams was given Mass cards for his service. Convinced that he was doing a kindness for the men and the girls, he would not take money. Martin Patton made a monthly stop to the rectory in Woeburne Heights to purchase indulgences for Hank as a regular part of his personal schedule. And Hank collected the cash the men gave him in the bottom of his black metal lunch pail. For twenty dollars a month, one of the mental defectives pocketed that pile of money when he washed the pails coming back to the kitchen from the orchard. Hank Williams had scratched a broken heart near the handle of his. In the evenings, Martin took a break from the management of his incoming calls to recoup the day's receipts on *Nebraska*.

At the end of Will's afternoon in the orchard, he got the tap. A young man stood at the bottom of Will's stepladder and shook the rung. Hey, man, Hank Williams wants you. Pronto. Will pushed away the branch. Hank stood just beyond the shadow of his chair, shading his eyes with his forearm, those eyes trained on Will. Will backed down the ladder and put his heavy shears on the ground. The grass was wet. He picked them up again and carried them with him to Hank.

What you gonna do with those? Cut off something? Hank smiled.

Did you want to talk to me?

Hell no. I want you to put your skinny self through that fence there and collect on the goodness that someone, not saying who, provided for you. You have got a friend. You just leave those clippers here with me. I'll keep an eye.

Hank Williams pointed to the left, and Will could see the tear in the fence. Just squeeze on through, you won't have no problem.

Will dropped the clippers in the dirt and wiped his hands on his pants. He pulled back the fold of metal, hot from the sun, and wriggled through, feeling the metal scratch all the way down his body. He did it twice more, in the two other fences, and turned back to look at Hank Williams. Who gestured, whole arm, to go around the side of the greenhouse. Will followed a path of pressed dirt along the east wall and around the corner. No bushes. But a field of grass and tall uncut weeds stretched out, and a path continued through it. The grass was nearly waist-deep. There was a smell of old urine. He stopped, turned back. Where you think you're going? a small voice shouted out, maybe twenty feet away in the grass. Back, said Will. He felt anxious, and stupid for feeling it. God knows he wasn't afraid of a hooker. The voice was the voice of a child.

Come on over here, let me see you. I heard about you.

Will pushed slowly through the ragweed toward the sound. Over here!

The path stopped abruptly. Nowhere. He looked out into a field.

You're slower than God. Get over here. And Will saw a small hand wave above the Queen Anne's lace. He walked toward that hand, separating the thick grass to get there.

Well. You're worth the wait.

Lying in a kind of mare's nest, the grass all tamped down in an oval shape, was a young girl in a yellow and white summer dress, big daisies tacked to the hem of each pleat. Will stared at her for a while. She wore thick pink shiny sandals. Her breasts poked out, small and round, like two eggs tucked into the bodice. What are you doing here?

Ought to be plain as day.

Will sat down. Dizzy all of a sudden from the heat.

What are *you* doing here? the girl said. She winked at him like a kid who had a secret already told. Then she made an unskilled grab at his zipper.

Wait.

No waiting. I don't have that kind of time. Then she laughed. Really convulsed with laughter. Then she started to cough. She gripped Will's knee with her hand. She had three tiny plum-colored bruises just above her wrist.

Will pointed. What's this?

Some people and their own strength. You can't believe. But you do, you know your own self. I'll bet on that.

Her face was so pale it took on the green of the grass all around her. Her eyes were dark, irises like a grainy wood. She had a tiny mouth. Her long, thin neck was rubbed with dirt near her daisy-petal collar.

What's your name?

Why would you ask me such a thing?

Will saw a movement in the grass, looked over.

That's nothing, a skunk or rabbit. No one'll come unless you stay too long. Or I blow my whistle. Look here. She reached into her square pocket with rickrack trim, and pulled out a silver guard's whistle.

What happens if you blow it?

I go home. Maybe for good. Means I can't handle my own security.

What's your name?

Loretta Lynn.

Will looked at the small greenish face. You any relation to Hank Williams out there?

Do I look like that old man?

No. Not a bit.

You gonna fool with me or not.

No. I don't think so.

Well, you're no fun.

You go to school?

I finished two years ago, what do I look like to you?

Will looked at her hands. She was pushing back the tip of her left index finger with her right thumb. All her fingernails were bitten down except this one, which was long, almost curled with length.

What's that fingernail for?

What do you think? She scratched a thin red line on the top of his hand. The nail was incredibly sharp. Imagine that was your eye!

Imagine. Will could see the blood but felt nothing, as if the cut was only a picture. Anyone ever blow that whistle for you? For your own good?

Who'd be that stupid. Who'd want to go and do that?

I don't know.

They'd be begging for trouble.

I suppose.

And I don't know if I'd get back here again after that. That would be a problem.

Yeah.

She plucked a grass shoot and severed it down the center with her fingernail. She chewed on a tiny sliver, head bent, the part in her hair exact and fine. Her hair, light brown, was cut in an uneven bob around her chin. Well, I'm not looking at you anymore.

Will picked up the whistle where it lay in the grass beside a folded yellow daisy on her skirt. The back of his hand had a thread of blood now. You need a license for that thing. He held the whistle between his fingers. It was lighter than it looked. You could go in the army, be a spy.

Do you think I'm still listening to you?

Do you play an instrument?

My head hurts, she said and shaded her eyes as Hank Williams had done, with her forearm.

Will took the whistle and rubbed the length of one yellow pleat from hipbone to knee and back up again.

There you go. That's the ticket.

I have perfect pitch, said Will. He touched the whistle to his lips.

Give me that thing. She held out her palm. Hand it here. She laughed.

Do you know what that means?

You want to see something funny? She fluffed the petals of her collar.

Will put his teeth down on the whistle, inhaled, and blew. Her brown eyes went flat. C sharp, he said.

He thought he would hear something. He thought there would be more time. But Loretta dropped her grass blade and stood up. Her legs were bowed and freckled. Just before the handle of Will's clipping shears came down on the top of his head, swung with an accuracy and a force that seemed nearly impossible from arms as old as those of Hank Williams, she looked down and said, I know that. I know that because I can sing.

~

Kay was getting used to things at the St. Regis. She lived on scrambled eggs. They came anytime she liked, and that didn't seem a luxury anymore. The St. Regis was the condition of her living, the place she directed the taxi to when she left the hospital. It took care of her dry cleaning, her laundry, it collected her phone messages. She could dial two digits, strong coffee and a decent Scotch arrived before she thought about it again. She was grateful for that and oblivious. She was oblivious too of the tab. Since Rita's sad visit a month ago, Roy had worked out a deal. Kay's father remarried for the second time, a woman he met on shipboard on the Baltic Sea, but from his honeymoon, he'd cabled Kay's bank a renewal on her line of credit. In another month's time she would be thirty years old.

Most days she felt excused from the demand to pay attention to her surroundings in any way. If a desk clerk looked as if she'd wept all night, or the elevator boy's hand shook, it happened beyond Kay's notice. Except at odd times, when a remark by a passerby would penetrate, something bizarre about Kay being a what? A gangplank? I'm on board, the woman crooned, pull up the gangplank. Or a whore. Had the woman in the yellow cape really called Kay a whore? Maybe she hadn't heard anything at all. That's when Kay would dial Merrill, when strangers started saying things she didn't understand.

Or Esther, or Gert, or Roy, or Dan, or anyone who could talk. Things were smooth, then a rupture, and everything was dangerous. Like the night she had a problem with the garbage. She couldn't reach a soul, she wasn't hungry, so walked outside to Fifth Avenue. She'd taken a turn, and another, and another. On the curbs, mounds of garbage were stacked high. On the side streets it formed barricades between the sidewalk and the street. She pushed on. She took more turns. Ahead there was a narrow tunnel shaped by piled trash, an empty building, the starless sky. Kay needed to walk through or go back the desolate way she'd come. Within the aisle of garbage, she felt certain a figure was edging toward her. The shape drew close. She screamed as if she'd been knifed. She opened her eyes, screaming still. She was all alone. The stench of grapefruit rinds and fish all around her.

With Merrill she played backgammon. The click of the disks, the padded thumping roll of the dice, Merrill's oval hand sliding things around, it was soothing. The truth was, she could call anyone. Randomly. She could dial the number of about a hundred households in Rumson, New Jersey, and the person answering would be generous and up to date. Kay could now count on the nuns, Gert, the pharmacist, the firemen, any number of people, to keep the town current. All she had to do was dial or go home. And that's why she stayed at the St. Regis. Even on the nights when she *could* go home. She couldn't stand to hear the bad news. The sound of her own sorrow, reflected back, got to her. Better to be here, where the scrambled eggs were always delivered by a ghost. And to play backgammon with Merrill, who had problems of her own. Or Roy. If the price was that she was transparent, that strangers whispered she was stupid and selfish, that was okay.

Kay had a routine. Awake by five. Three cups of coffee, black. Hair. Makeup, then shower, her face poking out between the curtains to steam-seal it. Powder. Dress. Toast. Last cup of coffee, cold, with first cigarette. Brush teeth. More lipstick. Pull up the spread on the bed. In the hallway, socked by lost perfume and last night's cigar smoke, she'd press for the elevator, slow to come. The lobby was quiet, always. On Fifth Avenue she walked to the cathedral. Behind the main altar, beyond the clatter of the day's preparations, she sat in the small blue chapel to the Virgin. She wouldn't kneel. She never lit a candle. She did not pray. She stayed until she was tired, as if some fight had gone on beneath her consciousness. She exited on Fiftieth Street. Hailed a taxi. Men in gray suits began to cluster on street corners, move in swift packs. Vie for the attention of the cabbies.

At the hospital, the rush was on. The metal cave of the elevator pressed twenty or more bodies. On the tenth floor, she moved, hip-checked, not hard but clear, she knew how to get through the quick-closing doors. She veered left. Room 1005. Bo was just finishing what breakfast he may or may not have eaten. His roommate was there or not there any longer. The day would begin.

This Tuesday morning Bo was awake, his breakfast tray pushed aside, not touched. His eyes were narrow as if the effort of looking at her was annoying him. Kay felt his forehead, traced her hand along his cheek, brushed back the fine white down on his scalp. What's up, sweetheart?

He closed his eyes.

Bo?

His lids flicked as if a small pulse of electricity jolted the skin. As if he was dreaming. Bo?

Can we get a new pack for the speedboat?

What speedboat, angel?

If it's here. His tongue sounded swollen. He opened his eyes and looked at her, furious. It's broken, he said. It's wrecked.

Honey, what are you talking about?

The boat. Bo looked like he was going to cry.

Did you have a dream?

Bo looked at Kay as if what she said was so ludicrous he couldn't parse it, then his eyes blinked almost shut. His mouth opened slightly, his breath coming in and out with trouble. He was sleeping, suddenly. She was still looking at him, still holding his hand. Jesus, what's going on? Kay watched him a moment longer; the circles under his sparse white lashes were so blue he looked like he'd been punched twice. Kay cradled his cheek in her hand, then went to hunt down Hollis.

Hollis was in a scuffle with a young redhead at the nurses' station. She leaned in to the high-top desk, her hip sticking out, her red cowboy boot tapping on the linoleum. Simple instruction. Don't get the foul-up here. Mrs. Clemens! I didn't see you, pardon-moi. Hollis pushed back from the desk and bounced toward Kay. Good! I've got some news.

He looks terrible!

Just a second. I'm sorry, Kay. Hollis went back behind the nurses' station to grab a clipboard. Are we straight here? she said to the girl, and didn't wait for an answer. Nodded herself. Checked a couple of things on the board in her hand.

Kay waited. She never greeted Hollis, her second self, the self she would be if she could know what Bo required here. But Roy took care of Hollis, she'd seen every show on Broadway. Kay had spotted other offerings from other parents, boxes of expensive chocolates, button-down sweaters, small pearl earrings to match a nurse uniform Hollis rarely wore. Did they all depend on Hollis the way she did? Kay had no idea. She never spoke to any of them more than once. One conversation to return a greeting and head off further communion. She did not want to know how their child was doing.

All right, so here's the news. It looks like we've got a donor in the father. Hollis glanced up at Kay, and then down again at the papers in her hand.

You're kidding.

For the transfer, for the bone marrow. Dr. Bronson thinks he can do it with Will Clemens's cells. It'll work, he thinks. He thinks it's worth a try.

Worth a try?

Hollis looked up at Kay. I'm sorry. You know? I'm really sorry. Last night, after you left, the new consult, Dr. Bronson, he came in, looked at Bo, studied all the backup documentation, all the workups and the history, your blood tests and Will's, and he thinks, and he's excited about it, that Bo can do the transfer with his father's stem cells. So last night, right away, Bo started on a high-test antibiotic. Take out any blood infection, which has been lurking, by the way.

He looks horrible. He's having nightmares.

Yes. It's nasty. But I've seen this work before.

I thought it was all brand-new.

No. Not the antibiotic. Dr. Bronson said he'd stop back late morning to talk to you. I can tell you what I see. But give me a couple of minutes, I've got a trainee. Just what I need, right?

Hollis?

Yes?

You're sure it's Will?

Yes, definitely.

Do you think this'll change anything?

Hollis watched down the hall as the young nurse with red hair tripped over a dropped paper cup. The girl stooped to pick it up with the tips of her fingers and walked to the nurses' station, left it in a crumpled ball on the high counter. Hollis looked back to Kay. I hope so, she said. I'll meet you down there.

What Kay could see without Hollis's interpretation: Bo's shoulders and head propped on three pillows stacked like a snowy slope, so, head elevated. His face and throat were slightly jaundiced, and the pajamas he wore, blue cotton, white piping, were some fantasy of what his father might wear. At home, Will slept naked, but Bo had wanted the idea and Kay had delivered it, three pastel sets from Best & Co. The pajamas were loose. One sleeve pushed to the bicep, and that arm was mounted, forearm taped in three spots to the stiff white foam card. Close to the inner elbow, but not in the crook, all veins had collapsed, worn out there, a new shunt was angled, taped, and a tidy bit of artwork: a drawing of Superman by Hollis mounted on top of the tape. Into the shunt a transparent length of tubing to the bag on the stand. In the bag, an amber-red liquid not yet in play. A second bag, clear liquid, hooked to a second line that transversed the first like a railroad connection. This was running, as far as Kay could tell. The second bed was empty. Hollis said she would aim to keep it that way until a private room came free. If they began the bone marrow transfer, they'd want him isolated. On the bedside table a black Matchbox 911T, a lidded plastic cup with a bent straw, a chain of hand-cut paper dolls (Rita), a blue crystal rosary (also Rita) wrapped in a spiraling snake around the base of the lamp and taped (Hollis, she was mixed on Catholicism), a Mass card facedown. In the corner, three large brown packing boxes crammed with cards, toys, gifts, caps. All for taking home. Kay leaned in close to Bo's face, studied the shape of his nose, the straight shaft of each pale eyebrow. Mouth open, his breath in this knocked-out sleep had the aroma of lemons too long in the fridge.

Hollis stood in the doorway, one eye on her trainee. So, the clear stuff is just sugar, amino acids, vitamins, the usual. The orange is the rocket fuel, the antibiotic, to kill any germs lurking around. A Mr. Clean of the blood system. He'll be on that all day, a slow drip, and it will make him very sleepy. They started him around ten last night, that's why he's so out of it. The last thing he wants to do is eat, but housekeeping brings the tray anyway. He's getting the equivalent of breakfast now. All day, we'll switch him back and forth. And if that works, and if they tap the donor successfully, day after tomorrow we'll start a seven-day countdown to the transfer. Of course, you'll have to sign off before they touch him.

You've already started.

This? No. It's a good prep. We could do this anyway, just for infection.

Could?

Here's our man of the hour.

Dr. Bronson pushed through the double doors at the end of the corridor, followed by a dozen doctors all in white.

Every floor at New York Hospital had a phone booth with the same bubble glass and the same occluded vista to the elevators. And it seemed to Kay she'd been in every one. Alice picked up on the eighth ring and Kay said, Go upstairs, wake up Mr. Cohn, it's an emergency. It must be, said Alice, and Kay heard the receiver crash against the desk like a dish breaking. Every phone booth had its own smell, this one smelled like camphor for babies, for their diapers. Kay wedged the door open so she could breathe. Dr. Bronson had been explicit. There was little time to waste. Ten minutes later—she kept a steady beat of dimes going into the telephone—Roy came on the line. Sweetheart. Kay explained. All right, all right. You need a judge's order, that's all. I can do that. Let me think for a second. All right. Give me an hour. Two, tops.

It was convenient for times when her room seemed too desolate that the St. Regis had a famous bar, not so crowded sometimes, cool and dark as a cave. Someone meandered on the piano keys, just tying notes together, enough to make a parched tune. The men who rushed off street corners in the mornings sometimes crossed long legs in the low leather seats at night. Kay drank a Scotch in a heavy tumbler, with lots of ice. The aroma was faint, delicious and elusive. She gathered up a top cube with trembling fingers, put it in her mouth and sucked. She was thirsty and hungry and hot. The waiter, silent, good man, offered a silver bowl with salty nuts, many Brazils. She ate half a dozen, one after the other like a prescribed medication, took a long pull on her Scotch, and the trembling subsided. Her father would be surprised to see her here in a bar alone. There was every possibility that Dan, Esther, Roy—especially Roy—Merrill, Frank might stop by for a drink. More nuts.

A man with a silver mustache, as silver as the bowl holding her nuts, nodded at her from the bar. A joke. She pivoted her head away and watched the face of the piano player. His mouth winced slightly just before each desiccated note. Another long sip. When she turned back to look for an almond this time, the man from the bar stood by the pushed-in chair, his hand resting flat along the wide top like a pale fish on a platter. I couldn't help but notice you, my dear lady.

Kay's eyes filled with the pressure to make a cruel remark.

May I join you? His cocktail napkin dangled from the bottom of his glass. It made him seem like a novice to Kay. She ticked her eyes toward the waiter, bartender, the businessmen at the next table. Okay, just for a moment, she said. Then I'm going upstairs.

So you are a guest here too. His hips scooped down into the leather seat. Kay hadn't noticed how anyone moved lately, except for Bo, but this dip registered. My son is very sick. Why didn't she just say that. My son is very, very sick.

In Lima, when a beautiful woman watches the musician's mouth, we say it's a sign of special sensitivity. For music, the mouth is more important than the hands. It's the hungry art, don't you think?

Kay looked at him a second, as if considering what he'd said. But she was thinking how Will would laugh if he were watching.

I've said something funny? The man had a wide grin with a tiny overbite. Two long teeth serrated the cushion of his lower lip.

No. But I made a mistake. Kay pushed back in her chair. She tried to signal the waiter.

Just a moment, give me a moment. I never know the proper words to say to Americans. But I like it here anyway. I always stay in the same suite, two-eighteen, big, yet close to the ground. I want to be a part of everything, yes? You understand this?

Kay frowned. She leaned over, reached for her purse.

And I like this management. Very thoughtful. Whenever I arrive, each time I am surprised again, how discreet, how private the Americans are. It's wonderful. A big surprise. Big one. He smiled, spread his hands flat on the table, examined his fingertips, then lifted his gaze up to her face. Kay thought of a trick Will had taught her. A joke about seduction. You lit a match looking down. And then before you blew on it, if you were a woman—or shook it, if you were a man—you looked up for a moment and let the flame show in your eyes. It was irresistible, Will said. And then there was the cat trick. You looked someone in the eye and imagined they were a cat, or better yet, a kitten. She was less sure how this worked, but Will said it was foolproof. Why not just look them in the eye and imagine you are fucking. Never works, said Will. It scares them.

Kay looked this fish man in the eye and imagined they were fucking. His shoulders were hard under her fingers, and he wanted to shove her into the padded silky headboard, she was a tight ball, her thighs pushed close to her chest, he rocked farther and farther into her. His skin was hot. His back was narrow. Her ass tucked right into his flat hands; when he came, he lifted her up and up. And when they were done, he left by the window, and she never saw him again. She looked him in the eye and she thought all these things.

He didn't look frightened at all. Every time, same suite, two-eighteen. I bet by these numbers. Horses. Dogs. I've been so happy here. No, he didn't look frightened at all, but she was, and when had that happened?

Kay stood up and knocked into the chair behind. Good night, she said.

It's too early for good night!

Good night. Kay sidestepped through all the chairs to the bar, dropped her drink there, and made for the stairs without looking back. She still liked the lifting-up part, repeated it a couple of times. Then repeated his exit out the window.

The housekeeper had already prepared her room for the night, turned down the coverlet on the bed she favored, replenished towels, tissues. Emptied ashtrays, removed glasses, dishes, trays. Kay lay down, face into the white pillow, and wished for a similar overhaul on herself. I'll start with my brain. She fell into a stone-dead sleep.

Half an hour later, she was awake, staring into the lit bulb of
the bedside lamp. Her body was sore all over. She pushed up to
sitting, felt her head throb behind her eyes, one eye, as always, a
circle of pain. Kay stripped off all her clothes and went into the
bathroom. In the bright greenish light she looked at her thighs,
she looked at the smooth length of her shins. She used to be a
woman with pretty legs. Technically this was still true. She opened
the shower taps and stood under the pounding water and hoped
it would disassemble the rocket now pushing off behind her eye.
Bo had terrible headaches. She wished she could, you know, the
usual, what all the parents wanted, take over the whole project.
She hadn't been able to reach Will all day, though she trusted Roy
had. The court order was already set. Kay would try to place the
call again. Go over the fine points. Before she signed anything,
she needed to talk to Will about odds.

It was nearly ten. Wrapped in her robe like a sarong, three pillows behind her, two beneath her knees, a Scotch poured neat. She
swallowed three aspirins, picked up the phone, and asked the hotel
operator to place the call. Just ring the number, please, I can request the party. It had taken her a while to locate the number Roy
had given her in case of emergency. Usually she spoke to Will on
Saturdays and only briefly, the scheduled call went through the main
prison switchboard to a designated phone. This was a direct line to
the guard's desk at *Kentucky.* Strictly rainy-day stuff, said Roy. In
her handwritten directory, she'd looked under W, Will, P, prison,
H, husband, and finally located it under R, for Roy.

A nice voice, relaxed and twangy, answered the ring. Did she
have the right number? Had she reached *Kentucky* at Woeburne?

Yes, ma'am, you have.

This is Kay Clemens calling.

Afraid I don't know the name. Are you that friend of Margaret
Jessup?

No. I'm Will Clemens's wife. I was hoping to speak to him. I
know it's late.

Will Clemens. Ha. That's a good one. How long have you two been married?

Excuse me?

You're to lay low there now, Loretta. This is no joke. You can't be talking to him, *Mrs. Clemens.*

I think there must be a misunderstanding.

You bet there is. Mostly in your dumb head. We'll talk later, when you settle down.

The line went still. Kay dropped the receiver to her chest. She held down the button on the phone with one finger when it started to whine. Loretta? Her breathing slowed down. She could hear her pulse in her ear like a saw. Room two-eighteen. Two-eighteen was Gert's birthday. Every year when they were kids, Gert got punch-bottomed Valentine candy from her brothers. She had a black Labrador retriever named Cupid who lapped the candy out of their palms. Now, Gert said, Red wasn't much better with the presents. Downstairs was a man with long, flat hands. Kay released the button on the telephone. When the operator came on the line she said, Yes, Mrs. Clemens, can I help you? Kay said, Try that number again, please. And when Martin Patton answered on *Kentucky,* laughing, saying, I'm warning you, *I'm warning you,* Kay said, quiet as a heartbeat, Officer, I'd like to know your name.

Timmy Mooney the pool boy had a bad attitude. So bad, the club manager said, that no matter how long Timmy's aunt and uncle had been sitting on the board of directors, next summer, by God, he'd have a boy skimming the bugs out of the Olympic-size pool and changing the chlorine who could be relied upon not to give a lot of lip and to show up just when those procedures were chalked on the schedule. In the meantime, Timmy had been demoted to the umbrella hut. That much he could handle. Locate the beach umbrella with the member's name Magic-Markered on the wooden pole, march it down to her usual spot, and stick it in the sand.

Now, during the popular eleven to one o'clock span, Timmy could be seen twisting pointed stakes up and down the long beach. He knew the boundaries of all the enclaves. Knew just how many paced yards the McHeffies needed to be from the McCarthys. He knew the Sullivan twins had their own Wedgwood-blue umbrella, apart from the greater Sullivan family, to match their unbelievable bikinis and the blue of their eyes. He understood just how far their mother needed to be from that vortex. And he always knew which family Lou-Lou Clemens had landed with. He could read the glaze of obligation in the mother's eyes.

A quarter mile down the shore, he spotted Lou-Lou's navy blue stretch one-piece and her belly, a round bump in the air, as she did an unspectacular half-gainer on the trampoline. No one watched her. The instructor, Lance DeMille, a blond half-wit with shoulders you could park a car on, gawked as the Sullivan twins adjusted in slow motion the tiny triangles of their bikini tops. But Lou-Lou never bounced high enough to be in real danger.

Lou-Lou Clemens had a thing for Timmy, a crush, he supposed, so he tried to let his awareness of her happen below her radar, which was very good, he had to say. But at thirteen, the public attention of a chubby nine-year-old was undesirable. Lou-Lou landed belly-down, then bounced up once more. Timmy watched her scramble to the edge, slipping and falling, now jumping off into the hot sand. She tiptoed, pranced her funny-looking legs to her flip-flops and her towel. All without a glance from the asshole Lance. The guy really should be fired. Not likely, though, he was too decorative. Timmy turned back toward the boardwalk before she saw him. She'd show up soon enough, no need to speed the inevitable. Lou-Lou was like a game of social hot potato, everyone tossed her around. But he kind of liked her, he did. He just didn't need that to be a known thing.

Lou-Lou was flying. Spiraling up into the air, a hairpin turn, a double somersault, a giant explosion, a boomerang against the sky, before her feet hit the mesh again of the trampoline and her turn was over. Up once more and amazing! The ocean ten million stars. She squinted up the beach, bodies floated on sand like souls on clouds. She reached the zenith of her last ascent, she spread her hands wide, her pixie hair flew up, hilarious, up higher she flipped and dropped belly-down. Her french fries and Tab made waves in her stomach.

Gert's sister, Mrs. Murphy, told her to be back at the cabana by three sharp, but that was hours away. She could go to the pool, she could lie on the edge of the ocean and let the foam accumulate on her legs. She could go back to Mrs. Murphy's umbrella. Mrs. Murphy had only boys, they were all older than Lou-Lou and mostly refused to acknowledge her. In the morning they'd gone into the cabana first, Sean, Reed, and Patrick. They came out in surfer bathing suits, and their mother said, Vamoose! Mrs. Murphy let Lou-Lou change with her, and that was hard. The cabana was big and whitewashed inside and smelled of baby powder and Bain de Soleil. Mrs. Murphy swept yesterday's sand from everyone's feet into a single pile. Later the cleaning service would come by and tidy up. The Murphy cabana was one of the grandest, situated just to the left of the high and low diving boards. While Mrs. Murphy swept and Lou-Lou unbuttoned the red plastic flower buttons on her blouse, the Murphy boys did screaming cannonballs off the high dive. The lifeguard shouted and threatened, Patrick Murphy, you're on thin ice there, buddy, but Mrs. Murphy looked like she was deaf. Once her boys were out of her sight, they were out of her universe, a theory about raising sons Lou-Lou had heard her explain to Gert on the porch over cocktails and hors d'oeuvres.

As far as Lou-Lou could tell, Mrs. Murphy always wore tennis whites. She had freckles and red hair. And as soon as she finished her sweep, she was out of those clothes, her mother belly poking out a bit like Lou-Lou's. Mrs. Murphy turned away. Through her white cotton underwear, Lou-Lou saw a hair streak like a tail, Mrs. Murphy had hair coming up from the crack in her bottom, little tags of dark red hair peeking over the elastic. Lou-Lou sat down in the chair by the door. She couldn't leave the cabana now, because then everyone in the deep end would see Mrs. Murphy's tail. The lifeguard trilled hard on his whistle. That's it, clown, outta the pool, Murphy. Now one of the Murphys would have to wait until after lunch if he wanted to swim again.

Lou-Lou missed, in this order: Bo, Merrill, her grandmother, her mother, her father. Then she rearranged the order: her father, she hadn't seen him the longest; Bo, he was the most changed; Merrill, because she was beautiful; her grandmother, because she was holy; and her mother, who could get along without her, she didn't like to understand that, but she did. Now Mrs. Murphy was ready to open the door. She had all her beach equipment, and her tail was tucked out of sight beneath the gold and black of her swimsuit. Lou-Lou looked for a bump in the back, but there was nothing.

Mrs. Murphy ignored Patrick, who sat huddled over, fake shivering, wet with pool water, his hair a greeny-blond slick. He stared at his bony feet rather than acknowledge his mother and Lou-Lou. On the way to the beach, Lou-Lou had been wedged in next to Patrick in the backseat of Mrs. Murphy's white Lincoln. Under the cover of her lowered eyelids, a technique she'd invented, she studied the swirl of blond hair on his legs. Now those legs were matted with water. How long do you have to sit there, Patrick? But her voice could not be heard, no sign from Patrick that she existed, and Mrs. Murphy was already up on the boardwalk, on the lookout for Timmy. And there he was, hauling her white umbrella with the long gold tassels.

Timmy, the demoted pool boy, was Lou-Lou's favorite person at the beach. She loved him. When she said, Hey Timmy, he didn't look at her either, but it was different. He was pretending, unlike Patrick Murphy, who really couldn't see her and didn't want to. If Merrill were here today, everything would be different. Like a parade. People would cluster around to have little chats with her, and Lou-Lou too. There she is! they'd say. When Merrill came to the Monmouth Beach Bath and Tennis Club, the members never knew what hit them. That's what Kay said. In *Man of La Mancha,* the actor who *was* the Man of La Mancha put on all his makeup so that everyone understood the trouble he went to and how he had the effect he had. Not so with Merrill. She wrestled hot curlers and ribbons and loofah, all out of sight, and told Lou-Lou about perseverance, dedication, and discipline. Words Lou-Lou had heard applied to reading and science, now directed at her knees and her belly, and the changes needed.

Lying facedown, cheek to her towel, in the shade of the umbrella Timmy had just erected, Lou-Lou had a crab's-eye view of a cluster of girls about twenty feet away. The girls all wore headbands to keep their shoulder-length hair out of their eyes. The tops of their two-piece bathing suits were bands too. They buried their Barbies head-down and poured sand between the pale legs until just a tiny oasis of Barbie calves and feet appeared in the distance. When the girls spoke to one another, they put their hands lengthwise across their mouths so no one could hear them.

The coolest, quietest spot at the club, cooler than the bridge room with its pink and green furnishings, cooler than the most exalted cabana, cooler even than the manager's air-conditioned cube, was the nest of two abandoned beach chairs secreted away in the very back of the umbrella hut: Timmy's hideout when the rush was over. Between one and four in the afternoon, he was rarely needed unless a sudden storm hit. He'd withdraw behind hundreds of umbrellas and blow smoke rings out to the ocean through the hexagonal window.

When Lou-Lou visited Timmy in the umbrella hut, some-times it took him a while to acknowledge her presence. She took refuge in the salty-smelling low-slung canvas chair. She curled her legs up and waited for a signal. Timmy stubbed out his Parliament and dropped it in the coffee can where he kept the old butts. His radio was small and red, with poor reception. It had sand in the grooves. Timmy stretched his arms up above his head and yawned, tiny tufts of ginger-colored hair showing in each underarm. His white chest looked like a perfect snow-drift to Lou-Lou, his nipples were narrow oblongs, like pale squished pennies with indents in the centers. As if a tiny knife had entered each and left a clean mark. Lou-Lou decided to tell Timmy about the plan for her bones.

She started out with just a word here and there, and he didn't stop her, he just lit another cigarette, so she told him everything. How a knife would go into her biggest bone and stir up the soft marrow in the middle, then a vacuum would be attached. She'd lie down on a white table in an operating room and Bo would be on another. The vacuum would scoop out whatever was soft in her skeleton and send it instantly over to Bo on his table. The strength in her bones would be transferred to his, and Bo would automatically begin to feel better.

Timmy looked at her hard in the eyes. He lit another cigarette. He watched her with the flame still burning in his hand, then dropped the match and stepped on it with his green flip-flop. There was a chance, Lou-Lou said, that things might not work out at the hospital. She'd lie there on the table after her bones had been vacuumed, and wait for spontaneous regeneration. She'd be like a lizard growing back a tail. But if they took too much, she might never move again. She'd have to live the rest of her life on the white table. And she hoped, she felt sick with hope, but she hoped that maybe Timmy would visit her if that happened, in case she couldn't come back to the beach club.

Timmy didn't answer. He looked down and frowned, took a long drag on his cigarette, sat back, crossed his legs, tilted up his chin, and blew a series of expert smoke rings, one opening in the air to capture the next. He stared hard out the hexagonal window for a long time. Finally he looked at Lou-Lou's face and didn't smile. She looked back, in the eye as her father had taught her was polite, waiting for the answer. Here you go, he said. The sound of his voice made her blink. He offered her the rest of his cigarette. You take it, he said. So Lou-Lou took the filter in her fingers and put her mouth where his had been. She didn't bother to do anything else with it and he didn't tell her how.

July 8

Is there something you're not telling me here, Dan? I mean, the guy is a doctor, why doesn't he live in Scarsdale, or Pelham, someplace reasonable. What's with the suite at the *Delmonico*? What is that? Roy banged the black receiver of his car phone against the palm of his hand as if it were a clogged pipe.

That's better, I can hear you now, before it was like the Atlantic Ocean was in my ear. So tell me, is it the same nurse we met? A new nurse? What?

I see. But do you think this might be a distraction? A wife can be persistent in a situation like this. I want this doctor to pay attention. If he sounds like his head is up his ass, I'm looking elsewhere. No skin off anyone's teeth. Find out and get back to me right away.

Yes, I'm aware of the timing. You think I'm not? I invented the timing here. Look, please, just do as I ask. Get the drift on the guy and his nurse, the level of distraction. He's got to be able to orchestrate this whole thing over the phone to people who barely know a hypodermic, much less a setup like this.

I know, I should have been a doctor. Tell Muddy. All right. We're in agreement.

I *already* talked to the warden. He's in my pocket.

Very funny. So he's in everyone's pocket. He's a big guy. Enough to go around. Listen, I'm hanging up. You know what to do. Call me right back.

Roy dropped the phone into the socket embedded in the upholstery behind his right ear. Strange design, don't you think, Peter? What do you think of the blue? Maybe black would look better.

The color gives a little extra life, Mr. Cohn.

You're so right, Peter. Roy rubbed his hand along the seat. he was glad at least he'd gone for the leather instead of plush. It smelled good, like aftershave, like someone's neck, like a thought that wasn't worth exploring because the five o'clock traffic on Park Avenue was a fucking zoo. The Delmonico. Peter, do you know anyone who lives at the *Delmonico* who isn't a crook?

Mr. Fumansor lives there, Mr. Cohn.

Oh. Great example, Peter. I feel much better now. The guy could fill several volumes of the penal code. You know what a gigolo is, Peter?

Of course.

Well, if only. I mean it would be a big step up for Mr. Fumansor, a display of some natural, harnessed and developed talent. A move toward a contribution to mankind and maybe womankind too. You know, I don't feel good about this.

What's that, Mr. Cohn.

Make a U-turn. Let's pick up Miss Horner instead. I'll wait before I pay any calls at the *Delmonico.* And Peter, a traditional route, please. Let's keep Harlem off the tour today.

Sir?

You heard me. So, were you inside at all today? Did you catch any of those boneheads in action? I'm surprised the jury isn't in a collective coma by now. Boredom as lethal weapon. They're wasting themselves. They could bottle up those personalities and spray Russia. Our problems as a nation would be over. But not mine. No. They'll bore me until I'm dead. That's the whole point.

All along the median strip on Park Avenue, heavy tulips bowed over. Petals splayed.

Boy. What a sight. Better just to have dirt. You can't expect a lot from flowers in July.

No sir.

Maybe that's it, can't expect so much. I hear that all the time. But you know what, Peter? That's wrong. Expect a lot. Expect the fucking moon.

July 9

An odd feature of the infirmary of Woeburne was the weapons cabinet. It looked like a hutch to Will, something his mother might have liked if old Jack Clemens had thought antiques were in any way useful. Will had been staring at it since he'd regained consciousness. The weapons cabinet had beveled glass inserts, with strands of twisted lead. Spindle shapes wound through the panes in a trellis pattern. It sent a subtle ripple so the glass looked like water. Will studied the effect for a long time while his head throbbed and the medication wore off. He counted the pistols inside. There were seven, all with metal cables snaked through the triggers. By the time a guard or nurse could detach a gun, the danger would be over, or they would be dead or hurt. But the security system at Woeburne wasn't Will's problem.

The sorrowful face of Arthur Schlenker, male nurse, attendant to any sick inmate, Tuesdays, Wednesdays, Thursdays, and alternate weekends, slumped over Will's cot to check on his own handiwork. He lifted a gauze patch the size of a small beret from Will's head and tapped around the stitches with a long wet Q-tip. Will flinched. That smarts, I'll bet, said Arthur.

You win.

You know what? Being just like that is what got you here to begin with. Arthur patted back down the loose gauze. This thing is already infected pretty bad.

Will had heard about the infirmary, mostly from Sammy, as an oasis for the discouraged. But the lights were blinding, and back at his desk Arthur Schlenker adjusted an audible neck crick. Five feet away Will could detect the hollow stink of poor dental hygiene. Will leaned over the side of the cot, feeling the urge to vomit. All along the floor beside his bed, little tufts of hair. All black.

What's this?

What does it look like.

Will brushed up a few strands with his fingers. He could feel the soap slick.

Hang down like that much longer, and those stitches'll burst.

Will tucked his fingertips beneath the edge of the gauze and felt the nubs of hair still left. He lay back on the sour pillow, closed his eyes, and hoped for sleep. One of the mental defectives carried in dinner on a tray. Meat loaf and mashed potatoes. Will retched on the first bite. When the overheads were finally shut off, Will could see the stars in the skylights to the north. The artists must have earmarked this place for their studio, for when they came back to live here.

He slept straight until dawn, a first for him at Woeburne. Will saw the morning reflected in the trellis of the weapons cabinet, the guns like lilies, the steel cables licorice he could bite through. And he thought, not for the first time, that the people who waited for him would be better off if he never came home. He sat up to assess the condition of his headache but found that, in his sleep, someone had handcuffed him to the bed.

On the second morning, he successfully swallowed oatmeal and a cup of weak sweet tea. Arthur Schlenker took Will's temperature and pronounced him cured. Twenty minutes later, Pasteur arrived to escort him back to *Kentucky*. Pasteur was in a pensive mood. He walked Will to his cell without speaking, unlocked the single door instead of the whole row, and told him he could rest there for now. Will would be all alone until the eleven o'clock head count.

In the last day or so, the accumulating solitude had become more frightening and electric than anything Loretta Lynn might have hidden in that petal skirt. His scruples, he thought now, had been ephemeral, the shock of the moment. He was, after all, a bad guy. And if he had fucked her, certainly he wouldn't be thinking now about the logistics of tying bedsheets. He'd still be working in the orchard outside, making hand signals to Hank Williams through the branches. Making a deal. The way the hangman game was played, Sammy said, they tried, not always successfully, to rig a release. Will didn't want or need that.

It was the coiled iron of the weapons cabinet that gave him the idea of *twisting* the strips of sheets, making a weave that wouldn't give out. An answer to one problem could be fitted to fix something else, Jack Clemens had been frugal with solutions that way. Roofing solved plumbing solved electric solved gambling debts solved a marriage gone dry. Will had always felt more versatile than that, but as he braided the strips of grayed sheets together, he thought of his father and understood him.

Will was at this for quite some time, had a tight unyielding weave three feet long when he realized Pasteur was standing in the closed doorway to his cell. Come with me, he said, and released the barred grill. Pasteur left, already walking down the catwalk to the guard's station. Just once Pasteur looked back, and Will saw such a profound weariness in those eyes that he decided to follow him, even though Pasteur had given him a second option. Just a year ago, another exec had gone right over the tier rail. The center courtyard and its checkerboard marble squares made a picturesque last moment. Sammy said this caused a lot of trouble with the mental defectives. They were sighting falling bodies for the next month.

Pasteur was reading a slip of pink paper at his desk. We're going to the warden's office, he said. Not looking up. Will let Pasteur lead the way down one staircase, through a long gray corridor, back up another flight of stairs, then across a glass and steel pedestrian walkway laced with razor wire in festoons, almost pretty. Over the turrets, across the fields and the orchards, from this high up, the railway bridge glinted red above a gray velvet river. Pasteur leaned hard on the metal door, as thick as a vault's, that led to the administrative offices.

The twenty-nine stitches Arthur Schlenker had configured in a scythe shape above Will's left temple itched like mad. He hadn't seen his head except in fragments reflected in the small glass panes in the infirmary, but now the grimace on Nancy Campanella, the warden's secretary, made him want to see what he looked like. She frowned at him, then glanced quickly away. Something that almost never happened to Will. Nancy Campanella had flame-red nail polish on short square nails. She scratched at her powdered chin as she asked Pasteur to wait a spell. You take a seat right there, he'll get to you soon as he can.

Nancy Campanella collected miniature semiporcelain waterfalls. A tiny, certainly rare, series of cascades lined up in frozen effusion behind her head on the bookshelves that stored telephone directories and boxes of stationery. Will had seen animals and people but never water commemorated in this way. Nancy wore a dress with anchors and nautical flags embroidered on blue cotton. He wanted to ask her about her artifacts, to catch her attention, but he was invisible to her.

Twenty minutes passed before the carved oak door whined open and the warden gave Pasteur a meaty wave in. Come on, Pasteur said to Will. Pasteur's cap hung so low on his bald head that his small sad mouth was framed and accentuated. Will felt he had hurt Pasteur's feelings in some way, which seemed ridiculous except when he thought about Emily. Pasteur's daughter wasn't much younger than Loretta Lynn, maybe the whole episode afflicted his sense of his daughter's safety. It wasn't Will's fault that the orchard was a cathouse with high school girls, but Pasteur was acting like it was.

Warden Flagmeyer offered Pasteur a seat by the huge mahogany desk, Will was left to stand. The warden took his own thronelike chair, looked down at his blotter, then up at Will. I hear you've been biting cherries over in the orchard. The warden glanced at Pasteur's serious face and suppressed a giggle. That's not nice.

Warden Flagmeyer spread his fingers along the edge of his wide desk. There is a place right here in Woeburne for perverts. Everyone all together. You won't need to chase children. You can all take care of each other. Isn't that right, Officer Pasteur.

Pasteur's huge hands capped his knees. He didn't answer. The warden looked at Will. I think an explanation would be nice.

There isn't one.

Beg pardon?

I was working in the orchard. I went to piss. I never saw what hit me.

I heard a different story. A little girl might have got hurt by you, and Hank Williams intervened just in time. He did the right thing. Warden Flagmeyer nodded, then picked up a piece of paper on his desk. One that had been folded and pressed flat a number of times. He rubbed the raised seal at the bottom. You know, Mr. Clemens, your smart friends can only help you so far. And that's not far at all. Isn't that right, Officer Pasteur.

Pasteur's full lips folded in.

But this is a court order, and out of respect for that office, I will comply. A judge was convinced that you should have a special privilege. But don't be encouraged. I can charge and punish you for what you did. Sooner or later, doesn't matter which. Later is fine with me. Warden Flagmeyer's smile crumpled into a swift hard cough. Okay. Okay. Take him upstairs, Pasteur. The doctor is already here.

He coughed again. Then banged on his chest with his fist. Summer's the worst, he said, opened his pen drawer and dropped the court order inside. Pasteur stood up. Thanks, Warden. He nodded Will toward the door.

What's going on? Will said.

Oh boy. I'm ready to start this day over. Go ahead. Take him up, Pasteur. The warden blew his nose into a madras handkerchief.

In the outer office, Nancy Campanella had the black phone tucked into her shoulder. Yup, he's here. I'm sending him right up.

Officer Pasteur, she said, they're waiting for you.

Thank you.

You know the shortcut?

I can go the usual way.

I'll take you. Give me two secs. Nancy Campanella picked up her blue straw clutch purse and a key attached to a large plastic reindeer. Little girls' room, she said, and went out a side door.

What's going on? Will said.

Back to the infirmary for you, mister. A doctor's come from New York to take some blood or something. Seems your son needs it. It'll go back with him packed in dry ice. Quite a production.

I haven't heard about this.

Been pending since around Tuesday, I guess, court order came by special courier. Takes a little time for the warden to fix up his ace.

Will looked at Pasteur.

Warden's not going to do anything for you without protection. He doesn't want to seem like a pushover. That's why you got the transfer to the orchard.

I don't understand.

Your child needs something from you. But the warden is not happy to have you here. He won't give you the time of day. He doesn't like your background, especially your Jewish friend. Nothing will go right for you unless the warden has the lever to make it go wrong. He installed that lever. That's what those stitches are in your head. That's Loretta's job.

Pasteur stared at his pressed-together thumbs. The room was quiet except for an oscillating fan blowing back and forth over the ceramic waterfalls. Funny little things, Pasteur said. He touched a small pink crest of foam. I never did get this kind of stuff.

Nancy Campanella returned with the shine on her nose canceled out and fresh dark lipstick the color of her nails. She dropped her blue straw purse in a file drawer and stood, chest high, very straight. I'll see you two gentlemen up right now.

July 13

His mother hadn't told him much. Hollis wasn't saying a lot either, which was unusual. The television set was off, to keep him from getting too excited, and the lights were low. He hadn't had a roommate in a week and a half, and a plastic curtain hung over the door that Hollis cursed at every time she came through with more juice, more fluid. She wanted him drinking all the time, to keep his mouth wet. Soothed, she said. And he peed into a plastic bottle with a long snout, so he didn't tangle the tubes on his IV trying to get to the bathroom. Every time he peed, Hollis gave the plastic snout bottle a shake and looked carefully before she dumped it in the toilet.

Hollis elbowed back the plastic curtain to get into the room. Idiots, she said. She had a nice apricot nectar in a blue cup with a straw. Now his mother was tired and quiet all the time. Hollis said today his mother had a cold. She put the nectar down on the bedside table and checked the line. Any burning feeling? Always that question. It was all she talked about. Any burn, how's his mouth, did he feel any pinch in his stomach. His mother had a cough so she couldn't come. But his grandmother would, in the afternoon, she would come to see Bo.

Yesterday someone brought Bo mashed carrots by mistake and he threw up all over his blanket. Hollis had an argument with the orderly and then with the doctor. She brought him something warm and chocolate, like melted brown chalk. Very sweet. This and the sugar IV kept him from getting the black-over in his eyes. He missed his mother. Every day his nose bled.

Hollis said what would happen would be very easy. It was just an IV, like all the rest. People were acting like idiots. Hollis told him that his father's blood stems would grow like flowers in Bo's bones and replace the cells that weren't working so well. He missed his father. It will be like your father's strength going into you. You'll feel better. Not so tired. When would that happen? Three more days, said Hollis.

This was the last day of chemotherapy, more in volume these last four days than Bo had seen in half a year. It made Hollis angry. It was frightening and dangerous, she thought. She was angry all the time now. She had to be careful what she said in front of Bo. I need to watch my stupid mouth, she said. Bo said that Hollis was smart. Tomorrow head-to-toe radiation. And the day after. Then his body would rest. Then his father's bone stems could be planted.

And then?

Then we watch you, my angel. That's the nice part. We just watch you get stronger and better. And then Hollis looked angry again. I need a vacation. I know, said Bo. Because Bo was tired too, tired of the whole day, and wished for a moment he was in his room with his boats. All the models were lined up on the blue painted shelf. And he fell asleep telling Lou-Lou not to touch anything because the decals and the glue were still drying. She would wreck everything. Hollis said, All right, I won't. And she kissed his foot through the new blanket, though it was strictly not allowed. Even Bo knew that. Lou-Lou's hand was almost touching the best boat, wrecking it, but then she heard him say Stop, and she said Okay, and she drew it away.

July 16

Esther wore a teal tweed suit—very hot this late in July—and a black silk shell, and low black sling-backs, because Frank had told her the news might not be good, to be prepared for trouble. She carried her gigantic black handbag. The mule, Roy called it, and she wedged it beside her in the courtroom so that no sweat-smelling gossip spy could cuddle down next to her and get the drift of her emotions. She wanted a little privacy. The bag helped, and the thick tweed helped, but the room was packed with those who were not well-wishers. Frank had warned her about that too.

Roy's new haircut was very good. From the back he looked like a sleek prince. His neck poked out of his collar, spanking-clean, tan from the sun's reflection off the Hudson River. Roy said when this was all over they'd go to the Bahamas. Maybe, said Frank. Don't pack just yet. And he laughed as if he'd said something very funny. Her nails were a wreck.

So much drama. How could people live like this day and night. The prosecutor's table looked like a funeral. Six pale men, sweating in their suits. Esther looked at them as little as possible. They made her feel sorry that men could curdle up that way inside. Like there was no real life in them. Imagination, your fatal flaw, Roy said. She was always imagining the sorrows of others. Strangers. In fact, she seldom thought up a happy scenario for a person she didn't know. The vulture, Roy called her. But that was inaccurate. Esther never benefited from the harm she saw happening all around.

Roy stuck his neck out like a baby bird, like something was jamming in his throat. Esther dug in her bag for a peppermint. She remembered this from the last trial, all the neck craning, the dry throat, the closed-off feeling. She could tell from where she was sitting, this day was a rerun. Except for the part with that poor girl. What a terrible story.

Roy had not wanted the girl on the jury from the beginning. Esther remembered that very clearly because there'd been a fight about it. During the lunch break over at Gasner's, a standing-room crowd, and Roy and Frank and Esther were at the center table, in the middle of everything, trying to create good relations. Anyone with eyes could see them. All morning the jury selection had been a frustrating exercise. And now Roy was angry because all the peremptory challenges were used up.

Empty pockets, he said. Just when we actually need it, we're spent. Not smart. Not smart at all. I thought you were a lot better than that.

Frank's head dropped down, and Roy's eyes popped out in an unattractive way. Frank suggested that just because the woman was a Negro she wouldn't, by definition, be against Roy.

Yes, like Hitler would see my good side. Given the right argument, he'd say, Sure, I see it your way now. What was I thinking?

Hardly the same thing.

Excuse me? said Roy.

Frank was quiet.

Excuse me? Roy said again. And people began to turn.

Esther touched Roy's wrist. You can't read people's minds, she said, you think you can, but you're wrong. Esther understood that Roy was terrible in that way. He never knew what went on behind anyone's face. It was a disability.

Roy stared at her for a moment as if trying to place her. You're right, he said, still staring, you're right. And he waved his steak knife in a spiral of forgiveness. All right. It's done. What's done is done.

And they could finish their meal in peace. Except now Roy didn't want his. He called the waiter and decided on something else, a baked seafood dish, which was a risky choice, but it calmed him down. Frank said they'd be late back to court. What does it matter, Roy said, we're already screwed. It's over, Roy said, and he nibbled on Esther's salty french-fried potatoes, nibbled them down to the plate.

But he was wrong. It wasn't over. Because when the case closed, when the jurors, including that poor girl, who had never once looked Roy in the eye, a bad sign, were in deliberation, there was a terrible automobile accident and the girl's father was killed. The judge brought all the lawyers into his chambers and Frank said, She must be told.

But the prosecutors were adamant because they thought they were winning, and it was probably a matter of minutes until the end. Just get the verdict, they said. She'll know, what—by this afternoon? He's dead, not sick. There's nothing she can do.

But Frank gave the compassionate side: A girl has a right to know, immediately, as soon as possible, that her father is gone from this world.

The judge agreed.

The same judge who was not inclining in Frank's direction in any way, something that Roy could not let up on, this failure of Frank's to charm the judge. He agreed. So the bailiff interrupted the sequestered jurors and had the girl delivered to the judge's chambers, and in front of Frank, the anticharmer, and the prosecutors, who were sour on this, the girl was told that a milk truck had jackknifed on the Long Island Expressway and her father in his Buick was killed instantly. The medical team had been able to determine that he had not felt any discomfort. The jury was dismissed. The trial was declared a mistrial. The girl was free to join her family. There were some horrible stories in the newspapers about the girl and her father. How he rarely drove, and if his daughter hadn't been detained by civic duty, he'd still be alive. Esther knew all that was nonsense.

Certainly things had gone better in the second trial. All prior mistakes were lessons learned, all tempers remained checked, at least on the defense team, at least in the presence of the judge.

Roy even had moments of romance here and there. A surprise. Esther sniffed the hot courtroom air. How could so much perspiration just hang suspended. It wasn't a gym. Presumably these people were bathing. Roy's tan neck, an oasis of good clean skin, Esther focused there to take her mind off the stink getting worse all around her.

Roy was experimenting with gratitude lately. He was thanking everyone he could get to stand still. It was scaring her a little, all this embracing of his fellow man. It made her think he was dying or something. That he was hiding some troubling intuition. But then, but then, she reminded herself, Roy had no intuition, so it meant, whatever, a mood swing. A pendulum slowly dipping into thanks. It would come back again when this was all over. Life would be normal, and they could stop listening to the creaks in the telephone line for clues of surveillance, and stop clocking the postman to make sure he brought what was expected. To make sure the monthly ransom note from Saks Fifth Avenue arrived on time.

And all those love letters she'd written. How many? It was a daily thing, at Roy's request. Write them, mail them, see if they get delivered. Her favorite: My schnauzer, You bring me the bone, over and over. Let's never cease the snarling. Your poodle. Roy loved dog references. So easy to please. And frogs too: My pond king, There are treats sweeter than flies. Sing low. Affection and warmth from one happy lily pad. Roy said she had not only the eye but the ear as well. He was delighted with these notes, and one or two arrived with Scotch tape that Esther had not applied.

Keep going, he said. Just a sentence or two gets the message across. They're like haiku, he said, Japanese poems.

And Esther said it was against her sense of patriotism to write a Japanese anything.

An approximation, Roy said, I'm just comparing. No need to worry. All sorts of ways these will not be mistaken.

And he was sure, so she didn't fight about it. But it made her nervous. The government reading her notes and possibly choosing to misconstrue her loyalties. She didn't need to remind him about treason.

I don't think that will be a problem, Roy said.

And one night, just two nights ago, come to think about it, he was expressing his gratitude on the aft deck of the *Wavemaker II*. A quiet cruise to Bay Ridge and back, she liked these evening roundabouts. And Roy offered her a Tab and sent the new first mate, Dirk, a weird gangly kid with a wide long throat, back to the galley. Listen, he said. Listen. Esther looked up and cocked her head just like Charlie Brown did when Roy called. Ha-ha, said Roy. Happy? he asked. He was standing up. Behind his head the bridge lights twinkled yellow-green as fireflies. Happy? said Roy. Think so, she said. Know so?

They were all alone, just Roy and Esther and the crew. What do I know about anything. Roy sat down, crossed his legs, took her hand. Thank you, he said. For what? I'm just getting to that. But then he was distracted by a lump floating in the water. A log? A body? Roy suddenly had everyone on board, Esther, Captain Peeko, Dirk, leaning over the rail shouting out what they could see, pointing flashlights and yelling. Darkness and a ripple and a long familiar shape, something like a water ski, floating away from them, that's what she could see. And Esther never got to say: Roy, you're very welcome. What else could I have done.

A lot of people wanted to know why they weren't married. It was on the tips of many tongues. And when she looked at all these men, these prosecutors, up front, huddling around like tired football players, drained like they had no blood left, Roy stood out. Nice hair, nice tan, nice hands that could be counted on to stay where they belonged. What more could she want, really? But deep inside she worried about some things, things she couldn't safely discuss with anyone. Even her mother had mentioned a word or two about Dora Cohn's little Roy. Esther should have been paying attention. Now her mother was dead and Esther had Muddy all to herself.

You owe her, Sylvia Horner had said to her daughter, and Muddy certainly acted that way, but for the life of her, Esther didn't know why. A little information her mother took to her grave. Esther asked Roy. She tiptoed around it: I have this feeling, I get this sense.

You and your feelings, he said.

But this one, this is something that happened.

We all owe Muddy. What can I say.

He was no help whatsoever. Muddy let Esther hang around, she'd known her mother after all. But she made it obvious that Esther wasn't what she had in mind for her Roy, Esther was marked in some way. And this was frustrating. You've got love, affection, a lifelong friendship, you have the roots and the background, the attraction to the nice things about a man, the fine shape of his hands, the back of his neck, the blue in his eyes, even when sun-burned, even shot red from the sun. You like all these things and are willing to provide a son. Think, with all your brothers, you've got to be loaded with boys. Esther felt she could have a dozen sons. And in this Roy was interested, when he could pay attention. But with the trials, now two, when one was hard enough, a burden, a nuisance, an assault on any kind of tenderness. And then Muddy with her nose that always seemed to smell something a little off when Esther was around, would point out the new hand soaps, for godsakes, it was a miracle they were still friends. Well, a lot of things were miracles.

Roy turned around and gave her a wink. He was adorable. Just like that, he cleared the air, made a promise. Okay. She had fingers crossed, toes, legs, they'd get out of here, he'd be declared innocent, and then the rest would be history. Esther twisted her ankles closer and hugged her huge black bag. This jury was taking a dog's age.

This business with Muddy. There was an odd day when Esther was a very small girl and her brothers were all in school, but she wasn't, for no particular reason that she could recall. What she could remember, right there, Roy's hair the same dark shiny brown, smoothed back like a helmet away from his face. Such a beautiful face. Esther's mother, a tall woman, a woman of grace, her father said. Imagine all those sons passed through those narrow hips, her aunts whispered; Esther watched her mother's surprising hips slip down into Mrs. Cohn's deep green silk brocade chair. She barely made a dent in the cushion. Esther thought of her own hips, little pins and sharp bones.

Her mother had a look on her face that made Esther want to go home. Mrs. Cohn was very small, big dark eyebrows quivered on her forehead like black moths, her mouth a serving-spoon shape, flat across, turned-down edges. Between us, she said to Esther's mother, I know these things, in my own family, my own brother had such problems. There are places she can go. And Esther with the sharp bones knew Mrs. Cohn meant her. Mrs. Cohn nodded at Esther. Send her into the kitchen, she said, as if Sylvia Horner needed special words to speak to her daughter. Words that Dora Cohn, with all her family experience, didn't know. Into the kitchen, precious, her mother said. Esther left the room to show she knew how to listen.

But she had no desire for the kitchen where an unhappy woman sat on a low stool polishing silver with a torn shirt. Esther looked through the door at the long, sad face. From the sitting room, she could hear her mother crying now. She went away from that sound too, down the hallway, through the special door to the area off limits to guests, the bedchambers of the family, to Roy's room, where the door was closed. She did not knock, merely twisted the knob, and inside, as she knew he would be, was the boy, as beautiful as he was today, his pajamas buttoned up, his feet in slippers, even on the bed. No books, no toys, nothing on the bed but him, he was watching her. She asked him if he was sick. He shook his head without lifting it from the pillow. She asked him what he was doing here all by himself on a sunny day. He said: Thinking. I'm thinking. And she felt safe. Everything would be fine. Even if her mother was crying.

She still felt that way. Now when she saw Roy was thinking, staring ahead, not giving anyone any heat, she felt safe, because his mind worked in ways hers did not, and hers worked in ways his did not, and that was a good thing. So why weren't they married? Time would tell. Already they were like inhale and exhale, weren't they?

You'd have expected a band or something, a little fanfare. But when it happened, everything went very fast and dry, like a rehearsal for a school play, a cast without talent. The members of the jury shuffled in, looking tired and unkempt. Roy tried not to look but could not help himself. No one looked back, a very bad sign, he said later on the steps outside the courthouse to a crowd of reporters all taking down notes. The whole jury, every single one of them, looked like they could use a vacation. Esther hoped the summer wasn't over for them. And then there was the back-and-forth walk, not a fraction of grace or hope from the bailiff. The judge coughed. He read the slip of paper without his glasses. The judge looked at no one but the bailiff. Another bad sign, Roy said later. And then the jury foreman stood, Esther didn't hear anyone say it was time. He read out the verdict like he'd lost interest in the whole damn thing. There was an indication in barely audible terms that yes, Roy was acquitted of all charges. When Esther understood for certain, she felt that thrill in her body, and she thought of him with his beautiful brown hair, and the boys they would have, and she would teach them how to sail, or find someone who could. While right away the prosecutors packed their briefcases and looked like men on an ordinary day when the office is hot and no one is happy, Roy put his head down and whispered something to Frank, who had his head bowed too. And when the reporters asked him later what he had said, what he had whispered, what were his very first words when he knew that he was a free man? Roy replied, God bless America.

July 19

Lou-Lou didn't like Andrew Maguire's bedroom, though Gert made a big deal about Lou-Lou sleeping there, sending Andrew to bunk with his younger brothers, Toby and Nathaniel. Gert wanted to save the guest room for adults. It was an all-lavender room with bed skirts and, in Lou-Lou's experience, untouched like the Virgin. From Andrew's stone-hard green plaid bed, Lou-Lou could see her stuff, all tangled up together under Andrew's desk chair. Lou-Lou liked to keep things concentrated here. Unlike home, where her mother was always on Lou-Lou to rein it in. Like Bo. Bo's room was a tight ship, her mother said. A place for everything; everything in its place. Here at the Maguires', Lou-Lou applied a related concept: Everything in the same place. Always in a place she could grab it all and go.

Gert didn't know this about her oldest son, but he was a pervert, that's what the Sullivan twins said. The Sullivan twins told Timmy Mooney they caught Andrew Maguire in the un-remodeled ladies' room at the beach club. The twins saw Andrew in the last stall, the one with the big cracks in the wainscoting, whispering really loud, Can you see anything? They never found out who he was talking to, but whoever it was didn't see much after that. No one went into the unremodeled bathroom now, except the mothers.

Andrew was the one who kept the fort down by the water. Lou-Lou was invited on a provisional basis, and then only allowed in the quarantine lean-to section with the dirt floor. The true club had a triangle patch of orange indoor-outdoor carpet. The two sides, quarantine and true, were divided by a beach towel. The walls of the fort were made of plywood, warped and buckled by rain. Through the wide cracks, the grass, trees, and water were visible. Inside Lou-Lou's part the floor was sticky and damp. When she sat, dirt caked onto her stretch pants.

Lou-Lou stamped on her floor to make it harder. Andrew opened the flap and said Lou-Lou had to leave now for good unless she wanted to come into his side and relax. Those were the choices. Lou-Lou saw a flush in his cheeks and around his eyes, like he couldn't make himself stop laughing, but he was not laughing. He lifted the flap until it was horizontal. Above the elastic of his surfer bathing suit, Andrew had his equipment out for an airing. Lou-Lou looked at the little brown nozzle, then looked up. Are you going to relax or what? Andrew asked.

Lou-Lou wasn't sure what he meant and patted down the damp dirt in a flower pattern of handprints. Her palms were brown with mud. I might relax, she said.

Well, then you should come in here. Wait. Look at this. He had some art papers stuck under the carpet. Andrew wasn't much of an artist, but he wanted her to see and held one up in front of his chest as if the nozzle weren't there. Can you do that? Andrew had drawn a picture of a fat girl naked, bending backward, standing on her feet *and* her hands. He made her breasts point up like a single rocket. You think you can do that?

Lou-Lou thought she could do that. Sure, she said. She had to start on her back, then put her feet and hands flat first and push her stomach up. She lay down on the dirt.

No, I mean naked. Can you do it naked, because it's more relaxing that way.

Lou-Lou considered this. She thought about how she would be different from the drawing. There were many people she knew who would have opinions on this idea, but she couldn't remember them. Something in Andrew's breathing close by, holding up his paper, the closeness of his naked thing, *was* sort of relaxing. Fine, she said. She unbuckled the strap on her sandal.

Andrew let the beach-towel flap drop. When he pulled it up again, his bathing suit was gone. His thing stuck sideways and up, the nozzle was dark pink now, and his brown pouch had a coat of white dust on it. Maybe baby powder. Andrew had a smell like a pizza. Lou-Lou held on to her sandal. Hurry up, Andrew said.

Lou-Lou worked the sandal off the other foot. She pulled off her shorts and underpants. Her pink sleeveless mock turtleneck was a little tight and got stuck going up over her head. Ouch, Lou-Lou said, get me out of here. Andrew threw a small dirt-bomb at her. It disintegrated and tickled her bare belly. She laughed, then he threw another that smacked her chest. Lou-Lou held still, she must be making some mistake, then another dirt-bomb hit her on the arm. She could hear Andrew panting for breath, and she kicked out a kind of fan kick, an exploratory kick, wide and slow in the direction of his breathing, and felt his weird powdered pouch with her toes. Gross, she said, and tried to pull her turtleneck back down so she could see. You killed me, screamed Andrew, you're trying to kill me. And he threw something hard at her, like a rock. Lou-Lou grabbed for her clothes, scrambled out of the fort, and ran up through the yard, bare-bottomed, and blindfolded by her mock turtleneck.

Andrew yelled after her, Get out, get out. He threw another dirt-bomb, which missed, but she heard it land. Lou-Lou hurled back her sandal, which was a mistake, now she'd have to sneak back down later to get it. She ran almost all the way to the house before she stopped, stepped into a forsythia bush, and yanked her mock turtleneck back down off her face. She looked out to see if anyone was around. Only the Ruddys' handyman, riding a mower in the opposite direction. Lou-Lou put her underpants and her shorts back on. Her belly had a round brown dirt mark, but her chest was cut, a tiny crescent scratch. The blood formed a small blotch now like a red Jujube on her mock turtleneck. When her mother came home, she would kill Lou-Lou for messing up her good clothes again. In the meantime, Lou-Lou would roll it up in her ball of stuff, and Gert would never see anything.

At dinner that night, Red Maguire was silent. Reflective, Gert called it, and the boys were in no mood to talk either. Gert smoked and sipped her Tom Collins, and barely touched the American chop suey or the iceberg lettuce with Russian dressing. As soon as *Bonanza* started, the boys were excused from the table to go watch with their father in the den. It was a ritual to watch the show about the Wild West father raising three sons, each apparently born from a different mother. All the mothers were dead and gone now. Let 'em fantasize, Gert said. She didn't get up to scrape the dishes, she lit another Winston instead. Listen, porky pie, I have a bone to pick with you.

Lou-Lou gave Gert her full attention, as Gert so often asked her to do.

Gert stubbed out her new Winston. She reached into the deep pocket of her lime-green capri pants and pulled out some white lollipop cotton panties from her pocket. Look familiar?

Yes, Lou-Lou said, they're mine. It was the only kind she wore, and pretty much the only color.

I thought we talked about this.

Lou-Lou was confused but at the same time not. From the serious expression in Gert's eyes, Lou-Lou had an idea of the subject, if not the cause. When she first started staying at Gert's, Lou-Lou made the mistake of going into the den during *Bonanza* and curling up on the sofa, right beside Andrew, so her body was touching his, much like she did with Bo when he was home. Gert happened to perch in the doorway for a second, saw Lou-Lou, and lifted her by the arm off the sofa and right out of the room. You're not pulling any of that kind of stuff here, madame. You can just forget about that.

But Gert didn't forget. The next time Lou-Lou's mother was home, she was very serious with Lou-Lou, just as Gert was now, serious about not letting boys touch her, ever.

Maybe you can give me a clue about how these turned up in Andrew's pajamas.

Lou-Lou felt very sad, because she didn't know. And that was an answer Gert generally didn't accept.

I think I deserve better than this from you, Lou-Lou. I think this whole family deserves better than this from you. Maybe you should get an early night. What do you say?

Lou-Lou looked up at the kitchen clock. It was six-twenty-five. Outside, it was still completely daytime.

Extra sleep never hurt anyone. I think this is for your mother to handle. Gert lit another cigarette. Exhaled a wide, flat ray of smoke. She picked up her drink, jiggled the ice. Yes, I'm going to pass on this. It's better that way. You go to bed now.

Lou-Lou stood up. The *Bonanza* theme was pounding out. She could hear Andrew giggle and say Shut up. Gert took a long thoughtful drag.

All right. I just want to say one thing. Maybe, just until your mother comes home, until she can talk to you, maybe you should just steer clear of the boys. Don't even talk to them. Okay, peanut? I think there's a little mix-up happening, and until it gets straightened out, that just seems the best solution. Do you think you can handle that?

I think so. Steer clear of the boys. You mean Andrew, Toby, and Nathaniel?

Right. Just pretend you don't even see them, leave them alone. Who needs 'em anyway. Right? It's better for everyone.

Okay.

Good. Good. Sweet dreams, now. Good night, lamb. Gert stroked Lou-Lou's cheek with her knuckles. Her hand smelled like smoke and lettuce.

In bed, in Andrew's room, even with the curtains closed, it was so bright, Lou-Lou could see all of her things perfectly. It didn't look like anything had been touched. It was a mystery, then, how her lollipops got into Andrew's pajamas. Maybe he bought a different pair for himself with his allowance. The sun made a milky line cutting through the curtain right down the center of the bed, right over her face, cutting her face in two. Always an asset wherever she goes, Mrs. Westerfield said, a young lady should be an asset, all the time.

Across the creek, that little girl from the house of woe was probably already in bed too. Lou-Lou put her hands over her own heart to determine how she was feeling. Better! it turned out. Much better. And Bo? Lou-Lou put her hands on her head, over her eyes. No headache. Bo was sleeping. Feeling okay. And Rufus? Her feet kicked away the stupid plaid blanket. Rufus was running hard, even in sunlight. Timmy was blowing smoke rings like hula hoops. And her father? He was sleeping, just like Bo. And her mother? Her mother was dancing. Singing and dancing, and twirling around in a beautiful pink dress, more beautiful than even Merrill had ever worn. And when her mother saw Lou-Lou? Even though Lou-Lou was wearing the ugly cowgirl pajamas that her grandmother had given her, even so, Kay stopped dancing, stopped singing. Tears of happiness dropped on both cheeks. Lou-Lou started running to her, running like a speed demon. Kay bent down to catch Lou-Lou, lifted her up, held her deep and strong. Her mother's neck smelled of warm pancakes. Lou-Lou tucked her face there and she listened hard when her mother whispered, You, my love, only you. Always.

July 23

Kay edged back into the orange vinyl seat, propped her elbow on the wood veneer armrest, and sank her cheek into her gloved fist. She leaned down and tried to rub the gray city ash off her white sandals through the plastic bag. She looked up to watch her son watch a television bolted into the wall. Long days of chemotherapy, three of radiation, the bone marrow transplant, which wasn't so bad in itself, and the aftermath, everyone suited up like they were in outer space, and here he was laughing at the Stooges so hard his eyes were tearing. Bo looked at her to see if she was laughing too. She grinned hugely behind her mask, and when he looked away, she watched him settle his round face back into the pillows. She watched to see if he had any trouble doing that.

Hollis came in, pushed back the plastic on the door. Greetings and salutations. She smoothed a hand across Bo's forehead. Cool. This man is cool as a cube.

As a cube?

Like ice. He's gonna get out of here.

Think so?

Yes, know so. A couple more days and no fever, no infection, we'll put him in a normal room. How's your mouth, Bo?

Bo opened his mouth for Hollis. With a wooden depressor, she touched his tongue as if it were the wing of a butterfly.

Are you sucking the ice chips, Bo? You look a little red in there. A small Styrofoam cup filled with ice sat on his bedside table. She peeled open the lid. Here. Keep at this. Bo tipped back the cup and took a few chips in his mouth.

What about food?

Tomorrow they'll try again with breakfast. Hollis took a long look at the catheter attached to Bo's chest. You all right here? But

Bo didn't answer, he stared up at the television. Looks okay. I don't see anything to worry about. Okay. I'll see you two on Monday.

Monday! Where are you going?

Can you believe it? I have the whole weekend off. I'm going on a mystery cruise.

You're kidding. With that Hetzler guy?

No way. I barely know him.

I thought that was the point.

Don't listen to your mother, Bo, she'll corrupt your pure heart. Hollis pecked the top of Bo's head, a kiss so quick, so shielded by the woven paper mask, it barely happened at all. The Three Stooges were in a fine mess. Bo laughed while Curly hit his own head with a frying pan. Hollis slipped out the door, unbuttoning the Peter Pan collar on her nurse's uniform as she went. See you Monday morning. And we'll start packing up your duds.

Around midnight, with Bo asleep for hours, Kay took off her scrub coat, her mask, her gloves, and plastic booties, made a small package to come back to on the chair outside Bo's room, and wandered down to the third floor of the west wing to see if the soda machine had been fixed yet. One machine for so many friends and relatives, it was an odd arrangement. But here it was, lit up and humming. Kay fished in her pocketbook for loose coins, dropped them in the slot. With a crash that echoed all the way down the long empty corridor, her Tab landed in the bin, lukewarm. Kay took it across the hall to the ladies' room and, without turning on the lights, went to the window, opened the sash, and lit a cigarette. She sat down on the wide sill, looked out over the empty street just below, no ambulances soaring in, so quiet. She could smell the river, the moon was bright, her son was getting better and maybe would be well for a while now. There was a big party tonight for Roy, she should make an appearance, but it was better to stick around here.

Kay liked this window, had found refuge here before on harder nights. She liked the big square tiles and the smoking as if in college. She felt almost happy. I'm in college, I could get kicked out for this. The moon was so high over the river it lit everything, the Dumpsters, the emergency sign, the yellow brick entrance. She hopped off the sill, flushed the cigarette down the toilet. She'd go for a walk around the block, she hadn't been out of the hospital in two days. A little fresh air wouldn't kill her.

Back on ten, there was a lot of action. She could hear it the second she stepped off the elevator, the squeaking running shoes, the loud whispers, the machines scraping along the floor. And she knew, before turning the corner, that it was Bo. Whatever happened was over, had happened while she was outside, dreaming of college. And the intern with the ass too small for his green scrubs was backing out of Bo's room with a machine on wheels. He's okay, he said, we didn't need it, and he winked at her and wiped his sweaty face, and Kay would have hit him if she could have raised her arm. Bo's bed was empty, and that terrified her except for the simultaneous understanding that if he were dead, the intern would be acting differently. Where is he? Where is he? Had she spoken out loud? The night nurse in charge, Clarissa, came back to find her. Your sweater, she said. She was very fat. She held Kay's cardigan by the top button. Bo had slept with it wrapped around his shoulders because he liked the smell. Where is he?

Intensive care. His fever spiked, happened so fast something beeped on our monitors. A mistake, actually. We read a code for his heart, and that's why all the hardware. But really it's just the fever. He'll be all right. We've been watching for this.

Why?

Well, it's not unexpected. We'll keep him in ICU for a day or two, let his system stabilize. It will help his throat too.

What's wrong with his throat?

Cankers from the chemo. So he's on a light morphine drip. Something for the fever, something for the pain. Didn't Hollis tell you? Dr. Bronson?

Yes. They told me. They told me it was possible. Show me where he is?

Kay followed Clarissa down the silent corridor, through a double set of doors, another corridor, now they were in a different building built in a different time, a left turn, a right turn, and they were standing in front of a glass partition, inside a small vestibule with a view into the pediatric ICU. All this had happened to Bo in the time it took her to drink a Tab, smoke a cigarette, and walk to the river and back. Clarissa handed Kay her sweater and said good night. Kay waved to the ICU nurse through the glass. She was taking Bo's pulse, reading numbers in an orange light. His eyes were closed. He looked asleep, exactly the way he had when she tiptoed out forty minutes ago.

The nurse opened the glass door and closed it quietly. He's doing great, she said.

He's okay?

You can see him in the morning. We'll let him sleep. The ICU nurse smiled. She had small teeth and red round lips. She had a mustache, bleached very yellow. You're welcome to sit in here. Kay took another vinyl chair and moved it around so she could lean her face against the glass. One of them had infected him. Either she'd done it or Hollis had. With some kiss or caress. She knew it.

~

Roy loved all the balloons. Esther's idea, of course. Red, white, and blue balloons taking a dive from the ceiling at midnight, just when the senator from Wyoming was making the fortieth toast of the evening. And the little boats, each a *Mayflower* carved from a baked potato loaded with caviar immigrants. Better a shtetl, said Muddy, or something useful. But Roy got the symbolism and it was good for him, it was right, and he was grateful for all the creativity. The sight of all his friends in red, white, or blue cummerbunds, it made him a little teary, he had to admit, and if his mother wore brown, that was her privilege. But Esther in the red sequins was a dream, and when they danced to "When the Saints Come Marching In," she laughed so hard and looked so pretty, he almost felt like he *would* marry her, why not, worse things had happened.

Frank whispered something to Merrill that made her blush. A frosty pink hit her cheeks, she blushed right down to the décolletage on her painted-on white gown. Fly on the wall, fly on her ear, what would he give to hear what Frank could possibly say to Merrill that would warrant a blush from her. Probably something about her taxes. She looked up and smiled like the million-dollar girl she was, and that other one, Million-Dollar Dolly, she was here too, with her friend with the death-defying tits, all in electric blue, to light up, to send electricity to the whole damn city if needed. Drop a bomb here tonight, you'd lose half the government, and a good portion of the other swanky citizens as well. When you win, everyone comes to the party. A fact of life. Lucky, he felt his luck like a snake winding around his feet, and that made him nervous for a second, even as they all lifted their glasses for the hundredth time that night, he was on the lookout for trouble, to find it before it found him. And that was easy to do: Kay. Where was Kay? She should be here. Weren't things going great? Wasn't this just where she should be, dressed in something fabulous?

Roy nodded and hugged his way to Frank and Merrill and bent down to whisper in the ear of the man who caused blushes: Kay, what gives. Frank frowned hard as if this thought had just occurred to him. But Merrill dipped two pink fingers into Roy's cummerbund and drew him to her. She's on watch.

She joined the army?

Ho, ho, Frank laughed, but not very hard, he was frowning, something big had slipped right past.

She's watching Bo.

For?

Just to make sure he's okay, she said she'd stop in later to celebrate.

Later, how later, it's after midnight.

Well, give her a chance.

Roy nodded and watched the lieutenant governor make a joke with the waiter.

Muddy was fading. Midnight and his princess had had it. So Roy said, I'll be back, he told Esther, and Frank, and Dan, and anyone who stopped dancing and talking and yelling and drinking long enough to ask. I'll be back. And he wrapped Muddy up in her long mink coat, in July for godsakes, holding it just the way she liked, and she was tired, didn't need to say a thing, and for once Peter was actually parked outside where he was supposed to be, it was a miracle, a night of miracles. And maybe it was time he should spread a little of this around.

Park Avenue sparkled with the night. Muddy was pleased and smiled at him and didn't mention anything about Esther or Merrill or anyone she usually liked to discuss after an event, except to say that blue wasn't Esther's color. She wore red, Muddy. Exactly my point, she did the right thing. What choice did she have, white on that skin? And blue? No.

Wait, Peter, I'm coming back.

Roy walked his mother in, all the way to the door of her bedroom. You're all right?

What else would I be?

True. True enough. Good night, dear, he said, and kissed her cheek, then turned to run down the stairs, happy, he was happy like a child. It was a sin to be happy like this.

Peter knew the entrance to the hospital where Roy could get in, and someone would get him up to the tenth floor, even if it was almost one in the morning. Roy had a hunch. And a hundred-dollar bill to the guard in the west wing had him standing in front of the right night-duty nurse. The fat one.

But she was impervious to his tan, his tux, which had cost a lot, now that he thought of it, was it really worth it for one event? How many Fourths of July could he dredge this up at, it was a onetime suit, and it still didn't move her. Money didn't matter, so he tried humanity. He told her, I'm a friend. And she said, And I'm the president of the United States, which gave him an idea, but then he rejected it. Too much. Roy reached into his pocket. I have this little flag, I'd like to give it to Mrs. Clemens.

The nurse, for reasons he would never fathom, except as a further sign of his incredible good fortune, which he needed to spread where it was most needed as soon as possible, stepped over to the phallus-shaped microphone on her communication system and called four numbers, Two-three-eight-six, over the loudspeaker. Am I getting the boot? Roy even asked that and smiled, a winning smile, a smile that said, *You want presidents, I'll give you presidents.* And a young man came scooting up the hall from wherever he'd been dozing, a pillow crease on his cheek. A cheek, Roy noted, the color of an autumn leaf, golden, lucky, he was so fucking lucky, and the boy took a sleepy seat where the fat nurse had just disembarked, and she said, Follow me, and Roy said, Thank you, thought, That boy's face is sweet. And it wasn't Roy's fault, no indication of his changing luck, when the boy got the ax the next day for pilfering in the fat nurse's purse while she was showing Roy the way.

Kay was sleeping too, but there was no crease in her beautiful face. Her cheek smashed against the glass, so if by sudden chance the glass lifted, she could go to her son. Sleeping or not, she'd be ready. Thank you, Roy said, thank you very much, and bowed like a courtier to get this fat nurse on the move. Give me the field here. Give me a chance. I'll be back, she said, and Roy thanked her again, and waved the little flag like a wand.

Roy could see Bo's face lit orange through the glass. Strangely, he looked not so bad, maybe it was his luck talking, but Roy could definitely determine that there was a kid with possibilities. Bo looked okay, looked positive, Roy didn't know why. He didn't necessarily want to wake Kay, who, even asleep, looked tired, looked clobbered by sleep. He sat down slowly in the chair beside her; the brocade of his jacket, maybe it was the embroidered stars, made a scratching noise on the plastic. He held himself suspended for a second, and then, carefully, let his keister hit the seat. She didn't stir, her face stayed mashed into the safety glass, and he looked at her crunched mouth and felt love, love like religion.

Twenty minutes later she was still asleep, and he was wide awake, with a list formed in his head of who he would call and who he could get. Roy had the time now and he had the energy. A mustachioed nurse wearing neon-red lipstick tiptoed toward him like a nightmare to wave him out of the ICU, but that was okay, his luck was holding. For Bo, this setback would be temporary, a poodle, a miniature poodle right around the bend. Esther was correct.

Back on ten, the golden boy had vanished, and a new nurse, cute with red hair, was counting sheets of paper. Roy handed her five one-hundred-dollar bills and stole a piece of paper from her pile. He wrote down his telephone number, the night line, where he could actually be reached. He knew she would take it. He could tell right away. She blinked, astonished, and he said, like he was teaching her a new prayer, the one that would change her life: Mrs. Clemens, whatever she wants, she gets. And then he made his way down the same back stairs he had ascended earlier, and miracle of miracles, Peter was right where he left him.

Back to the party, Peter, he said, it can't possibly be over.

When Pasteur first dropped the hint of his release, Will was losing so badly at hearts, he didn't hear it. He couldn't concentrate on anything because his hip throbbed as if a miniature jackhammer drilled the bone. A week and a half after a minor procedure. He thought it might be infected. At the card table, he shifted and rubbed and irritated the other players. For christsakes, Clementine, take a bath or something, said Ray Spofford, always a bad sport. You're making me itch.

You better get someone to take a look at that, Pasteur said.

I'll take a look. You want me to look, Clementine?

Pasteur pressed his creased newspaper flat on his thigh. He glanced at the wall clock. Twenty-five to five. Clean it up, he said. We'll break early. Just add up what you have.

Good work, twitch. You won me a Bundt cake.

Yes, well. Last chance for that kind of help. Soak it up while you can, said Pasteur. Let's go now. He jammed the newspaper into a back pocket. Come on, I want to get out of here.

Who doesn't? Sammy Finlandor sneezed into a closed fist.

Let's go.

Will folded his hand reluctantly. For one bright moment he was doing so badly he thought he might shoot the moon. Recoup his losses. See young Emily again. Win himself a cake.

Just after breakfast the next morning, Will was shaving turnips when Nancy Campanella tiptoed into the kitchen, lavender skirt swinging back and forth over empty cans on the floor. Chef Brodie was muscling some dessert into shape for dinner. Cling peaches and oiled stale bread, stirred together with a bag of sugar. One egg leavened the whole thing. Nancy watched until the orange batch was poured into vast tins and set in the oven, then she handed Chef Brodie a pink slip. He nodded as he read it, wiped his hands, and read it again. All right, I'll tell him. But after she left, Chef Brodie got distracted by a rust situation around the handles of his two best fry baskets. He placed an angry call to the supply clerk.

By ten o'clock Pasteur was standing beside Chef Brodie. You think I don't have enough to do?

Take him, go ahead, Brodie said, and picked up the wall phone again and dialed.

You need more help down here?

Brodie gave Pasteur a squint. Needing help and getting it, two different animals. Listen, I have something to do. You take your man. We'll still eat. Chef Brodie waved Pasteur off and started yelling into the phone about the waste of his time and talent, the danger in shoddy equipment.

Pasteur moved slowly through the kitchen to Will's sink. You can let that go now. Will just looked at him, not sure what he meant. I said, You can put that scraper down and follow me.

Will spent the next half hour filling out forms on Pasteur's clipboard. They wanted a full accounting of his next intended decade. Will sat on the edge of his cot and tried to imagine anything at all about what might be ahead. His mind worked like a toy with a spring action, rejecting each obvious idea. He'd see his family. He'd find a job. Just thinking such things made him sick to his stomach.

All right, that's enough. Pasteur had a short stack of clothes, Will's suit from the courtroom rolled in a ball, a pair of black loafers, and a new green plastic satchel. Get dressed. There's a car outside for you. I'll walk you down to the gate, but I don't have all morning for this ceremony.

Sammy Finlandor had been trying to get a cold tablet from the infirmary for two days. He'd been stuck working in the laundry because his nose wouldn't stop running. Will could hear him sniffing all the way down the row. After the head count, Will shook out his suit. It smelled like cat piss. His eyes started to tear for no reason. Sammy walked by the open door.

What's going on? Sammy sneezed hard, doubled over and stood upright again. What are you doing?

I don't know.

What do you mean, you don't know. You're leaving, obviously. That's amazing. Just this morning they told you?

Will nodded.

Christ, look at you. What are you, crazy? You cry when you arrive here, not when you go.

Will squinted down into the green plastic valise.

Come on. Sammy started to cough again, deep in his chest. Come on. I'm dying here. That's something to cry about. Will put his hand flat over his eyes.

Sammy took a look both ways down the catwalk, then stepped inside. What do you need to do here. What are you going to do with all this shit.

Leave it. You take everything.

Like I want a can of letters from your wife. Be real. Sammy pried open the tin flap on the cherry can. Wow. She's got a lot to say.

Will sat down on the cot again and tried to untie his oxfords, but now he was sobbing, like a seizure.

You are a mess. I'll help you. Sammy squatted down and tugged off each shoe. Okay, you're all set. I'm just going to take these as a memento. Sammy slipped his hands into the shoes. He clapped the soles together. A cuc-a-racha! Come on. Come on. Come on. It's over. Sammy tapped Will's shoulder with a shoe. Come on. Take a deep breath. Isn't that what they always say. This is the time for all that crap. Sammy leaned over. You hear me in there? Will opened his eyes and nodded. I hear you. Sammy kissed Will, suddenly, on the lips, Will jerked his head away, then Sammy stood up coughing, lifted a shoe to cover his mouth. Will sat way back, Jesus Christ, then he started to laugh. Stupid faggot.

Good. Now get the fuck out of here. And Sammy left, slipped out the open door and away down the catwalk. The sound of his choking pinged off the glass roof.

In the courtyard, Pasteur did a lot of handshaking with Peter as if it were a transfer-of-custody situation. All right now, time to look on the bright side, he said to Will, but did not shake his hand. Don't let your mind visit here too often, that's key. Then the rest of you won't come back either. When the long blue car pulled out under the first twist of razor wire, Pasteur waved once, then went back inside. Will's loafers felt cold and stiff and thin on his feet. The leather bit into his toes. He asked Peter to turn off the radio because the speakers jabbed his ears. The soft seat felt like sticky wax, and his face burned with a fever he hadn't felt before. He rubbed his mouth. His hand smelled old. They passed nothing on the road out to the thruway but scrub pine and dirt and weeds. Will didn't see a single other car or face. Peter said he would drive Will to the hotel, after that he kept quiet.

Sometime late Monday afternoon, Kay came to believe she could go home. She would find a taxi downstairs at the front entrance, easily, and that taxi would take her to the train, from the train she could find another taxi, and then she'd be in Rumson. She'd be inside her own house, step into the laundry, reach into the dryer and pull out the nightgown that had been there for how many weeks now. She'd let Carmen go over a month ago. She wouldn't eat, or wash, she'd just crawl into her own bed, her side softer than the other, and she'd be there by nightfall. She began to count on that. She held Bo's toes through the blanket.

Hollis launched herself into the room, carrying two canned sodas. Her face worn with aggravation. Don't blame me, she said.

How could I blame you? How could I blame you, Hollis? And he's better now. He's back. And you'll be here tonight. Is that for me?

Yes.

It's freezing. How do you get a can this cold?

I keep them in the lab fridge.

Smart.

Yes.

You are. Everything. Hollis. He's okay.

Yes, he looks okay. Hollis read all the gauges, then the clipboard. A quick surge and now he's okay. He just got a fever. And now it's gone.

Kay nodded. Now it's gone.

That Clarissa is a pain in the ass, but she did the right thing.

Think so?

Definitely. A night in the ICU whips everyone into shape. We'll be watching him like the sun rises and sets on him for a few days now.

Kay cracked open her soda. Bo's eyelids fluttered, then he turned his cheek away from her and sighed in his sleep.

I might go home now.

Sure, why not. He'll rest until dinner, anyway.

No, I mean home home.

Oh.

You don't think that's such a good idea?

I think it's okay. Hollis was back to examining the label on the IV. She turned away, opened her own soda.

Dr. Bronson's coming in about ten minutes, and then I think I'll go home.

Hollis nodded. Okay.

And I'll come right back tomorrow.

Fine. Good.

Kay watched Hollis's hand. Fingers to wrist, taking her own pulse, a funny nervous habit.

Sure, she said again, why not.

Dr. Bronson looked a bit like a piglet to Kay. He wore a pink shirt, had pink skin and black wires of hair on the backs of his hands that pressed like trapped insects against his rubber gloves. He took the plastic drape in the doorway and looped it over a chair as if he needed some fresh air. Seven doctors followed him into the room silently, all dressed as if for surgery. They lined up against the windows. Dr. Bronson stepped to the bed and gently lifted each of Bo's eyelids, he unbuttoned the pajama top and felt all around Bo's neck and chest, then he covered him up with a blanket and went back to wrestle again with the drape. Bo never woke up. Dr. Bronson nodded to the assembled doctors, All right. And they all left shaking his hand as they went. Now he leaned in the doorway, patted his round stomach, he was ready for her.

Kay followed Dr. Bronson down the hall. He motioned her into the play-nurse's cubicle, swept a pair of trolls off the desk to the floor. Drive me batty, those things. I can't stand to look at them.

Kay took a seat. She couldn't keep her eyes off the fallen trolls.

So, said Dr. Bronson. We're making history.

Kay stared at him. He's barely been conscious for two days now.

I see a very minor setback, completely well handled, by the way. Out of ICU fast. That's good. We've already got some positive test results. His blood looks very good. I think if all continues to go well—the doctor flexed his small articulate hands twice—I think we're going to see a remission.

Do you really think so?

I do.

Kay bent forward and picked up the trolls. Straightened their hair, dropped them in her lap.

Dr. Bronson frowned at her. You look tired.

I am tired.

Go get some rest. This is a big change for the better. From here on, it's just cheering him in to home plate.

And what about later?

We'll keep him feeling well.

Dr. Bronson shifted his weight in the social worker's bucket chair. Maybe you don't understand what's happened here? This is unprecedented. Really unheard of. You know that, don't you.

Kay nodded, handed him the trolls. Dr. Bronson laid them on the desk. Is there something you wanted to ask?

One of the new nurses stuck her head around the corner. They're all waiting for you, Doctor.

Be right there. Mrs. Clemens?

She shook her head. No. I believe you.

You're just tired. Who wouldn't be? Dr. Bronson stood, led her by the arm out of the cubicle. You know what? I'm going to call you in the morning, okay? We'll talk more, he said, then signaled to the waiting nurse to show him the way to the conference room.

Kay walked back to Bo's room, remasking. She held his ankles through the white cotton blanket. She rubbed her hand along his shins. He almost always slept on his back now, to accommodate all the monitors, the Hickman, and the tubes. She gave Hollis a quick smile, then headed out to grab the elevator, untying the lab smock, stuffing her mask and gloves into her pocketbook as she went.

Right away she found a cab, but as soon as she was settled into the back and the cabbie was careening down York Avenue, looking for a cross street not choked with traffic at five o'clock, she changed her mind. She couldn't make the trip after all, it was too far and too long to go home. The St. Regis, please, she said. The cabbie gunned his engine at the red light, as if now they were in business. It meant another day before she saw Lou-Lou. She'd call Gert as soon as she got into her room.

It was after six by the time they crawled the twenty steaming blocks downtown, and inside the lobby of the St. Regis, it looked like Mardi Gras. A hundred people, at least, in black tie and ball gowns. Wasn't it early for this? Kay flipped open her purse and plucked out her sunglasses, the ones that covered half her face. She hadn't touched a lipstick in a day and a half, and she'd slept in her dress all weekend. She wriggled through the crowd.

The elevators were all at the penthouse. She pushed all the buttons, not one would budge from the top. The women in their crinkling gowns and the men with too much cologne and their cigars waving pressed into her, they wanted the elevators too. She took the stairs. By the eighth floor, sixteenth landing, she was sticky with sweat and needed to cry. And so angry she felt she would knock over the next person who got in her way. Kay pushed through the fire door onto her corridor which, empty, smelled of new paint. Maybe they were renovating this floor, maybe that's how Roy cut the deal. Her doorknob still had the sign on it. Don't trespass, don't come near me. It had been a week, at least, since

she'd let the maid service clean up her room. She treated almost
everyone now as if they were carriers of a deadly virus. When did
that happen, when did she start becoming so hateful. All the
partygoers looked like ghouls to her. She remembered Gert in a
strapless gown once, with so many freckles on her shoulders it
looked like a translucent lace shawl. And Kay had loved that, the
strangeness of it. What had happened to her.

Kay stuck the key in the lock, turned it, stepped inside the tiny
foyer and out of her sling-backs. In the sitting room, her eggs from
three days ago still sat a yellow mess just where she'd left them.
She felt a sick relief to be here, out of anyone's sight or hearing,
and then immediately a smack of fear. The bedroom door was
closed. She never closed it. She thought to call the manager, someone, but it was a free-for-all in the lobby, who knew how long
they'd take. She could see her hands were shaking. But inside she
went still, still and angry.

She wrapped a cold trembling hand around the crystal doorknob, turned and pushed. It was dark in the bedroom. Almost
like the sun had set rapidly from one room to the next. The curtains were drawn closed across the window that overlooked the
air shaft. She pulled aside the fabric. Through the window, sooty
drafts carried the scent of hors d'oeuvres. In her bed, in her dirty
sheets, was her husband, dead asleep. A streak of gray across his
shoulder, his head covered in stubble patches and a long red scar.
She looked at him, face turned into her pillow, hands tucked
around his neck, fingers cradling one cheek.

Kay felt an odd stricken calm, but her hands still shook and
she went to shut out the smell, the nasty smell of hors d'oeuvres,
and spotted the back of a woman in a gown, ready to go, in the
window opposite. She pulled the window shut, dragged the curtains together, drowning out most of the light. She could still see
her husband's face sunk into the pillow, and the rise and fall, very
slight, of his breath in his back. I miss you, she thought, looking
right at him. That seemed true now. She could not move. She sat

at last in one of the low boudoir chairs, wide-bottomed, low-slung, good for putting on difficult shoes. She sucked on the remains of a warm, flat soda in a bottle. She unclasped the stranglehold of her dirty stockings and she unzipped her dress, untangled the straps of her bra and slid it off her chest. Felt the heat of the airless room and felt the weariness of her husband like a radio broadcast to her bones. And her own weariness and her own anger, and she slid off her panties and felt the slick satin of the chair, and how dirty her own body was, sweaty, smelling of the hospital and the cab and all the cigarettes she'd smoked in disinfected toilets, and how her breasts pulled down heavy like a sickness, and she took this body and went across the room to her husband and lay down, she curled into his back and put her mouth to the base of his neck, her breasts touched his skin where the strange gray ash streaked beneath his shoulder blades, she dropped her left hand to the base of his spine. She would lie there just this way, her body against his cool cool skin, until she could breathe and think and feel anything that made sense again.

August 1

Lou-Lou glanced sideways at Timmy Mooney, the demoted pool boy, in the light shimmering off the Atlantic Ocean. Sparkles like stars flashed from the water to his face. His calves were drenched by low foamy swells. He was watching and waiting.

Lou-Lou had been avoiding Timmy, hiding out. She'd never gone back to New York to get her bones tapped, as she had said she would. She knew he would think she was a liar. Maybe she was a liar. All the rest of July, Gert sent her to the beach club only twice, and each time Lou-Lou stayed far away from the umbrella hut. When she saw Timmy sticking umbrellas in the sand, she froze until he finished and moved away. She felt so sad when he left, but she couldn't do anything differently.

Now Lou-Lou listened closely in case Timmy spoke. They stood this way, side by side, near the jetty, at the end of the half-mile strip of beach that was the private property of the Monmouth Beach Bath and Tennis Club. The water was rough today, with huge breakers. Timmy was going to give her some tips on bodysurfing.

That morning Lou-Lou got creamed over and over. She crashed, then wobbled upright, clumps of sand stuck in the bottom of her bathing suit. The lifeguard finally beached her, blew his whistle and ordered her to sit for an interval in the shadow of his big white chair. After digging in some encampments, Timmy strolled over and said, Look, it's just not that hard.

They were waiting for the perfect curl. Timmy squinted out to the horizon line, and there a small bump began to form. All right, here we go, Timmy said. Now just watch. He began corkscrew running, swiveling his body to cut through the water, fists at chest level, elbows straight out from his shoulders, until he was thigh-deep, then he took a dive. The water crept higher and higher, gathering a thick green bottom and a thin top like frosted glass. The foam around her feet was sucked away suddenly with a hush. Timmy reversed direction and let his body be pulled up into the top, up higher until he was part of the crumbling lip, he put his hands out in the air as if grabbing on to something, to keep climbing for the last full reach, and then, swimming like crazy, Timmy's body slipped down into the crash of white bubbling water, swallowed up in it, fingertips heading right to her.

Far down the beach, the lifeguard's whistle tooted shrill and fast. Lou-Lou turned to see the guard waving at her. Whistling and waving. And now Gert was running along the wet sand in a shocking-pink muumuu. Gert had promised she wouldn't pick Lou-Lou up until dinnertime, now she was ruining everything. Lou-Lou looked down at Timmy, just about to glide in beside her. Lou-Lou! Gert shouted out, and Timmy scrambled upright, water pearling all over his shoulders. He laughed, breathless. Easy, totally easy, he said. And Lou-Lou smiled at him, as if she still saw the whole thing in his eyes.

Lou-Lou! Gert was panting. Didn't you hear the loudspeaker? Come on. Let's go. We have to hurry. Gert took her by the hand, and together they raced back up to the boardwalk.

What's the matter?

Nothing's the matter, your mother called and she wants you in the city, pronto. She's sending down Uncle Roy's car. Peter will be here any second. So let's go.

But why?

You need a why? Your mother wants you. Gert unlocked the door to Mrs. Murphy's cabana. No time for a shower, here are your shorts. She tossed Lou-Lou her Danskins.

Is it for my bones?

Your bones? Gert poured Mrs. Murphy's baby powder into her hand. She puffed it onto Lou-Lou's damp chest. Honey, your bones are just perfect.

The green stripe of the awning made an odd chartreuse shadow on Gert's face. She held Lou-Lou's hand tight. The long blue limousine pulled slowly through the clubhouse gates. This is good, said Gert, this is what we've all been praying for.

Lou-Lou didn't remember Gert praying. Did Gert want a limousine?

Now, don't get too excited. Just take it slow. Lou-Lou wanted to ask about these instructions, but now Gert was waving to Peter, flagging him down. Here we are! Peter pulled the car to a stop and hopped out.

Mrs. Maguire, Miss Lou-Lou. Peter removed his stiff cap and opened the back door. A block of cold air rushed out. Newspapers covered the carpet. Huddled under the leather puff of the seat, a miniature silver poodle whimpered and scratched. For you and your brother, Miss Lou-Lou. A gift from Miss Horner.

Oh. Kay's going to be thrilled.

He's crying.

Just scared, Miss Lou-Lou.

Now, get going, you two, said Gert. When Lou-Lou was settled in the backseat, the little dog turned his nose to the corner. Gert leaned in and patted Lou-Lou's cheek. Be good, angel, no matter what. Then she backed out of the car. Angel. Now Lou-Lou was worried. Maybe she wouldn't see Gert for a while.

Peter poured her a small ginger ale on ice from the bar, then closed the door. Gert rubbed at her nose and watched from under the awning as Peter made the slow wide turn out of the club. He drove the ocean road to the highway. The tiny dog ignored Lou-Lou and his little silver bowl of food, ate the newspaper, and threw up on the back of the blue jumper seat.

By the time they reached the end of the Lincoln Tunnel, the puppy had rested his nose on Lou-Lou's flip-flop once. Peter cruised up the West Side Highway and down the spiral ramp to the Seventy-ninth Street boat basin. At the bottom he slid to a smooth stop. Peter reached through the open divide with a silver leash. Here you go, Miss Lou-Lou. You might want to put this on. He's never seen the water before.

The *Wavemaker II* was docked at the end of the first pier, engines running. The tarp on the Boston Whaler rescue boat was peeled back. Captain Peeko fiddled on the bridge. Lou-Lou put the dog on the ground, and he ran in uneven arcs back and forth in front of her as she walked along the path holding Peter's hand.

Uncle Roy came running down the gangplank. What took so long? Sweetheart! What do you think of our friend? But Uncle Roy already had the poodle up in his arms. The dog gave a yowl, jaw trembling, teeth exposed. Uncle Roy tapped his nose and the dog stopped crying, panted instead. I thought you'd never get here. He sent her up the gangplank first. Hold that rail!

Esther came up on deck from the salon. *Bonjour, bonjour, chérie!* She nuzzled Lou-Lou's hair with her cheek. Esther smelled like melted vanilla ice cream, and Lou-Lou's face was tickled by the white taffeta roses of her bathing-suit top. *Comment vas-tu?* What do you think of our French *ami?*

Oh, *merci beaucoup.*

Ha! Esther laughed. Ha! She shook her head back and forth very fast. *Très bien!*

Roy dropped the dog. Okay. Let's get out of here.

He gave a swooping wave to Captain Peeko. The engines roared, and a tall boy, not beautiful like Timmy, ran to toss the ropes and release the gangplank. The poodle shrieked like a tiny fire alarm.

It's all right, Esther said. She lifted the poodle and cradled him in the fabric rosebuds like an infant. She smiled at Roy and rocked the dog. *Pauvre chérie.* Poor little boy.

Maybe you better put him downstairs, or we'll get it from both ends.

Okay, mademoiselle. We'll take this little guy where he can be comfortable.

In the salon, Esther scattered Roy's fresh *New York Times*. The poodle combed the periphery of the room and finally leaped up into the leather ottoman, tucked his nose into his paws, and closed his eyes. Calm at last.

Well, he knows good furniture. Darling? A life jacket?

Back on deck, they all watched in silence as the *Wavemaker II* pulled out of the basin and into the full channel of the Hudson River where the ocean liners sailed, then Uncle Roy introduced her to Dirk, the first mate. Excellent math skills, said Uncle Roy.

Lou-Lou shook Dirk's hand.

Give her the tour, go ahead.

Lou-Lou had been on the *Wavemaker II* many times, but she took the tour. She followed Dirk below. He showed her the blue wavy satin bedspread in the stateroom that looked like a small oblong sea, he showed her the tiny shower with a curved ripple-glass door, and the galley where boxes of Florida red grapefruits stacked in the corner smelled like medicine. He showed her two pink shells mounded with caviar, and chopped eggs and white whipped sour cream under cellophane in the narrow metal fridge. Gross, said Dirk. I guess your father's some guy.

Business, said Lou-Lou.

You're lucky. Dirk sighed. My father's a jackass. Then he took her up to the bow and let her hang off the front tip when Charlie Peeko wasn't looking.

It was a fast trip to the Statue of Liberty and around the bottom of New York City, already they were coming up the East River. Charlie Peeko steered closer and closer to the highway, past the heliport, past the houses that almost leaned over, terraces dripping off them, past the tunnels like long caves, going faster toward a low square building right next to the water, with silver wires jutting out from the top and a tiny dock, like the dot on a question mark floating on the water.

On the dot she could see two people; the man held a bundle. The wind flapped Lou-Lou's hair, and when she cleared it, they were that much closer and she could see her mother and her father and the sack that was Bo. Hey! Hey! she yelled.

They can't hear you, said Dirk.

She could see them, though, her father was there, with short hair, and his face tipped into Bo's cheek. And Bo was laughing. What's so funny?

Lou-Lou's mother stood up now, shielded her eyes, the wind snapped at her pale skirt, it flicked like a flag, she held it down with the other hand. The *Wavemaker II* slowed and pulled in closer, engines grinding and reversing, but still they were a long way off.

Uncle Roy came racing up to the bow, Esther behind him. Dirk! Dirk, don't just stand around gawking, get this thing in the water. He motioned for Charlie Peeko to do something, and the engines sputtered into a lower gear. Esther threw her arms around Lou-Lou's life jacket and squeezed.

Dirk and Roy lowered the Boston Whaler off the winch and into the channel. Dirk climbed down and pulled the crank to start the motor. Roy swung both legs over the side and dropped into the Whaler. He held tight to the seat and looked ahead, his shoulders straight, deep brown from the sun. Lou-Lou could smell the coconut of his lotion in the air. She watched them skim fast across the channel, Dirk steering with one arm stretched behind him. The bow lifted up like a tipped plate.

Lou-Lou watched her father in the distance, as if watching a movie. He kissed the top of Bo's head and Bo tilted away, then back for more, like normal. The Whaler sped toward the dock and rocked a little in the wake of a big barge chugging past. Seagulls whirled and screeched.

Dirk scrambled out of the Whaler onto the dock, and then, after Roy yelled something, lay down flat on his stomach, reached with both arms, and held the ropes tight to keep the boat steady. Lou-Lou's father held Bo close to his chest and carefully, making a kind of basket of his whole body, lowered Bo down. Roy grabbed

Bo around the middle and sat abruptly, put two life jackets on him, one in the normal spot and one around Bo's legs like a blanket.

Her father backed down into the Whaler. Her father with a haircut just like his picture from the marines. Opened his arms to her mother, who went down backward too.

Champagne! Esther danced back toward the salon. Watch her, she hollered to Charlie Peeko on the bridge.

Dirk untied the ropes and made a big leap into the boat. Roy shouted something, but Lou-Lou couldn't hear it. This time the Whaler didn't fly along the water. Something slowed them down. The channel was smooth now, but they barely moved. Bo was at the front end in her father's lap, her father's hands made an umbrella over Bo's face to block out the sun. Lou-Lou leaned as far as she could out over the bow and waved. But her mother scanned the water, looked back toward the Statue of Liberty as if she were watching for something. It's okay, thought Lou-Lou. It's okay. The Whaler hobbled a tiny bit closer. Roy held the tiller on the engine. And Dirk sat, hands folded, beside him. Not so far, thought Lou-Lou, it's not so far, and by watching, she was helping. They moved a little closer. That's good, she thought. She was bringing them to her, with all of her natural abilities and all of her hope. Her mother and her father and her brother, she was helping them, bringing them to her little by little, and now they were almost there.

Acknowledgments

My thanks to Rick Moody for his impeccable attention. Susan Cheever has my devotion. Donald Antrim gave kind-hearted, clear-eyed guidance. Melanie Jackson is a wonder woman.

Thanks to Elisabeth Schmitz for graceful and judicious editing. I am grateful for the fortifying wit of Molly Boren and for Andrea Schaefer's gentle, wry lucidity.

Thanks to my family: Hugheses, Beesons, Shoemakers, Theeses, McKennas, McCranes, Wirstroms, Shaheens, Hetzlers, and McCarthys. Especially my sister, Paula V. and my friend, Catherine A.

Sara Beeson, Alex Busansky, Brent Spencer, and Judith Kuppersmith offered expertise and clarity. My lasting thanks to all.

Thanks to The Corporation of Yaddo and to the people who work the daily miracles there. Thanks to my friends at the Writing Seminars of Bennington College, and those at the July Program, too.

I am indebted to a number of authors and artists: Robert Neese's *Prison Exposures* (his "prank" photo inspired Persephone's cherries), Murray Kempton's essay "Undertaking Roy Cohn;" Jonathan Demme's film "Roy Cohn/Jack Smith," performance by Ron Vawter; *Fool for A Client,* Roy M. Cohn; *McCarthy by Cohn,* Roy M. Cohn; *Citizen Cohn* by Nicholas Von Hoffman; *Autobiography of Roy Cohn* by Sydney Zion; and *Point of Order!,* the documentary by Emile de Antonio.

Most of all, for his infinite generosity, I thank Duke Beeson with all of my heart.